P9-CQD-919

BEIJING PAYBACK

BEIJING PAYBACK

A NOVEL

DANIEL NIEH

ecco
An Imprint of HarperCollins*Publishers*

Nieh

HarperCollins books may be purchased for educational, business, or sales promotional use. For information, please e-mail the Special Markets Department at SPsales@harpercollins.com.

FIRST EDITION

Designed by Suet Chong

Library of Congress Cataloging-in-Publication Data

Names: Nieh, Daniel, author.
Title: Beijing payback : a novel / Daniel Nieh.
Description: First edition. | New York, NY : Ecco, [2019]
Identifiers: LCCN 2018033459 (print) | LCCN 2018033746 (ebook) | ISBN 9780062886668 (ebook) | ISBN 9780062886644 | ISBN 9780062886651
Subjects: | GSAFD: Suspense fiction.
Classification: LCC PS3614.I35626 (ebook) | LCC PS3614.I35626 B45 2018 (print) | DDC 813/.6—dc23
LC record available at https://lccn.loc.gov/2018033459

---

19 20 21 22 23 LSC 10 9 8 7 6 5 4 3 2 1

TO MY TEACHERS, ALL OF YOU

三人行必有我师

NOTE ON LANGUAGE

Any dialogue in this story introduced with Chinese transliterations is spoken in Mandarin Chinese, and all subsequent dialogue between the same characters can be assumed to be in Mandarin unless otherwise indicated.

The Chinese names in this text are rendered in the pinyin transliteration system, which is standard in mainland China but not phonetic. The meanings and pronunciations of many Chinese characters vary with context, and the following nonexhaustive guidance is solely intended to assist the reader in becoming acquainted with the Chinese names in this novel.

Xiao (小), a common character in given names, means "small" or "young." It is pronounced, roughly, as "shee-ow" (ɕi̯ɑʊ̯). *Zhou* (洲) means "continent" and is pronounced, roughly, as "joh" (tʂɤʊ̯). Thus, Victor's Chinese name, Xiaozhou, sounds like "shee-ow joh."

Lian (莲) means "lotus" and is pronounced as a diphthong: "lee-enne." *Ying* (英) means "brave." Juliana's Chinese name, Lianying, sounds like "lee-enne ing" (liɛn iŋ).

Sun (孙) is a common surname that can mean "descendent." It is pronounced as "swuhn" (su̯ən).

Syllables ending in *-ng* have a soft, nasal vowel sound. *Peng* is pronounced "Pung" (fəŋ); *Ouyang* is pronounced "Oh-yahng" (ɤʊ̯ i̯ɑŋ); *Dong* has a long *o* sound and is pronounced "Dohng" (tʊŋ).

I wiggle my fingers, wiggle my toes, will blood into the frigid appendages of my body. I heave deep breaths to jump-start my lungs and diaphragm. *Where am I?* Wherever I am, it stinks of urine. Thanks to whatever the Snake Hands Gang injected me with—was it ketamine?—my neck feels like I spent a week on a roller coaster wearing an iron helmet. I winch my eyes open for a fraction of a second, then quickly squeeze them shut again. The white light above my head is too bright, the space too tight, and I can't change the position of my body. My clothes are still wet from the rain, so I must not have been unconscious for long.

I replay events in my head, searching for the signs I missed, the turnoffs on this winding path that could've precluded this outcome. Maybe Jules was right: Maybe my loyalty had blinded me. I had seen my choices too simply, seen only what I wanted to see. Maybe I shouldn't have come to Beijing at all.

Maybe it's too late to be having second thoughts.

This isn't the end, I tell myself, rocking my chin from side to side, scrunching up my face, expending major willpower to suppress the urge to cry. I knock my forehead against the frigid metal like I'm hitting the side of a TV, trying to change the picture. *You'll get out of this.* Snake Hands won't want the attention that comes with killing an American. The police will catch up with them. Sun Jianshui is already on his way.

Dad didn't send you to China for you to die in this hole.

PART ONE

UNITED STATES OF AMERICA

SIX DAYS EARLIER

1

Bounce bounce squeak squeak—the only sounds in the dark arena are the little meetings between the glossy wood floor and the round orange ball, the wood floor and my sneakers. Twice up and back spin moves, twice up and back crossovers, twice up and back behind-the-back dribbles.

I go through the routine like I have every day for a thousand days, not thinking at all, just doing the drills. My mind is empty except for the rhythms of the ball and my shoes. In the dim green glow of the emergency EXIT signs, I roll out the Shoot-A-Way gun and position it beneath the rim, its giant net stretching upward like an open talon, a mechanical maw. I shoot threes from the top of the key, and the gun fires the ball back to me every three seconds, two hundred shots in ten minutes, until my forearms start to ache. I move on to floaters, the little man's shot, the hardest in the game: floaters from the paint, floaters from the foul line, soft banked floaters off baseline drives. I miss, I calibrate, I try to relax: "*Cóngróng zìruò, cóngróng búpò*—Find yourself, don't force yourself," Dad would say.

The lights come on when I'm up in the nosebleeds running the steps. Andre is waiting for me. When I step to the free throw line for the last part of my routine, he stands under the basket, rebounds as I hit two foul shots and a hard drive to the rim. Five times in a row, all ten foul shots all net. At 5 feet 9 and 155 pounds, I may not be a lock for the pros like Andre is—"*Yěxǔ nǐ xiāntiān tiáojiàn bùzú*—Perhaps your innate characteristics are insufficient," Dad once told me, laughing—but that's not because I miss free throws.

After I swish the last one, my workout is over. But I still feel like someone's holding a live wire to the base of my skull. I'm not finding myself; I'm not finding anything. I'm fighting away thoughts about last Friday night, the game in this very building, and then, as I sat wrapped in a towel in the boisterous locker room, the phone call from the police. The yellow tape across the front door of the house I grew up in.

Andre flicks the ball back to me, and I hurl it into the stands with all my strength, all my fury. Without saying anything, Andre dutifully walks into the stands to retrieve it. When he comes back, I'm lying supine on the hardwood.

"Number three add guac?" he says.

"Okay," I say. "Let me shower first."

After breakfast burritos, Andre drives me to meet Dad's lawyer in West Covina. We make a couple of U-turns on Glendora Avenue before we figure out that the law office of Perry Peng is signlessly tucked between a boba tea café and an Asian supermarket in the corner of a U-shaped strip mall, one of the hundred such strip malls that line the wide boulevards of the most Chinese part of Los Angeles County.

"You want me to pick you up later?" he asks.

I shake my head. "I'll ride home with Jules."

He pulls away, and I get comfortable leaning against the mall building, a tan stucco horseshoe. The February sun hangs low in the southern sky, casting jagged reflections off the pristine windshields of the late-model minivans and family sedans in the parking lot. I start a game with myself guessing how late my sister will be, counting down from 444, but she exceeds expectations: I'm somewhere around negative 250 when I spot her little Japanese hatchback a block away.

Juliana parks, then steps out of her car and slings a messenger bag over her shoulder in one fluid motion. Jules has always dressed herself well, and most recently she's nailed grad-student chic: flowy natural fabrics, minimal makeup, disordered cloud of layered black hair. Even though her eyesight is fine, she has taken to wearing thick-rimmed eyeglasses, which, combined with the upturned nose she got from Mom, tend to lend her an inquisitive look. The sole other member of our halfie-halfie tribe, Jules has the same skin as me, smooth with no hint of pink, but her eyes are lighter, more hazel, more confusing. If our parents were here, it would make some sense, like: Oh, hey, white mommy and Asian daddy, I get it. But they're not. They're dead.

"Hey, Jules."

She hugs me, then holds me away at arm's length and smiles up at me. Puffy eyes, white teeth.

"Are you ready to inherit some restaurants?" I say.

She glances down at her hands, inspects her fingernails. "I was kind of hoping you would take care of that."

"You had a more senior position when we worked there in high school."

"As a hostess?"

"I mopped the bathrooms. And stirred the duck sauce."

Jules's chin begins to quiver, and she blinks a few tears out onto her cheeks. She pulls me back into a hug. "This sucks so unbelievably much," she manages to say, her voice breaking.

I wish I could think of something to say back, something

better, something comforting. But I can't find the words, so I just frown back my own tears as hers soak into the shoulder of my shirt. I stand there with my arms around Juliana's small frame, my eyes squeezed shut, and wish with all my willpower for some other reality to present itself when I open my eyes.

But when Jules's breathing evens out, when she steps back from me and I have no choice but to open my eyes again, the same shitty reality is still right here. There's nothing to do but dab our cheeks, blow our noses, and push through the tinted glass door into Dad's lawyer's office.

The waiting room is clean, carpeted, and hospital bright with fluorescent light. Mr. Peng is perched on the side of his receptionist's large white desk. He walks over to us with some special sympathetic expression on his face, his hands out wide.

"*Liányīng, Xiǎozhōu, jīngwén lìngzūn císhì, wǒ shēngǎn tòngxī*—Lianying, Xiaozhou, I am very sorry for your loss."

"*Duōxiè, Péng lǜshī, ní hěn ānwèi wǒmen*—Thank you, Lawyer Peng. You comfort us."

The corners of the lawyer's mouth flicker at the not very fluent register of Jules's formalities in Mandarin. Perry Peng is a sleek vision in grays and silvers—short gray hair, trim gray suit, shiny silver tie clip—and he has a comforting, familiar odor, bay rum or beeswax. He leads us back into his immaculately feng shui'd office. In front of his large desk, two beige sofas face each other across a low glass table, and we sit on these. Long scrolls of calligraphed poetry hang on the walls beside classical ink wash paintings: mountains and forests, poet-hermits drinking from gourds. The receptionist brings in a pitcher of hot water. Peng plucks an enameled canister from the elegant ceramic tea set on the glass table and starts scooping silvery green needles into the pot.

"*Wǒmen xiān yìqǐ hē bēi chá*—First, we'll drink tea together," he says. As we sip the jasmine brew from small porcelain cups, Mr. Peng offers his condolences for our sudden loss, saying how shocked he was by the violent tragedy and how unfortunate it is to have to discuss trivial matters of estate at such a sad time. And so on.

Then he puts on a pair of rimless reading glasses and clears his throat.

"As you probably know, medical bills absorbed most of your parents' savings—"

"Excuse me," Jules pipes up. "Can we use English? I'm afraid my Chinese is a bit rusty."

The lawyer glances up at her, then back to his papers. "Certainly. As I was saying, most of your parents' savings were absorbed by medical bills during your mother's illness. In addition to that, your father refinanced your house at the time. The house and his remaining savings will now belong to you, Lianying." He hands Juliana a thin sheaf of papers.

We look over the summary on the first page. The numbers are decidedly unsexy. Dad was thrifty but not quite financially literate, and he had perfectly mistimed the housing market.

"We should sell it," Jules murmurs to me.

"Fortunately, that is not all," Peng interjects. "Your father also had a life insurance policy through the parent company of his restaurants." He hands Jules a thicker sheaf of papers, this one printed in Chinese.

Jules glances at me, then back to Peng. "Did you just say 'parent company'?"

The lawyer nods. "I recall that he said you might not know he did not own the restaurants. You see, there were other investors in the Happy Year Restaurant Company, people in Beijing who took on risk in the early years of the business. Vincent Li was the chief executive, and the company paid his salary."

"But Mr. Peng," Jules says, "our father *always* acted as the owner of those restaurants. He built each one of them, he designed the menus, and he trained all the managers and the chefs. What you're telling us—I can't even—it comes as a complete shock."

Mr. Peng's mouth forms a tight line. He removes his rimless glasses. "As you know, your father and I worked closely for many years, and I am intimately acquainted with his affairs. I can assure you that these arrangements are exactly as he intended. Please review the life insurance policy. It includes instructions for filing a claim."

With that, he stands up and bows to us once more.

My teacup is still half full, and I'm staring dumbly at the jasmine sediment. Taking the hint, Jules nudges me and stands up, too.

"We understand, Mr. Peng," she says coolly. "Thank you for your time."

As we pass through the waiting room, Peng takes me by the elbow and steers me aside. He pulls an envelope from the inside pocket of his suit jacket and hands it to me.

"This is something your father wanted you to have in the event of his death," he says. "Xiaozhou, I know you and your father were close, and this is a difficult time. Please rest assured that you and your sister have nothing to worry about."

Nothing to worry about. Parent company. The words enter through my ears, bypass my brain, and travel straight to my stomach, where they begin building little nests of confusion and anger.

"Thank you, Mr. Peng. We're just a little mixed up right now."

The lawyer smiles and waves his hand between our faces as if to whisk away any idea of a misunderstanding.

"Think nothing of it," he says.

Out in the heat on the other side of the tinted glass door, I follow Jules to her car. She puts the key in the ignition, but she doesn't turn it.

"What the hell was that?" she says.

"I don't know. It doesn't make any sense."

"A parent company. Just like Dad to fail to mention that for, like, our whole lives. Classic Asian parenting move."

She pulls the insurance policy out of her messenger bag. "Can you read this? My Chinese is so shitty."

I stare through her windshield, seeing nothing. "I'll do it later."

"Victor, this is important."

Important? The insurance policy is important? Last week Dad was alive, and now he's dead. *Nothing to worry about.* I want to demolish Mr. Peng's tea set, tear Jules's car apart with my fingers, my teeth. Instead I clench my jaw shut, lean my head back, and close my eyes. A raw silence fills the car until Jules quietly says, "Fine."

She starts the engine. I allow my eyes to fall open, gaze out the window. We cruise along Badillo Street, wide lanes lined first by single-story stores and offices, then by big houses and apartment buildings built too close to each other. The street is partially shaded by fan palms and holly oaks, the sentinels of planting strip and median, which seem to ignore our loss, or buffer it. And then we're back at the house Mom and Dad bought when we moved to the States, a sterile and carpeted subdivision McMansion with all the comfort and predictability of the slow deaths they'd both been denied. Porch swing, gas grill, big fish tank. Jules parks in the wide driveway next to my regal old sedan, a high school graduation present from Dad, its battery probably dead now after a winter of disuse. We let ourselves in and go cry in our own bedrooms, comforted by the proximity of the other, perhaps, but in no mood for company.

And then I remember. I pull out the envelope and tear it open.

Inside there is a thick plastic card with a hole punched in it, a thin leather cord running through the hole. Also attached to the cord is a small wrought-iron figurine of a monkey. The card is blank except for some scuff marks and a little round sticker. A sticker with the number 14 written on it in ballpoint pen.

I take another look at the envelope, and this time I notice Dad's tiny handwriting in one of the corners: "Chateau Happiness Spa, Temple City."

2

I call Andre for a ride, and he says he'll leave right away. Andre's been my best friend since the summer before seventh grade, when we met at a basketball camp. We weren't the two best players, but we were the two most intensely competitive, and our first matchup led to a tussle that might've ended in biting had the coaches not pulled us off of each other.

Basketball was the center of our sullen lives. We were those teased children compelled by fretful parents to bring home stellar report cards, craning our skinny necks on the fringes of middle school life, worrying the hems of our T-shirts with our fingers. In the absence of other diversions, we exhausted ourselves on the street in front of my house, playing H-O-R-S-E, bump, tips, crunch, and endless games of one-on-one. Then we went inside, made peanut butter and jelly sandwiches, and resumed our endless deathmatch on my video game consoles.

Andre Osipenko didn't have a console, a tablet, a television in his room, or even a phone of his own. His parents ran a housekeeping service. Infertile immigrants from Warsaw, they adopted

Andre when he was a runty two-year-old and seemed to live solely to feed him, to kiss him, to envelop him in warmth. But grade school tested their steely family bond. Being a shrimpy black kid with a Polish accent and steamed beef tongue in your Pokémon lunch box just wasn't a recipe for popularity. And Andre craved acceptance. He chafed against Lucjan and Halina's highly contagious uncoolness. For him, like me, the court was a refuge.

Then, during our first two years of high school, he stretched out to six feet ten and moved from shooting guard to center. And as he stretched, he mellowed. He became that slow-moving man-child in sweatpants and huge headphones. He still did his schoolwork if he was enjoying it, but he didn't read textbooks that bored him when he could be lifting weights, watching tape, or balancing on one foot with his eyes closed, visualizing made free throws. Or napping—he was always napping, about to nap, just finished with a nap.

If anything, Andre's growth spurt allowed us to grow closer, to complement each other better both on and off the court. We helped each other improve, watching hours of YouTube videos, dissecting Chris Paul's spin dribble and Chris Bosh's mid-post step-back. I know some people think I only got a basketball scholarship to San Dimas State University because of Andre, but I don't let that bother me. He wouldn't have set the district scoring record and been written up in *Sports Illustrated* our senior year of high school if I hadn't been tossing him all those pretty lobs.

Now, in our final season of college ball, Andre's leading the Cal-10 conference in points, rebounds, and blocks. He's got a separate phone just for the agents and pro scouts who shouldn't be calling him yet. As for me, I ride the pine behind Howie Miller, our bigger, faster, stronger starting point guard, even though he's a year behind us. At least I did until last week.

"So where did you say we're going?" Andre says as I climb into his Detroit-made truck, an aging juggernaut, hula girl on the dashboard. He's finishing one protein bar and unwrapping another. Andre hasn't treated me any differently in the past week, and someday I'll figure out how to thank him for that.

"A massage place in Temple City. Look at this. The lawyer gave it to me." I show him the contents of the envelope.

"What's with the monkey?"

"I dunno. Dad and I were both born in the Year of the Monkey."

"So what does that mean?"

"Monkeys are supposed to be clever and stubborn. If you believe in that sort of thing."

"Clever and stubborn, huh? Sounds like you on the court."

"It doesn't mean anything to me. Half the people I know were born in the same year. Including you, and all you do is dunk on people."

Andre splays his hand on his chest in mock indignation. "I'd like to think I dunk on people in an intelligent way."

Andre starts the truck, and Regime Change, his latest conscious hip-hop obsession, pounds out of his stereo system.

Hypocrite give a shit about material things
Fur collar, faux baller, illegitimate bling
When the shit hit the fan boy that ice don't swing
'Cause you can't see me and your bird can't sing

"So would you believe me if I told you that my dad didn't actually own any of his restaurants?"

"For real? I mean, your dad *is* those restaurants."

"That's what the lawyer just told us. Jules is worked up about it. But I can't muster two shits about anything. I can't think about anything but—" I grasp at something in the air with both hands. "I guess I'm still in shock."

"Well." Andre checks his mirrors, hops the curb to pull a sweeping U-turn. "*I'm* still in shock."

"He always said he had sold a restaurant back in China. We came here and he started setting up Happy Year right away. I never thought twice about it. We had an English tutor, and Jules went to private school. Turns out it wasn't his money. I mean, who shows up fresh off the boat from China with a fat wad of U.S. dollars?"

Andre contemplates this new fact. "I guess I always assumed it was your mother's inheritance or something."

I shake my head. "Her parents aren't dead, at least as far as I know. They run a megachurch in Missouri. They basically disowned her when she decided to marry Dad."

"Cuz he's Chinese?"

"Uh-huh."

Andre lets out a low whistle.

"I thought I'd told you that before."

"Maybe you did and I forgot," Andre replies, nonchalant, as he coasts into the middle of two parking spots.

"Can you wait here?" I slide out of the car. "I'll be quick."

Chateau Happiness is another squat stucco establishment that shares its chunk of suburban sprawl with a Taiwanese shaved ice shop, a martial arts academy, and a travel agency. Cheaply printed posters advertising the spa's various services—massage, facial, reflexology—cover the windows completely. The Southern Californian sky above the short buildings is stupid azure blue, huge, breezy.

In the middle of the afternoon on a Thursday, the whole block seems deserted. Glancing from one empty storefront to another, I wonder how these places earn enough to stay in business. And then I see a guy standing in the window of the shaved ice shop: a slight Asian guy wearing a Lakers cap and a black T-shirt, standing halfway concealed by the window frame. Looking right at me. I glance around to see whether there's something worth viewing behind me, but it's all the same, the spectrum of worn taupes, tans, and asphalts of the San Gabriel Valley, without a soul in sight.

When I look back, the guy is gone.

I push through the door of Chateau Happiness into a shallow reception room with a desk, a watercooler, and some folding chairs. There are more posters on the walls: Chinese diagrams of the nervous system, the spine, the foot. There's a waist-high plastic fountain decorated with tiny bodhisattva figurines and colorful LED lights. The permed hair of the bespectacled woman behind the desk is dyed a light-suckingly matte shade of black.

"Massaji?" she says.

"Uh, no, thank you. I'm here because I found this." I pull out the cord and hand it to her. She peers at the card, then the monkey, then pulls off her glasses and examines the card more closely.

"Where you find this?" she demands.

"I—" But as I start to talk, a wave of pain crashes over my guts, and I shut my eyes for a second and put my hands on the desk to collect myself. "I'm sorry. It belonged to my father, Vincent Li. I mean, Li Renyan?"

Her face falls when she hears Dad's name. She heaves a sigh and cocks her head at a sympathetic angle. Then she rolls her wheely chair over to the beaded curtain beside the desk, sticks her head through, and hollers something in Cantonese.

"Ailan will help you," she says to me.

On cue, a petite woman in slippers, a fitted red V-neck, and silky white pajama pants slips through the beaded curtain. She looks a few years older than me, with clear, quite white skin and straight hair that falls nearly to her waist. The lady says something to her in Cantonese, and Ailan's curious smile turns into one of those sad faces I can't seem to avoid.

"*Jiéāi*—I'm sorry for your loss," she says to me in Mandarin. "Your dad was a really kind person." She has a cute southern Chinese accent to go with her cute southern Chinese everything else.

"It's okay," I reply, just to say something.

Ailan has me remove my shoes and don slippers of my own,

and then she leads me down a dim, narrow hallway with dingy walls. She stops in front of an unmarked door.

"This is the VIP changing room. Your father's things are in there."

As she turns to go, her words replay in my head—her voice, her tone—and something makes me wonder who it was that she knew as Vincent Li, and how well she knew him.

"Ailan? Did my dad come here a lot?"

She turns back to give me a tight-lipped smile and a one-shoulder shrug.

"Yeah," she says in English, and then she walks away.

The VIP changing room is a squarish space with two benches and a wall of wooden lockers with numbered doors. A shower turns off in the next room, and a tall, thin guy walks in. He's wearing a robe and slippers, and he's got a card on a cord of his own hanging from his wrist. Ignoring my existence, he passes the card in front of a locker, which pops open with an electronic chirp.

I sidle into the adjacent bathroom to pee while the guy gets dressed. I wash my hands and then spend a moment catching up with myself in the mirror, running a hand over my buzzed hair. Dad looked at himself in this same mirror and saw the same dark eyebrows, small mouth, and high, sharp cheekbones. For the first time in a week, mental activity is flickering around between my ears, cutting through the snowstorm of negative emotions and numbness. How often is "yeah"? Did he have a secret massage habit, or was this some other part of the Happy Year business, which I now know that I know nothing about? The tall guy is whistling. He spends a short eternity perfecting his comb-over.

Locker 14 is in the bottom row. When the dude is finally gone, I sit on the bench and wave my card, and what do you know, the little door pops open. The first thing I see is a tote bag of clean clothes, neatly folded. Dad was always planning ahead. I dig around in the bag and feel something hard at the bottom: a rubber Casio wristwatch. It's pretty worn—I'm guessing it predates the Swiss wrist candy he was wearing when the cops found him on the floor of his office. With my cell in my pocket, I've never felt the need to wear a watch, but I strap on the Casio just to see what it feels like.

Then I notice the flat aluminum attaché case leaning against the locker's back wall. I set it on my lap, flip up the twin latches, and lift the lid. The sides are lined with dense black sponge in an egg-crate pattern. Inside, resting on a row of neat stacks of hundred-dollar bills, is a gun.

3

Is it loaded?"

"No."

"May I?"

"Sure."

Eli picks up the pistol, inspects it in both hands. Andre and I requested each other for roommates as freshmen and ended up in a triple with Eli Henochowitz, an Orthodox Jew from Brooklyn. At least he was raised Orthodox. He has a kippah, but he only wears it for Skype purposes. Eli started exploiting what he calls "Internet arbitrage opportunities" when he was an eighth grader. At this point he's heavy into cryptocurrencies, freelance SEO, and all sorts of other inscrutable online endeavors—he likes to call himself a webusinessman. Once, blackout drunk on Jaegerbombs, he boasted to a roomful of basketball players and Tri Delt sisters that he was a senior member of a secretive antifascist hacking collective. Nobody was really interested.

Eli's nominally enrolled in college as a COMM major to prevent his parents from wigging out. He applied early decision to

SDSU, he told us, "for the weather and the hos." After an occasionally awkward adjustment period, Andre and I came to love Eli for who he really is: a borderline genius with the heart of a saint, the imagination of a twelve-year-old, and the libido of a bonobo.

"Victor," he says, "why the fuck would your dad leave you a gun?"

"That's not everything, either."

"Is there a crossbow, too?"

"Look at this stuff." Andre gestures toward the case on the table.

Eli sets the gun down on the coffee table and flips through the little burgundy passport with my name in it. "Since when are you a Chinese citizen?"

"I'm not. I have American citizenship, and you can't have both."

He fingers the cash. "How much is this?"

"Fifty grand. And one hundred thou in renminbi. Chinese yuan. It's like fifteen grand in dollars."

"Fuckin' A, Victor."

"No kidding."

"So that's it? No note or anything?" Eli asks. I shake my head. "And you have no idea why he would leave these things to you?"

I don't, I tell him, but I recount my experience at the massage parlor, how Ailan gave me the feeling that Dad had all kinds of secrets. I also tell him about Jules's and my meeting with the lawyer, and how it seemed like he wasn't giving us the whole story. "Not like he was lying, but like he was just telling us the parts we needed to hear. The whole thing felt rushed." I shake my head, stare at my hands. "Or maybe I'm just imagining things."

"Do you think he knew what was in the locker?"

"The lawyer? I dunno. Possibly."

"I thought your dad was killed by a burglar."

"I thought so, too."

We sit there for a moment and stare at the money, the passport, and the handgun on the table. Mostly at the gun. It's a Walther PPQ, which according to Google is the finest striker-fired 9-millimeter on the market, whatever the fuck that means. The three of us went to a shooting range on a Groupon once. I shot pretty well. Eli was terrible. Andre made it look easy.

"So what do you guys think this means?"

Eli puts a gentle hand on my arm. "A lot of time when people keep secrets, it's not necessarily a bad thing. My parents know nothing about my life here, and trust me, that's for their own well-being. Like, I eat pork now and then, but it's not like *every* Tuesday is a coke bender."

Andre clears his throat pointedly.

"Anyway," Eli says, "my point is that, if I died, I'd probably want my folks to know who I really was. So what's a good reason that your dad would have a gun and some stacks of cash? Like maybe he's a police informant. Or a spy for the Chinese intelligence services. And he's hidden that information from you for your own safety, but now he wants you to know because you've got all this untapped potential, right? And so now you—"

"Whoa, okay, Henochowitz! Back up the trolley," Andre cuts in. "Vincent Li befriended stray dogs. He meditated twice a day. Somehow I doubt he was narcin' on dealers after his long shifts managing four restaurants. Look, Victor, this stuff is crazy, I mean, money and a gun? But maybe your dad left this stuff to you as some kind of emergency kit. There're no indications that he wanted you to *do* something with it. For now, what you've gotta do is take it easy and take some time to, you know, process and stuff. Right? Am I right?"

I sort of nod. *Take it easy:* the path of least resistance, a classic Andre position. I know what he's saying is true. But having something to do would really hit the spot right now.

In Andre's car we are quiet. After a while Andre asks me what I'm thinking. I tell him how much I hate staying at the house.

How I wouldn't go back at all except that Jules says she can't fall asleep there if she's alone. How I hear her getting up in the night to double-check that the doors are locked, and she's got a hammer sitting on her bedside table.

How I lie awake at night and watch different versions of Dad's murder in my head, over and over.

"I wish I could comfort you," he says. "But if it were my family and my house, I'd probably feel the same way."

For dinner Jules and I pick at takeout that someone from one of Dad's restaurants sent over. I ask Jules about how design school is going, but she gives me a short answer. Then, as if to be polite, she asks me about college, but I find that I don't have much to say, either. Given that she's already having trouble sleeping, I decide to wait until the morning to tell her about the gun.

After dinner I wash the dishes. Dad always did the dishes, even when it was his turn to cook. He got a big kick out of doing the dishes and singing show tunes at the top of his lungs while Mom sat in the breakfast nook trying to read a magazine or do the crossword. Sometimes she would give up, come into the living room where we were watching TV, snuggle up with Jules and say something like "Six hundred million Chinese men and I marry the only one who has memorized *Cats*."

I'm lying on my bed, staring at the ceiling and fighting down the persistent bubble of misery rising in my stomach, when Jules knocks on my door. I tell her to come in. She sits on the side of my bed and says, "Hey."

"Hey," I say back.

Her forehead is crinkled up, and her eyes are wet and shiny. She makes little tiger fists in her lap and examines her cuticles. She turns her face away, addressing herself to the wall. "I seriously can't feed the fish. I can't go down there and feed all those stupid tropical fish without thinking about how it was like the greatest joy of his life to feed his fish."

"Uh-huh," I say. For a while there is no sound but her sniffles and her tears pit-patting onto my bedspread.

She finally breaks the silence: "Play me in Ping-Pong?"

"Sure."

We descend to the basement and play a best-of-five. I play conservatively, returning neatly, trying to work her toward the corners, but she sends it all back with big looping spin shots that put me on my heels. I get one game off her, but only because she's less focused than I am. A million years ago, a prior version of Jules won state in tennis. Whooping up on me seems to put her in better spirits.

"I guess you're still my bitch," she says as we wipe down and fold up the table.

"Mmhmm."

"How about I teach you some basketball, too," she suggests brightly.

"Okay."

Upstairs, in the hallway, she leads me to her room.

"I need to show you something," she says.

The walls of Jules's childhood bedroom are white and bare, but every inch of the floor is covered with clutter. I poke a half-unpacked suitcase with my shoe. "It's like a tornado hit Madewell."

"Shut up. It took me an hour to read this insurance policy. Seriously? China needs an alphabet." She hands me the stack of papers from Perry Peng. "I need you to tell me I'm understanding this correctly."

The cover page has just one line in the middle of it: "*Xìng Nián (Běijīng) yǒuxiàn gōngsī,* Happy Year Co. Ltd., Beijing."

"Holy shit," I say after a while.

"Right?" Jules is slouched against a pile of bedding with her nose in some weighty hardcover.

"This policy is worth twenty-four million renminbi."

"Yeah."

"I mean, holy shit."

"I know." Jules sets the book down on her bed and flicks her bangs out of her eyes. "I feel like such an idiot for questioning the lawyer guy like that."

Silence sets in as we process. *Four million dollars.* Two students, ages twenty-five and twenty-two, with four million dollars.

"Does it mean anything for you?" I ask her.

She tips her head to one side, brow furrowed.

"I don't know, Victor. I guess I could drop out of design school and open a boutique. Or travel around the world. But I'm not ready to think about using this money. It just doesn't feel right. I'll file the claim and we'll figure it out later."

"So you know, it might be tricky to convert it to dollars because there are some restrictions on the yuan. You might be able to buy Chinese equities— What?"

There's a little smirk on Jules's face. "So that's who you're gonna be, huh?" she says.

"What is?"

"An *economics* major." She says the word like it's a synonym for *necrophilia*.

"I am an econ major."

"You know what I mean."

"I guess so."

Jules's gaze strays upward into her imagination of my future. "I know Dad was all about it, but I just can't picture you sitting in a conference room while people do PowerPoints about corporate synergies or whatever. For like forty years of your life."

"Yeah, well. Not everything is fun and games."

She sits forward again, starts talking with her hands. "I'm just saying, you don't have to follow whichever track Dad laid out for you. I mean, have you read a newspaper lately? What's the point in putting your nose to the grindstone when we're on the fast track to extinction anyway? Dad slaved away like Sisyphus at those restaurants, and look what it got him. Everything can disappear, just like that."

"So? You've got a solution to that problem?"

"No solutions, Victor. I just want do an original something, be an interesting someone. And at the end of it all, feel like I lived on my own terms, even if I lived in a shit world. I mean, seriously, Victor, you're still really young. Don't you even care who you become?"

I have never shared Jules's negative appraisal of the world we live in, which has been pretty good to me aside from the pair of obvious whammies. Dad was born in the middle of an epic Communist disaster, and all that he did—immigrating to California, the restaurants, everything—it was all so we could have a nice life here at the top of the food chain, a life I've always intended to accept. So what if stuff's a little boring sometimes, and the news is depressing? The news is never not depressing.

But I know better than to argue with Jules when she's in a righteous mood. One time she tore into me for a whole hour for letting my teammates call me "Rice," which I admit is a bit racist but was basically just a hazing thing that she didn't understand. Tonight doesn't seem like the night that we resolve the questions of "Isn't the world fucked?" and "Should Victor conform?" So I play defense by diverting the conversation to Jules's weak spot: herself.

"Sure, I think about that stuff all the time. I really do," I say. "But I don't have any bright ideas. What do you actually want to do? Design clothes for rich ladies? Or go back into advertising?"

"I don't know." She's inspecting her cuticles again.

"You would make a great lifestyle blogger," I say, suppressing a smile. "I mean, if you really focused on curation, you could have a superpopular Pinterest board."

She flops back onto the bed. "Please stop talking."

"Well then."

"Blow it out your butt."

"Okay."

After a minute she sits up and recrosses her legs. "I'll be the Ping-Pong champion of the galaxy. And you will be my noble steed."

"Uh-huh."

"We will travel from planet to planet, spreading a Ping-Pong message of peace. I'll feed you on Thursdays."

"Good night, Jules."

Lying in my childhood bed, I can't help thinking about the way this house used to be, when Jules and I were nothing more than rowdy kids and Mom and Dad were nothing less than heroes: breathing, singing, hugging grown-ups, not yet a set of cooling memories, reasons to go to church or visit a lawyer. I want to go back to then, I want to go back to them, I want so much to go back and not take it for granted. Not guilt-trip Mom into buying me Jordans, not slam my bedroom door on Dad when he was trying to give me a pep talk after a bad game, but just bask, bask, bask in all that warmth.

My nose wrinkles up and my eyes fill with tears. This goes on for a while until I sit up and find my phone and my earbuds and cue up a Mandarin news podcast from the VOA bureau in Beijing. Feuding political factions. Villages where everyone has cancer. Import tariffs on solar panels. The world's workshop, pollution and population, propaganda and pandas—the newscasters speak Mandarin impossibly rapidly. I understand about half of it, as usual, and as usual, it lulls me to sleep within a few minutes.

4

Double move, spin move, fake spin, head fake, pump fake, ball fake, figure eight, spider dribbling, two-ball dribbling. Jump stop, up-and-under, big twenty. Pull-up, step-back, finger roll. *Bounce bounce squeak squeak swish.* I narrow my mind to the moment, see only the court, feel only the rhythm of the ball and the footwork. "*Bǎwòzhù dāngxià shì zuì zhòngyào de*—The present comes first," Dad preached.

Some of my earliest memories are of watching Kobe Bryant on TV at the height of his Lakers career. The Black Mamba—he was a single-minded winning machine, a grand master of his craft. Then there was CP3, Melo, Flash, King James, the Durantula, now Steph Curry—the Baby-Faced Assassin. I'd be shooting at the hoop in the street after each game that I watched, dribbling in my bedroom after dinner until Jules made Dad make me stop so she could "read in peace."

Basketball became my true home, the language I spoke more fluently than Chinese or English, the realm I navigated better than anyone else because I knew the timing of each streetlight and pothole. On the court, the rules were simple and explicit, as opposed to everywhere else, where no amount of effort could help me make a girl smile or discern which British boy band was lit. So I studied the game like a fiend, honing my body and my mind until I could sense ten men on the court with my eyes closed, assess infinite unfolding possibilities as a reflex, and by instinct choose the action best suited to my strengths, my limitations, my squeaky sneakers and medium-small half-Asian hands.

And that's why I'm here now, hiding in the place I'm most comfortable, rehearsing a role that I was last asked to play during high school. I doubt the SDSU coaches have even noticed that I haven't been at practice in a week.

I plant the rock at the foul line and hit the medicine ball, kettle bells, and jump rope. I stay focused throughout my strength and plyometric routines, but when I'm running the steps, I allow thoughts to enter my head and distract me from the burn in my quads, calves, hamstrings. "*Yǒuxiē shì nǐ wúfǎ gǎibiàn*—There are some things you cannot change," Dad used to say. "But you can decide to not think about them. You can control your own mind."

Those nights when I came in from shooting in the street, he would make me sit against the wall for as long as I could, my knees bent to a ninety-degree angle. Jules called it Chinese Wall Torture. "*Bié qù xiǎng nǐ de tuǐ téngbùténg*—Don't go thinking about whether your legs hurt," he would say, his hands clasped behind his back like a general reviewing his troops. "*Jīntiān nǐ wǔfàn chīle diǎn shénme ne?* What did you eat for lunch today? Would Kobe Bryant give up so easy? Huh? What are you going to buy your sister for her birthday? Answer me."

After I collapsed onto the floor, rubbing my thighs and sucking in air through my clenched teeth, he'd look at his watch and say, "Almost nine minutes, not bad," with an insouciant raise of his thick eyebrows, and I would run at him, tackle him, swing little fists at him, and cry, "*Shénme búcuò? Kàn nǐ néngbùnéng zuò jiǔ fēnzhōng!*—Who's not bad? Let's see if you can do nine minutes!"

Andre is sitting on the bench when I return to the court, and he rebounds for me as I hit my foul shots. He's shown up every morning since Dad died, toward the end of my workout, to run me through some shooting drills and drive us to breakfast burritos. Even though I didn't stay at the Quad last night, he knew he could find me here around this time.

"You been driving, outlaw?" he asks.

I shake my head no, nod toward the stands, where Jules is lying on her back on the top row, holding a book above her face, a sweatshirt tucked under her head. Andre sticks his pinkies in his gums and gives her a shrill coach's whistle.

She looks down at us, waves a hand, starts down the steps.

"Is she smoking a cigarette?"

"That appears to be the case."

"She pick that up from that dancer dude?"

"Performance artist." I rattle in my last shot. Ten out of ten. "He's done, though."

"Jules nine," he snickers. "Art boys zero."

I stagger over to the bench, sit down by my gym bag, and mop sweat from my forehead with a towel. The nausea blooming in my stomach lets me know I pushed myself close to my limit. Almost hard enough to pass out and attain oblivion. Almost.

Andre's in front of me, idly balancing the ball on the back of his hand.

"What would you say to coming to practice today? Might feel good to get back on the grind."

"I dunno, Dre. I haven't been there in a week."

"Every streak must end. Plus Coach says you can play tomorrow if you practice today."

"Huh. Okay."

Andre puts his hands on his hips. "Okay like 'Okay, I'll be there'?"

"Yeah."

Jules flounces up with a big grin on her face, but it's not hard to tell that she's been crying.

"Hi, Dre." Her eyes scan the rafters. "Hi, Dre. Hydrate. Victor, you should hydrate."

"Officer on deck," Andre announces, and they salute each other, a ritual of origins long forgotten.

I finish changing my shoes, straighten up. "Jules, I need to show you something at the Quad."

"Have you ever watched this guy train?" she asks Andre, ignoring me. "It's like the montage from *Rocky IV*."

"Yeah, sure," says Andre, "but which half of the montage? Rocky or the Russian?"

"Well, he's methodical like Drago, but he's short like Stallone."

"Thank you. Here, you can carry this." I roll the medicine ball into her twiggy arms.

When we arrive back at our triple in the Quad, the door to Eli's bedroom is closed, and some kind of awful butt-rock is emanating from it.

"*Uch,*" Jules says, flopping onto the couch. I go to my room and retrieve the case from under my bed. When I come back to the common room, Andre is arranging hummus, pita chips, and cans of coconut water on the coffee table.

"And voilà. Snack is served." He bows like a maître d', one forearm behind his back.

"I mean, OMG." Jules touches the palms of her hands together. "Do the little coeds who make it this far just pee themselves in delight?"

Andre makes a thoughtful face. "There was one girl who did that."

I hang back for a moment, watching them munch and joke around, satisfying their animal needs for companionship and nourishment. Jules has known Andre so long that she can be her weird self around him and put Dad out of her mind for a while without feeling guilty. Andre slept over most Saturday nights of our childhood, years in which the three of us were fixtures in the breakfast nook, passing the cereal and watching SNL sketches on Jules's laptop. Stuff like that doesn't happen anymore now that we're allegedly adults, and it strikes me how death has brought my only version of family together for this moment.

Perhaps Dad would be touched.

"Jules, Perry Peng gave me the key to Dad's locker at this massage place in Temple City. I found this briefcase there."

I put the case on the table, pop the latches, and open it up. "He said Dad wanted me to have this stuff, but he didn't say why."

It takes a second for Jules to register the contents of the case, to identify these objects so incongruous with our environment and our lives. A look of total dismay spreads across her face, and she brings a hand up to her mouth. She lifts the PPQ out of the box with her thumb and forefinger like it's a bag of dogshit and places it on the table. Then she flips open the passport.

"What is this?" She looks at me beseechingly. "Victor, what the fuck is this stuff?"

I shrug, helpless. "I don't know. There wasn't a note or anything."

She sets the passport down and sits still for a minute with her hand back over her mouth. She breathes deeply, her other hand on top of her head, and we watch her think.

"Those cops who took our statements—we should tell them," she says.

"But this passport is some kind of fake. What if that gets Dad in trouble?" I say.

"Gets Dad in trouble?" Jules's eyes flash. "Victor?"

"I mean, I don't know, the insurance policy? Jesus, I have no fucking idea, Jules!"

She stares at me for a quiet second, then looks down, and I know that my voice was too loud, my rage is showing.

"Neither do I," she says to her lap.

We sit there for a long moment, and silence settles over us like a quilt, our minds roving over memories and questions as our eyes rove over the dorm carpet. A little piece of me feels good that it's the same for everyone—we're all lost here together—but the rest of me is unaware of anything except the pain bubble and the bottomless pit, the one Dad will never come back from. Then the music unmuffles as Eli's door swings open and he walks out of it, unshaven, in sweats and a Bluetooth headset.

"Whoa, hey," he says, and disappears back into his room. The butt-rock stops and then he returns. "Hey Jules. I'm really sorry about your dad." He comes around behind me and starts massaging my shoulders. "You two hanging in there okay?"

"I guess so," says Jules.

My eyelids flit closed.

Eli circles back around the couch and scoops up some hummus with a pita chip. "Are you playing against Lafayette tomorrow?" he asks me.

"I think so."

"Because, if you recall, some time ago we were talking about having people over tomorrow night. But it's totally cool if you don't want to." Eli shifts from foot to foot. "I mean in light of the circumstances. I would one hundred percent understand."

"A jock party, how droll!" Jules exclaims, dabbing her eyes with a tissue. The devil-may-care mask returns to her face as she bundles away her grief and confusion. "Can I come? I could do with some binge-drinking."

"For sure you can come," Eli says. "If it's cool with Victor for us to do it."

"And if you come to the game," Andre adds.

"No offense to your lifelong passion or anything?" Jules lights up at the opportunity to express an opinion. "But I'm not superkeen on group glorifications of mock combat, with all the grunting and charging and shrieking bimbos. It just makes me think of Rome. Did you know humans are the only species that celebrates violence? There's no fighting for sport in nature."

"There are gang rapes, though," Eli points out. "Penguins gang-rape each other all the time."

"Pardon me?" Jules pauses with a pita chip halfway to her mouth.

"I saw it on the BBC. They do it to the guy penguins, too."

"Okay. *Anyway,*" Andre cuts in, "we're not having any penguins or gang rapes at this residence unless it's cool with Victor."

Three faces turn to me. *Who gives a fuck,* I want to say, but instead I say, "It's fine." I put the money, gun, and passport back in the case and close it. "I'm gonna take a walk."

Even February is flip-flop weather in San Dimas, but the pleasant sunshine feels wrong on my skin, an insult to the icy numbness within. I pop in my earbuds, head out of the Quad, stroll the tree-lined streets of the campus. The carefree people around me are flirting over iced coffees, tossing Frisbees, making plans for weekend nights filled with racy possibilities, while anguish nags at me like a strobe light in my peripheral vision, a clawing in my stomach that just wants to grow and grow. How long until it goes away? When will the latest little good news outweigh the big old bad news? When that day comes, Dad's death will be no less upsetting. Just less vivid. I'll just have moved on. I'll be an ordinary guy who used to live in a personal hell but now feels pretty normal. Seems bogus.

"It's only life," I mutter to myself. Only life stretched ahead of me: graduation, some job, some girl, some kids. True love? My father was stabbed to death. Mom and Dad would have loved grandkids. Would I love kids? Until two weeks ago I was only interested in the rest of the basketball season. That mock combat that Jules was ranting about gives me purpose when I get up in the morning. The apparent thinness of my life makes room for a fat sense of despair, but I can vanquish it with a shrug. Would it be better to love more things? More things to love, more things to lose.

As I make my way back to the Quad, my mind makes its way to the aluminum case stashed under my bed. I try to comfort myself with Andre's assessment: I can't act without more information. There's nothing to do, and I'm hungry. I want lunch. Maybe this is what happens. Maybe someone kills your dad, and the pain throbs and throbs, and then you eat a hamburger. But the black fury inside me pushes back, sets my teeth against each other, and I squeeze crescent marks into the calluses of my palms with my fingernails.

The San Dimas air is dry, clean, and citrusy, and above my head some tardy swifts wing south in a V. On the sidewalk by the door to the Quad there is a tall, barrel-chested man wearing an Angels cap, a Hawaiian shirt, and khakis. As I walk up, he flicks away a cigarette and sticks out his right hand. With his left hand he flashes a badge.

"Victor Li? My name is Richard Lang. Detective Lang. San Dimas Sheriff's Office. Can I ask you a few questions?"

5

As we stroll around the Quad, Lang asks me mostly the questions you'd expect: where I was on the night of the crime, had I noticed anything unusual at the house, and so on. He seems pretty relaxed about interviewing me about Dad getting killed.

"So you have a sister, Juliana, right, who's twenty-five. And your mother—?"

"Died of stomach cancer. Nine years ago." I helpfully finish his sentence.

"Right." Lang shifts uneasily, and I see him inhaling my pathetic parentlessness before he regains his track.

"So, Victor, I want you to give this question a minute before you answer. Think about the times you saw your father in the recent past. Did he say or do anything that seemed strange?"

The PPQ, the passport, the money flash into my mind. *That's not what he asked about,* I tell myself, but nonetheless I feel a hot tingle at my hairline, an incipient dampness in my armpits.

"Not that I can think of," I say.

"Was there any change in his routines? Such as, did he start any new projects, for example, or make any new friends?"

That jogs my memory a bit—I tell Lang that Dad had recently been spending a lot of time writing on yellow legal pads. Whenever we asked him what he was up to, he claimed he was writing stories.

"And did you ever read any of the stories he was writing?"

"I can't read handwritten Chinese. He said he'd type them up and I could read them when he was finished."

"Do you know where these legal pads are now?"

"I would guess in his office somewhere."

My nervousness turns into curiosity as I watch him write in his little notebook with a golf pencil. His movements are slow and deliberate, and the pencil seems too small for his wide, fleshy hands. "LEGAL PADS," he writes in big capital letters, and then underlines them.

I find myself wondering how many homicides he has solved during his tenure at the San Dimas Sheriff's Office.

Lang flips the notebook closed. "Look, I know you and your sister are going through a lot right now, and I don't want to disturb you by sniffing around your house. Plus my Chinese is not the best. So if you could take a look around his office for those legal pads . . ."

"Sure. Look, Detective?" I stop walking and turn to face him. "I already gave a statement last week. What's going on?"

Lang looks at me carefully, like he's deciding how much he should tell me. "In your statement, you said that your father didn't go to your basketball game that night because he was expecting a business call from China. We know now that there was no call to your house from China or anywhere, answered or not. At least not that night. But there were a couple of calls to and from China in the days leading up to his murder."

Murder. This cheerful guy in a Hawaiian shirt and Angel's cap is filling me in on the details of Dad's murder as college students walk through the dappled shade of eucalyptus trees, across the manicured grass from one faceless sandstone building to another, texting as they make their way to their next class.

And then, over Lang's shoulder, I catch a glimpse of a slight Asian guy in a Lakers cap. Black T-shirt, black jeans, black backpack. The guy who was watching me from the shaved ice shop by Chateau Happiness. Or was he? Probably just some guy in black walking through a college campus, I tell myself.

"Maybe he was supposed to make the call, but the burglar showed up first," I say.

"Right. Maybe. But here's the thing; this kind of case where a burglar kills someone, it doesn't *never* happen, but it's uncommon. A smart burglar quickly realizes that someone is home and gets out of there. Someone's home?"—Lang slides his hand through the air demonstratively—"See ya later. Now, a confrontation occurs when you have a dumb perp who doesn't know what he's doing and maybe a young, aggressive homeowner with some kind of weapon, which is not exactly who Vincent Li was, but the point is this. These dumb burglars who get in fights and maybe commit assault or homicide? We find them. They're sloppy. They leave blood, prints, clothing fibers. They're desperate individuals, head cases, nut jobs, junkies. Or whatever. You get me?"

"I think so."

"Anyway, whoever killed your father was *definitely* not a dumb burglar. The house is clean. No fingerprints, no footprints, no clothing fibers, no skin under your father's nails. And he kills him with two precise stabs in the chest and a clean slash across—well, anyway, he does it neatly, so the victim didn't, ah, you know, spend a long time bleeding to death."

It's like there's a permanent wince on Lang's face just from looking at me. He tucks the notebook into the breast pocket of his Hawaiian shirt, pulls off his Angels cap, and scratches his bald spot.

"Look, sorry. I didn't need to say that. What I mean is, also, there's a thousand-dollar watch on your dad's wrist, and our perp doesn't touch it. And he kills your father in his office, which was probably not blocking his exit from the house. So what I'm saying here is that the forensics guys, they're saying that this criminal's behavior doesn't resemble that of either a smart burglar or a dumb burglar."

"The San Dimas Sheriff's Office has forensics guys?"

Lang sighs. "Not exactly. They're on loan from the Orange County Crime Lab through this interagency collaboration program. I wish I could say it's going well, but they don't really share our priorities."

"Is that why we weren't allowed back into our house for four days? Because you couldn't get these guys out to San Dimas?"

"Victor, I'm not gonna bullshit you. These interagency collaborations, they're not all roses all the time. But now they've assigned us a team, and I think they're gonna start acting more serious about it because they're telling us that possibly, possibly, we're talking about an experienced killer."

I stare at him, unblinking, unsteady, my hands clenched into fists. "So do you have any leads?"

The wince deepens. Lang puts a big paw on my shoulder. "Look, son, I understand how you feel. Trust me, there's an ongoing investigation here. But for now, you've gotta sit tight and do your own thing, get back to a normal routine as soon as possible. Okay? And, legal pads, right? Here's my card. You can call me on my mobile. We'll talk soon."

I start to speak again, but then clamp my jaw shut as something inside me says don't—don't tell him about the gun. *Sit tight and do your own thing.* So I just bow my head, take the business card from his outstretched hand, and thank him for his time.

"Hey, no problem," Detective Lang says. He claps me on the shoulder again and ambles off toward visitor parking.

6

The whistle blows. "Run it again."

"Utah! Utah!" Howie calls the play at half court, then brushes Andre shoulder to shoulder on the screen, then hits him with a pocket pass as he rolls to the rim. Andre throws it down with a little extra swag, swinging his legs and slapping the backboard, because practice is almost over.

I'm standing on the sideline with the rest of the reserves, replaying my conversation with Lang in my head. *Possibly, possibly, we're talking about an experienced killer.* The timer on the clock hits zero and the buzzer sounds.

I stand in the shower with my forehead against the tiles, letting the water cascade off my shoulders and down my body, flicking the handle back and forth between almost too hot and way too cold. I want to take a breath without feeling pain, to claw free of the thick envelope of my shock, to hear a piercing, clear voice in my mind that tells me what to do. But I don't know how to mourn. After Mom died, Dad never cried. He never talked about her. He took us out to fancy restaurants on her birthday and told us that she would want us to enjoy what we still had rather than dwell on what we'd lost.

But now I'm not sure what I still have. I don't have the willpower to help myself, to help my sister, to win basketball games. I want to find those yellow legal pads because they're a thread that I can follow back into the past. I'm not interested in the future. I want to wrap my mouth around that Walther PPQ and wake up in an alternate universe, or not wake up at all.

But I know that Dad left it for me for another reason, and if I can manage to want anything at all, I want to know what that reason is.

I'm getting dressed when our head coach, Francis Vaughn, wanders into the vicinity of my locker, looking at the ground, a sheet of paper in his hands. He scrunches up his face and rubs his temple with his forefinger.

"Hey. Victor. The coaches and I, we're glad to have you back," he says. "I was really sorry to hear about your dad. He was a terrific guy."

"Thanks, Coach," I say, silently praying for him not to attempt to console me.

"And we all know we can count on you to give every last bit of effort."

I can tell there's more coming, so I just look at him. He hands me the sheet of paper.

"This is our scouting report on Jason Maxwell. You're going to put in some minutes on him tomorrow night. He's a tough cover, likes to attack the basket. I don't want you to try to beat him with your strength. You're gonna have to be crafty, feel his rhythm and disrupt it. You can't be a cannonball at all times. Sometimes you need to be a jellyfish. Or whatever. Are you getting me, son?"

A shimmer of resentment tightens my jaw. So he doesn't know I've already read the notes on Maxwell half a dozen times—that for four years I've been getting the scouting reports for every player on every team we play from the assistant coaches.

"Oh, and Victor? One last thing."

"Yes, Coach?"

"Take it easy on the sauce, okay, son?" He's squinting at me like Lang did—like he's talking to a recent amputee. "I mean, you're a senior, you can do what you want. But don't be too proud to hand over those keys."

I grit my teeth, close my eyes for a second, compose myself. "Like I told you, Coach, it won't happen again. I don't have my license back yet, anyway."

"Great, Victor. I have complete faith in you."

"Thank you, Coach."

"See ya tomorrow."

Andre's talking through the game plan for tomorrow as we walk across the vast parking lot outside the arena, and I'm in my head, asking myself where I would be if I were a yellow legal pad. The wide sky is still lit blue by the remnants of the day's sun, and after the humidity and closeness of the locker room, the cooling air feels exquisite on my soap-cleaned skin.

I'm climbing into Andre's truck when I catch a glimpse of purple and gold floating past the end of the row of cars.

Muttering obscenities to myself, I shut Andre's door and crouch-run as quietly as I can to the last row of the parking lot. When I get to the end, I poke my head out, and there he is: the guy in black clothes and a Lakers cap, walking right toward me, his thumbs tucked into the straps of his black backpack.

I take a deep breath, set my jaw, and step out in front of him. I don't say anything. I just block his way and show him with my expression that he's not going anywhere before he explains himself.

The guy comes to a stop with a surprised smile on his face. "*Ò! Nǐ shì Lǐ Xiàozhōu, duì ba?*—Oh! You are Li Xiaozhou, right? I am Sun Jianshui." He starts to bow, then changes his mind and sticks out his hand.

My hands remain at my sides, clenched into fists. "How do you know my name?" I ask the man in Mandarin.

He looks at his hand, shrugs, and sticks it into his pocket. "I worked for your father, Li Renyan. I just arrived from China."

Andre jogs up and comes to a stop beside me. "What's going on? Who is this guy?"

"What do you know about my father? Why have you been watching me?"

The man's eyes dance rapidly back and forth between me and Andre. Then he looks away and puts a hand on the side of his head. "I am here to help you. But maybe it's better if we can talk somewhere else," he suggests.

"Help me with what?" I ask in Mandarin.

"Help you with your father's work."

"Victor, who is this person?"

I translate for Andre, tell him I have no idea what to do with this guy, and we confer in whispered English as Sun Jianshui grows increasingly agitated. Finally, he fishes under his collar with both hands and pulls out a thin leather cord.

"He tell me, I can give you a look at this," he blurts out in English.

On the cord there's an iron monkey figurine. Just like the one that was on the cord with the Chateau Happiness keycard. Andre and I look at each other.

"You speak English?" Andre says, loud and slow.

The guy bobs his head. "English."

"Cool. I am Andre." He puts one huge hand on his chest and sticks out the other for Sun Jianshui to shake. "You eat tacos?"

7

Once we're at RoboTaco, Sun insists on treating us with a crisp hundred-dollar bill. He's a lean, watchful type with flat cheekbones and no depth at all to his eye sockets. I guess he's in his late twenties, maybe early thirties. We let people cut in front of us while he spends a minute holding the laminated menu about six inches from his face.

"Maybe it better you do for me," he eventually concludes, handing the menu back to Andre.

Once we're situated at a booth in the corner, I ask Sun Jianshui why he's been following me.

"Following you?" Sun says.

"I saw you yesterday at the shaved ice shop by Chateau Happiness. And again today, on campus, when I was talking to that cop."

Sun looks down at the table and smiles. "Old Li talk about you sometimes. He say you love to play basketball, that you clever and you have good eyes, like me. You see, we work close together. His enemies are my enemies. So I must behave very careful. I wait until

I can find you alone. Sorry"—he nods to Andre—"but since Old Li die, I am like"—he wrinkles his nose, searching for the word—"*jiànbudào de*."

"Invisible," I say. "Are you saying that you know who killed my father?"

Over the course of the next hour, Sun tells us his story in the janky English he says Dad taught him: hard to follow at times but pretty impressive for someone who claims to have just arrived in the English-speaking world for the first time in his life. He tells us that he worked for Dad—"Old Li"—as his personal assistant and general gofer. That Dad and three other men formed a brotherhood in Beijing more than thirty years ago, and that the brothers did a lot more than run restaurants.

"Mr. Ai, Mr. Ouyang, Mr. Zhao, and Old Li," he recites their names. They were teenagers when they met, basically street kids. In thc uncertain years following Mao's demise, they carved out a niche in the gray market, wrangling permits for street stalls and running discreet errands for officials. Then, when China opened up in the 1980s, the brothers scored big by bringing Western goods in through Hong Kong. Microwaves, handbags, cordless phones—China's nouveau riche scrambled to pay inflated prices for the limited supply.

"Are you saying they were smugglers?" Andre asks.

Sun looks at me.

"*Zǒusī*—smuggling," I translate.

"Ah, smug-ling?" Sun tilts his head to the side as he considers. "Yes. It is smuggling. But it is not, you know, pirate ship, middle of night, dadadadada"—pantomiming a tommy gun. "More look like normal ship, but pay bribe, cash money, easy time through the, uh, *hǎiguān*."

"Customs."

"Customs, yes. And in the end, customer is government official. So." He sticks his palms out like the scales of justice, weighing them up and down as if to say, *Who am I to judge?* He's a good storyteller despite the language barrier, so affable and unassuming that it's easy for me to nod along, even as my skin goes clammy, my heart sinks into my stomach, and I realize that Lang's forensics guys must have been right.

When Dad started a family and decided to move to the United States, Sun tells us, his so-called brothers agreed to use the company to help him set up a restaurant business here. But not all of them were willing to let him make a clean break.

"China-America trade is number one big business," Sun explains between tidy bites of the *al pastor* special. "Big big cake. For some of Old Li's partners, whatever is not enough, they always wanting more. Two men, Mr. Ouyang and also Mr. Zhao"—he shakes his head, makes a disgusted face—"they are, you know, greedy, *kě'è*?" He looks at me.

"*Kě'è?* Despicable. De-spic-able."

Sun nods gamely. "De-spic-able, yes. They think, why not eat some more cake? Mr. Ouyang and Mr. Zhao, they try to use Old Li to get into some American markets. Sometime Old Li say yes, and sometime he say no. And there is Mr. Ai, too, he take Old Li's side in Beijing, argue for them to leave Old Li alone. Many years go like this, more and more fighting between the brothers, but not open fighting. Then Mr. Ouyang and Mr. Zhao have an idea to bring something dangerous to sell in the United States. Something they are calling 'Ice,' but I do not know exactly what is 'Ice.'

"Old Li decide that Ice is very bad idea, terrible," Sun says, scowling. "Mr. Ai and Old Li, they oppose Ice together, but Mr. Ouyang and Mr. Zhao insist. Now the fight is open. Old Li start to worry, what if his position is in danger? So he make a preparation."

"So these men, Ouyang and Zhao, my father's business partners, they—" I can't speak the words aloud to finish the sentence.

Sun nods intently, says this is probably what happened, but he doesn't know for sure. Maybe they conspired to kill Dad, or maybe one of them acted alone. Either way, it's a tragedy, he says. They used to be the closest of friends. He looks at me, and his eyes show pain and sincerity. He switches to a formal Chinese.

"*Lǐ Xiǎozhōu, nǐ fùqīn bù yīnggāi yǐ zhèzhǒng fāngshì líshì*—Your father should not have died like this, Li Xiaozhou."

His words sound muddled, reaching me through a thick buffer, finding me somewhere deep beneath the surface of consciousness. My palms are slick, and more sweat beads out of my underarms and the back of my neck. I look away from Sun, look around the restaurant, look down at the Guisados Sampler that remains untouched on the plate in front of me.

"Hey, Victor, hey." Andre slides a plastic cup toward me. "Wanna drink some water?"

I shake my head, blink a few times. "And what about you?" I ask Sun, trying to speak in a normal voice. "Who are you exactly? How long have you been working for my father?"

"Basically, long as I remember. I live on the streets when your father hire me. After that, I live in his office. You see, a kid can be useful for, ah, 'smuggling'? Sending messages, delivering packages. And also, the kid is a mask, everybody trust man with a kid. Then, when I grow up, Old Li find other ways for me to help him."

A slight smile drifts across Sun's face. "Old Li, you know, he had a warm heart. He see me like his family, the only family I have."

I want to say, so what does that make us? Sun's story is beyond the realm of anything I'd considered, even after finding the gun. And yet I somehow sense that every word of it is true because his gestures, his mannerisms, even his halting English—it all reminds me of Dad.

"If you knew him so well," I ask him, "then what kind of pets does he have?"

"Easy," says Sun. "Old Li always love tropical fish."

I manage to say, "Can you guys give me a minute?"

Outside I breathe in heaves, one hand against the brick wall of the building. I feel people coming in and out of the restaurant, glancing at me and quickly looking away. I wish we had a real winter right now, with some frigid weather that would cool the bonfire in my brain, but it's still balmy, and the last traces of daylight silhouette the low, wide campus buildings on the western horizon.

A day ago I lived in a different reality, one in which Dad got killed by being in the wrong place at the wrong time, but now I've learned that he knew what was coming. That he practically allowed his own murder without informing me, that he had a whole life he never told me about. How could I be so clueless? My father, my sole parent for so long, the person who taught me more than anyone—he had hidden so much about himself. And Sun—who was this mild-mannered shadow who appeared out of nowhere? Who'd known Dad longer than I've been alive? How come he knows all about me, and I've never heard a word about him?

My stomach lurches; I taste bile in my mouth. The pain is crushing up into my lungs, spreading through my veins, coiling around my spine. But I know that inside of it, between my heart and my stomach, is this stone about the size of an egg but denser, harder, smoother. "*Nǐ hàipà de shíkè, nǐ bù zhīdào zěnme jìxù de shíkè, zhuāzhù zhè ge shítóu*—When you doubt yourself, when you don't know how to go on, grab hold of that stone," Dad said to me, holding a quivering fist between our faces, and so I always have, when my lungs are burning, when my body begs me to stop. And now again, as I scrape my knuckles back and forth against the coarse brick wall just to feel something, the stone is my anchor in the storm. It steadies my breath, quiets my mind until there is space between my thoughts, enough space for my sight to swivel inward: Do I have more? Do I have enough? The answer is always yes. The stone reminds me of who I am. And who made me this way.

8

"What are you doing in here?"

Jules pokes her head through the French doors into Dad's office. I'm kneeling over a filing cabinet, flicking through health insurance handbooks, car maintenance records, tax returns.

"Oh, hey," I say. "There you are."

I tell her about Detective Lang and the yellow legal pads, leaving out the part about smart burglars and dumb burglars.

"I told him I'd look around the office." A second later, she's still standing there, so I say, "You wanna help?"

She gives a little shrug. "Sure."

"I haven't searched any of those shelves."

Jules stands in front of the bookshelves for a while. "I hate being in here," she says.

"I'm not trying to think about it."

"Yeah. Aren't you smart." She starts pulling books off the shelf. "He's got some weird stuff here. A Chinese-English edition of *Les Misérables*. Who knew *that* existed?"

"Uh-huh." I tap the flashlight app on my phone, hold it in my mouth, and crawl between the cabinet and the bookshelf.

"Oh no. I found the dedicated shelf of shithead books. *The 7 Habits of Highly Effective People. The 48 Laws of Power.* Oh my God, *The Fountainhead.* Really, Dad?"

I crawl backward into the middle of the room and take the phone out of my mouth, wipe it on my shirt. "I liked *The Fountainhead,*" I say.

Jules makes a pukey face.

"That's because you're still unreconstructed, Victor."

I'm in his desk now, a huge, handsome chunk of blond wood with big deep drawers and a hutch that rises almost to the ceiling. Printer paper, binder clips, Japanese gel pens, little boxes of staples, everything in its right place. Dad was quite the neat freak. I find a yellow sticky note attached to the floor of one of his drawers: "The test of a first-rate intelligence is the ability to hold two opposed ideas in mind at the same time and still retain the ability to function."

I pass it to Jules. "Look at this."

"Hey! I sent that to him. F. Scott Fitzgerald. It was a couple of years ago, some snotty email I wrote him about wanting to go to design school. I was still at that branding company, playing grown-up and walking around in smart shoes all the time, but I really hated feeling like a corporate pawn. He was trying to persuade me to do an MBA program. I think he thought I'd meet a husband there." A snort of indignation. Jules and Dad got along better after she left home for college—as long as the subject of conversation wasn't her life decisions.

"Anyway, he was saying, why do you want to make expensive clothes when you despise the people who buy them? He didn't understand that it was about the creative challenge for me, wringing beauty out of materials like sheep fur and cowhide. So I sent him that quote."

A gloom falls over Jules as she stares at the little yellow square covered in Dad's meticulous handwriting. Of course he'd given in eventually. Of course she'd written a brilliant application essay and earned admission to a selective design program in San Francisco. Of course he'd agreed to fork over tuition and living expenses for Daddy's motherless little princess.

"I didn't realize he was taking notes," she says.

A few minutes pass in silence as I picture Dad, middle-aged and finally going gray, squinting at his monitor and recording Jules's self-justifications onto a sticky note with one of his fine-tip Japanese gel pens. Then I see him thirty years younger, at the helm of a yacht, sneaking Marlboro Lights into Shanghai, or Ningbo, or wherever.

"Do you feel like you knew him really well?" I ask her.

She rolls the question around in her head. "We didn't have a magical bond like how he would watch you play basketball and give you motivational speeches for like a zillion hours a day. Sometimes I got tired of watching the Dad Show. He had this old-fashioned idea of how he wanted everything to be, and that idea could be very inflexible."

"Uh-huh." All gripes I'd heard a thousand times before.

"But he was a fun guy, and he had a big heart. He was a pretty great dad in a lot of ways." Her voice tightens up at the end.

I close the last desk drawer. "I don't think those yellow legal pads are in here."

"I guess not."

"Jules, what if you had a chance to speak with him before he died, and he asked you to do something sketchy for him. Would you do it?"

"Does this have something to do with that gun?"

"Just tell me. What would you do for him?"

After a moment, Jules says, "I would consider his request very thoroughly. We had our share of disagreements, but I loved him a lot, and of course I'm not ungrateful for all that he did for us."

She searches my face, then cuts her eyes back to her cuticles. "Anyway, I don't have anything else to do. He was right: I don't give two fucks about fashion design."

That's an awful lot of candor from Juliana, who is ordinarily too busy critiquing everyone else to admit that she herself has never fully committed to anybody or anything. I've been dreading her reaction to Sun's story, but I also know that keeping it from her isn't an option. So I tell her everything he told me: the four brothers, the company in China, the bridge Dad wouldn't cross, and the price he paid. We sit there, on the floor of the room where he was stabbed to death, and I tell her that maybe it wasn't some strung-out burglar who did the stabbing. Maybe it was his oldest friends—people he chose never to tell us about.

We sit there quietly for a while and she looks at the floor, letting her hair shield her face from me as her shoulders tremble, until finally she tosses her head back and squints at me with wet eyes.

"Do you think we can trust this person?" she asks.

"I don't know. I mean he evidently knew Dad well. If there were any resemblance, you'd think he's our half brother. But he's not family. He's Dad's employee. And he shows up with all this information we don't have, all these instructions for us—"

For a second I'm lost in thought, trying to picture Dad's other life in China, another boy tagging along at his heels, soaking up his attention. Helping him commit crimes. And my ribs ache as I try to reconcile the love with the lies.

"Victor?"

"Yeah, sorry. You'll have to meet him and see for yourself. Anyway, he has another iron monkey like the one Dad left me."

"But you got that monkey thing from the lawyer, right? What if it weren't really from Dad?"

"Well, shit, Jules. I don't have all the answers."

We sit there in silence for a minute. Then Jules says, "So what does he want us to do?"

I tell her the plan.

There are still trophies on a shelf in my old bedroom, dusty trophies from grade school that commemorate my participation in various basketball teams and camps. Most of them are the kind of meaningless trophies that everyone gets—Victor was on the team! There's even a "Most Improved Player" trophy, that dubious award handed out by coaches to the untalented gym rats who stay after practice to practice more. Because they've got nothing better to do.

I hurled that cheap piece of gold-painted plastic into the garbage can in the kitchen after my disappointing sophomore season in high school. It wasn't until my senior year, when I was making space for the only trophy I ever cared about—All-Conference Third Team—that I discovered that Dad had fished it out of the trash, sneaked into my room, and tucked it onto the shelf in the back.

Jules used to have trophies, too. Debate Team, Model United Nations, and, of course, her big one for winning state in tennis. She also had a cello, a guitar, and a saxophone, each of which she'd stopped playing after a few years despite showing what her teachers tended to call "unusual promise." But during her senior year of high school, she donated her instruments to charity and threw her trophies away, along with most of her clothes and everything on her walls. And to replace them, she used a thick black Sharpie to scrawl on her wall in block letters: NO DOCUMENT OF CIVILIZATION IS NOT ALSO A DOCUMENT OF BARBARISM.

Two weeks later, she painted over the quotation. She threw out her bed, put her mattress on the floor, and painted every surface white. The only remaining decoration in her bedroom was an old photograph of Mom tacked to the inside of her closet door.

I have a picture on my wall from the same roll of film, Mom and Dad together on the Great Wall at Mutianyu, toothy grins on their faces, their hair flying around in the breeze, their arms wrapped around each other. I'm staring at this photo at one in the morning, unable or unwilling to fall asleep, asking my dead parents what they want me to do. Mom, with her religion, and Dad, with his conviction, each had their ways of making the world simple: every decision a choice between right and wrong. But now their smiling faces are mysterious to me.

I heave a sigh, locate my headphones, and flick off the light. All Sun wants for now is for Jules and me to have lunch at the original Happy Year restaurant and see if anything's out of the ordinary. Jules agreed with me that we have no good reason to refuse to do that. Perhaps now is not the time to search for answers. Perhaps now is the time to sleep.

I crawl into bed, cue up another Mandarin news podcast, and sink into my plush down pillow. I turn up the volume, drown out my imaginations of masked men prowling through the downstairs hallway. Of what it feels like to get stabbed in the chest. "Today's main stories are: Hong Kong stocks decline after democracy protests turn violent. Premier Li Keqiang announces next phase of massive 'One Belt, One Road' infrastructure initiative. The Tibetan yak is upgraded from vulnerable to endangered by the International Union for the Conservation of Nature. Please stay tuned for detailed reports."

Before long, I'm lost in my dreams of the past.

Dad leapt up into the driver's seat of the Subaru and tossed two zippered bank bags—one red, one blue—into my lap. We were making the rounds of his restaurants, collecting cash to drop at the bank. It was a sunny August day in the San Gabriel Valley, pushing one hundred degrees, and the trees, the foothills, even the roads seemed thirsty. I was eleven years old, sitting up front next to Dad, tapping a rhythm against the seat with my heels.

"*Méiyǒu rén bú'ài chī zhōngcān*—Nobody doesn't love Chinese food," Dad said with a grin, rolling up his sleeves, revealing the wide, jagged scar on the back on his right wrist. When I asked him about the scar years before, he told me he had sliced himself on the edge of an aluminum takeout container at the first Happy Year restaurant back in Beijing.

But that's not really what the scar looked like.

"I'm a little tired of Chinese food." Jules was sitting in the back with Mom, devising a plan of attack for back-to-school shopping. A couple of years ago, she never would have sassed Dad like that, but now that she was fourteen, it seemed impossible for anybody to do anything that she didn't find annoying.

Dad gave me a wink and reassured Jules that he'd shortly drop us at the mall on his way to the Happy Year branch in Rosemead.

"I still don't see why we had to do all this other stuff first," Jules said.

Dad flicked on his blinker and cautiously merged the Subaru onto Foothill Freeway. He reminded Jules that the current plan meant less driving during rush hour, less gas wasted. And what's so bad about spending a few extra minutes in the car with her family? Maybe visiting Daddy's restaurants was a good reminder of where the money came from for her nice back-to-school clothes.

Jules didn't say anything. She stared out her window with an irked look on her face. She had grown to vocally scorn the sun, the mall, the palm trees; she seemed to despise everything in the San Gabriel Valley except the botanical gardens at the Huntington Library, where she probably longed to be on that August day, reading Salinger in the shade of a gazebo instead of driving around with us.

"Maybe after I pick you up from the mall, we can all go to Cold Stone," Dad said. "Does that sound fun to you, *jiějie*?"

Juliana sighed. She reminded Dad that she was not a little kid anymore and would not be bribed with sugar. Didn't he know that stuff could give you diabetes?

Dad laughed and said, "Okay, *jiějie,* whatever you say." I could see that his neck muscles had tightened up, and so had his grip on the steering wheel. His knuckles were mottled white like the scar tissue on his wrist. Before our last stop, he and I had been eagerly debating whether Shaq would really leave the Lakers. I wanted to return to that topic, but I could tell that Jules had spoiled his good mood.

"Now then, Juliana," Mom said. "I think it's fun being all together for a little while. Don't forget that Daddy works very hard at his restaurants most evenings."

Then she coughed a few times. She'd been coughing into little white handkerchiefs all week. *Something must be going around,* she kept saying, even though none of the rest of us had gotten sick.

"Ice cream sounds great to me, *bàba,*" I said.

That set Jules off. Maybe I had known that it would.

"Hey, Fido," she said, "when are you going to evolve from canine to human?"

"When are you going to start taking Prozac?" I retorted.

"Victor, that's *enough,*" Mom said firmly.

"Why do you always take her side?" I whined.

Dad slammed his hand down the steering wheel. "Don't talk back to your mother!" he shouted at me.

For a moment, the only sound in the Subaru was the steady blow of the full-blast air-conditioning. I pulled my knees up in front of me and hugged them. And then, very slowly, very quietly, I began to cry. I knew I was too big to cry, and I tried as hard as I could to fight back my tears, but I couldn't help it. The afternoon had been ruined, and there I was, crying in the car in front of my whole family, with no way to escape and nowhere to hide. I hunched my shoulders and tried to make myself as small and as quiet as possible.

Jules reached up and touched my arm, but I jerked away from her and turned my body to face the window.

"I'm sorry, *dìdi,*" she said. "I didn't mean it. Really."

Then Mom started coughing into her handkerchief again. Her coughs were as harsh and dry as the parched southern faces of the foothills that loomed above us. Except then they were no longer dry, they sounded wet.

And she said, "Oh, my goodness."

I heard Jules gasp.

9

The day after she found out she was terminal, the day after she came home from the clinic, went straight to the backyard without even looking at us, and lay on her back on the lawn for the whole afternoon, Mom taught me to cook my own breakfast. In the nine years since, I'd repeated the recipe with such consistency that Jules dubbed it "Eggs Victor." This morning—Saturday, Lafayette Game Day, eleven days after Dad was stabbed to death in the next room—I modify it to serve one-and-a-half Victors:

Start the toaster oven and put three eggs in a pot of water and cover it and set it on the stove. Set stove to medium.

Fill the electric kettle with water and slide three pieces of bread into the toaster oven.

Spoon coffee grounds into the wide glass beaker until the grounds are three fingers deep and then pour hot water from the electric kettle over the grounds (make sure none escape the deluge and float dry to the top).

Pour two short glasses of orange juice and sip from one. Thumb through the sports section.

Put your palms on the counter and clench your eyes shut for a minute as a tsunami of sadness washes over you. Picture the life gushing out of your father's body. Did he think of you, did he say your name? If you were there, what would he have told you? Stir the coffee in the beaker.

Take the pot with the eggs off the stove. Set the table with two bowls, two forks, one knife, two mugs, the full glass of orange juice, one paper towel torn in half in the role of two napkins, and a jar of jam.

Use the lid to drain the water out of the pot of eggs and then refill it with cold water and put it on the woven trivet on the table. Press the coffee and put that on the table, too. Send a text message up the stairs: "Eggs Victor now."

Tear one slice of toast into pieces in a bowl, peel two of the soft-boiled eggs, mash them into the toast with your fork.

Sprinkle salt and pepper. Hear footsteps on the stairs.

Jules pads in: sweats, slippers, and froofy hair. "Yay, Eggs Victor," she says, tearing up her piece of toast. "And the worm for earliest bird goes to . . ."

I pour the coffee. "Are you going to wear that to the restaurant?"

"I'll bring stuff and shower at your dorm before we go. Is that okay with you, Herr Victor?"

"Look, I just—I'm sorry." Take a deep breath. Spread jam on the last piece of toast. "I don't do this every day."

"I know," she says.

Since it's game day I do a shootaround with Andre instead of my usual morning workout. We move methodically, serious, working our sweet spots and weak spots. At the end, by the time we're winded but not beat, we take turns shooting foul shots and yelling at each other.

"A whole troupe of Vegas showgirls," Andre waves his arms spastically. "Shagging on a spaceship!"

I swish the shot anyway. "*Xiān bié qù xiǎng guòqù de nàxiē hé wèilái yào zuò de shì, bǎ zhùyìlì jízhōng zài dāngxià*—Busy your mind not with what you have done or what you will do but with what you are doing right now," Dad used to say.

"Final event," says Andre, stepping behind the basket. He squints up at the rim, squeezes his eyes shut, and then lofts the ball neatly over the backboard. It falls through the net.

"Oh, booyah. What's up now, huh?" Andre dances a few beats of the Ghostbusta.

I retrieve the ball, play along, make a bored face. As I'm lining up the shot, the far doors bang open and the sounds of Women's Volleyball spill into the arena: fresh sneakers, nets and uprights on rolling carts, brassy chatter and laughter. I close my eyes and release; the ball takes two bounces around the rim and falls in.

"Ooooh, Victor Li! Are you showing off for us?"

Holly Michaels, All Cal-10 libero, sashays up to us with a thousand-watt smile on her face, tanly, symmetrically, gorgeously terrifying. I'm mumbling some explanation when she cuts me off, turning to Andre with her hands on her hips.

"Do you have any idea how much this guy is in here?"

Andre grins. "The hardest-working man on the team. You coming to the game tonight?"

"I shouldn't, because none of y'all ever come to any of our games."

"I'll be at the next one," Andre says.

"Uh-huh." Holly drops her chin, looking ravishingly unconvinced.

"Hi, Andre!" A towering blonde waves her whole arm at us from across the court.

"Oh hey Jamie, what up girl!"

"That's Jeanie," hisses Holly.

"Oh." Andre smacks himself in the forehead. "Look, Holly, why don't you and Jeanie come to the game tonight and then come to our after-party at Irving? Four-oh-two."

Blueberry eyes narrow. "I'll consider it. Good luck tonight, Victor." She chucks me on the shoulder and runs off to help her teammates set up the nets.

"She likes you," Andre says.

"After what happened at that party? No way, man."

"That was two *years* ago, bruh! When are you gonna let it go?"

Jules finishes tromping down the bleachers. "Who was that fresh little package?"

"Seems like we're done here," I say.

"The monk," Jules says. Andre gives me a look, pulls off his sneakers, slips into his slides.

Back at the Quad, Andre sits on the counter and massages the arches of his feet with a lacrosse ball as I scoop supplements out of little plastic jars into a blender filled halfway with soy milk and bananas. Creatine, whey protein isolate, branched chain amino acids.

Just as Jules comes out of the shower wearing my towel, there's a knock on the door, and she detours to open it.

"Hey, you must be Sun. I'm Juliana," I hear her say, and then he's following her into the room. It looks like he's wearing the same clothes he arrived in last night.

"I am very sorry to meet you," Sun says haltingly, looking embarrassed. "I am saying, in such a rotten time. Your father has tell me many nice things about you."

"Thank you, Sun," Jules says. "What a gent. Okay, boys, I'll go put on some clothes so Andre can regain control of his eyeballs."

"Ignoring a half-naked woman is impolite in some cultures,"

Andre calls after her. "Hey, my man Sun. Where have you been all morning?"

"RoboTaco. I wake up three o'clock, big jetlag. I don't sleep again. So I walk there, twenty-four-hour operating."

Andre narrows his eyes. "You've been at RoboTaco since three in the morning?"

"I am walking around all San Dimas. So cool and quiet. So clean air. So much space, so much trees. Old Li have always say to me that America is the most beautiful place." Sun sighs with admiration.

"So you've definitely never been to the States before?" Andre asks. "Because your English is pretty damn good."

Sun combines a wry smile with a shrug. "Old Li always love to watch American films," he says. "That how he teach me English. We watch everything in Happy Year office. I think his favorites are Robert Redford and Vin Diesel."

Except when he says it, it sounds more like "Win Dieser." Sun closes his eyes in concentration, then reopens them and deadpans with true Dom Toretto gravitas: "'I live my life a quarter mile at a time.'"

Andre and I look at each other and share a surprised laugh.

"Dad did have a Vin Diesel thing," I point out.

Jules emerges from my bedroom in black slacks, black tank top, and wet black ponytail. We leave Andre to his foot massage, gather around the table, and go over the plan in Mandarin. As he reiterates his instructions, Sun's manner is grave and steady again. Jules and I will go to the original Happy Year restaurant for lunch and visit the main office at the back of the restaurant. We'll keep an eye out for any conspicuous changes, and we'll try to find out if the safe in Dad's office has been tampered with or moved. And, of course, we won't be saying anything about the gun, the passport, or the taco-loving man from Beijing camped out in my dorm room.

It's in a grim mood that we head down the stairs and out to visitor parking, and for once Jules has nothing to say. The midday winter sun is warm and mild, and the noontime breeze seems to carry a hint of salt, even though we're fifty miles from Santa Monica. I think back to the last time I saw the Pacific Ocean—it was about six months ago, in August, when Dad drove us out there to celebrate what would have been Mom's fifty-fifth birthday. The ocean always mesmerized Dad, made him go all soft and sentimental. He could stare at it for hours on end without saying a word. That evening in August, we ordered *omakase* at a hole-in-the-wall Japanese place, toro sashimi and blue crab hand rolls. I remember walking along the beach afterward, Dad and I ambling along in quiet content, our faces bathed in the setting sun, as Jules pattered ahead to trace sine curves in the wet sand with her bare feet. It was a different ocean then, a different family who saw it.

10

Ground Zero: the San Dimas Happy Year Chinese Restaurant. There are three other Happy Year restaurants spread around the San Gabriel Valley, each of them newer and larger than this one, but the San Dimas location is the granddaddy, home base. On Saturday at lunchtime, the parking lot is a bit of a shit show.

"I hope we can get a table," Jules murmurs. We're lurking in her hatchback as we wait for three generations of a Chinese family to pile into a minivan. A honk sounds from the growing line of vehicles behind us, and Jules thrusts a middle finger out her window. That numb mood has come over me again, the one in which I keep reconstructing the last night of Dad's life, replaying various scenarios in my head, now with additional detail: *two precise stabs in the chest and a clean slash across*— Lang didn't finish his sentence, but I have a good guess.

It's not until we're walking through the automatic sliding doors that I realize how uncomfortable this situation will be. The two young hostesses rush up to us as soon as we step inside the waiting area. Wearing long faces and pink *qipao,* they ask us in their chirpy

Fujian accents if we're holding up okay, if we have everything we need. They tell us how things aren't the same without Dad around. Blood rushes to my face as the twenty-odd people waiting for tables perk up and bend their closest ears toward our conversation.

Rick Yin shows up to save us. Tall, handsome, and fluent in English, "Slick Rick" Yin has worked at Happy Year almost as long as Dad, I guess because his acting career never took off. Dad valued him enough to pay him nearly twice as much as any of his other employees. Technically he's the front-of-house manager, but Dad often had him on the phone with the bank, the utilities, the Chamber of Commerce, and so on, and not only because he speaks perfect English. Slick Rick can wheel, deal, and wheedle. On the rare occasion that someone orders a bottle of wine, he makes them feel like they're at a Michelin-starred restaurant just by how he opens it.

"*Xiǎozhōu, Liányīng, nǐ zǒngsuàn lái le*—You're here at last," Rick says, as if we were turning up late instead of unexpectedly, and he wraps the two of us into a big hug like he'd been doing since we were in grade school.

"It's really nice to see you, Rick," I say, meaning it.

"How's business?" says Jules.

"Oh, business is great, really, super. You know your Dad, he trained us pretty well! A new guy came over from Beijing to help out, Mr. Rou. He's back in the office. You'll want to meet him. Kind of a character," and Rick laughs like he said something hilarious. He seems a little antsy beneath his Chinese Elvis veneer. I thank him and tell him that we'll go back and see Mr. Rou now.

"We can't eat here," Jules says hoarsely as we pass along the seafood-tank side of the vast dining room, and I nod my agreement. Through the saloon doors, in the kitchen, everyone is too busy with the lunch rush to notice us. I'm beelining it to the office door at the back when Jules grabs my arm.

"Hey, slow down. You cool, Cato?" she asks.

She's right—I'm not. I take a long breath, try to unwind the key between my shoulder blades a few clicks. The kitchen is intense with the heat of the gas stoves, the sounds of chopping and frying, the competing odors of sesame oil, cilantro, and Sichuan peppercorns. My eyes reflexively drift to the back doorway, where Dad would stand with his arms folded over his chest and supervise his underlings. He started me working here when I was thirteen, five or six hours each weekend at minimum wage, wrestling the mop and bucket around the bathrooms or mixing the duck sauce in an industrial-size garbage can. Three cases of applesauce, three jugs of white vinegar, two boxes of white sugar, half a bottle of molasses, and one big jar of plum sauce, which Dad had shipped in from China by the case. No ducks. If you didn't stir it fast enough, the sugar would clump, but if you stirred it too fast, you'd end up with sticky brown goo all over your pants.

My eyes dance over to the extra sink Dad installed by the chopping station for velveting the meat, presently filled to the brim with bloody skirt steaks, corn starch, and diluted Shaoxing wine. Old Jiang, Dad's indispensable knife man, spears a steak with a barbecue fork and begins shaving uniformly thin slices off of it with concise, rapid motions. He handles his ultrasharp blade with mesmerizing efficiency, standing over his work with an athletic flex in his knees, an unlit cigarette dangling from his expressionless lips, as he flicks bits of gristle and fat into a separate bowl.

"*Jīngtōng gèshì jìnéng, zhǐ shì biǎomiànshàng sìhū bu fèilì*—Masterful skill appears on the surface to be effortless," Dad would say.

I take Jules's hand off my arm and give it a squeeze. "I think I'm okay."

"Play dumb."

"Right."

"Don't flip out."

"Right."

We slip through the back door into a fluorescent hallway, a bright dream of thin white walls and rough corporate carpet, eerily serene after the hubbub of the restaurant. Dad's office is the second glass door on the left. We peek through the glass and see a sturdy Chinese guy with a shaved head and cauliflower ears, sitting at Dad's desk and talking on the phone. He's wearing a loose black button-down, tucked in, like a corny stage magician. I tap on the glass and the man looks around. When he sees us, some kind of resolved calm spreads across his wide face.

"Yuck," Jules whispers.

The man rises and unlocks the door, which requires more steps than I remember. Only then do I see another man getting up from the sofa behind the door, a muscular young Chinese guy with deep acne scars on his temples, a long black ponytail, and what looks like a life-size tattoo of the human nervous system running up and down his arms and legs.

Shaved Head ushers Ponytail out the door, and as he steps past us, he scans me with an expressionless look that feels like an icy hand on my chest. Then he strides purposefully toward the exit at the end of the hallway that leads to the back of the parking lot.

Shaved Head waves us into the office, speaking Mandarin: "You must be Lianying and Xiaozhou. I saw you at the funeral. My surname is Rou. I am called Rou Qiangjun."

He stands up to shake our hands; his is coarse, calloused. His shoulders are broad and powerful, his muscular neck almost as wide as his head. I notice a tattoo on the inside of his right wrist, but it's mostly concealed by his magician shirt, so I can't tell what it is.

"Please, sit. I've worked for many years for the Happy Year company in Beijing. After the company heard the terrible news about your father, they sent me here to help. Since I arrived, I have learned how much everybody loved your father. Please accept my sincere condolences."

His southern accent is not the same as the hostesses' Fujianese inflections—more like the thicker, heavier Mandarin spoken by people from Hong Kong.

"So you previously worked at the restaurants in Beijing?" Fishing. I figure he has no idea what we've been told about the company.

"That's right. It is all very different here in America." He smiles at me without showing his teeth. "I learn a lot each day."

He's a decent liar—no stuttering, no fidgeting—but I can sense him taking measure of me as I look around the room. Nothing much seems to have changed, except for the new locks on the door and a small lockbox sitting on top of the bulky drop safe in the corner. I scan the untidy desk, the stack of papers on the filing cabinet. No yellow legal pads.

"Is everything going smoothly?" Jules asks.

"I assume you heard that someone broke into the restaurant a few nights ago. No? They cleaned out the registers and broke into the office. You see, your father was the only one who knew how to open the safe, so the employees have not been dropping cash into it. So a lot of cash had accumulated in the drawers. You haven't heard anything about that, have you?"

"I'm afraid not," I say, and Jules shakes her head, but Rou keeps his gaze on me, watching me keenly, and I find myself imagining him stepping through the broken window in the breakfast nook, peering around with his small, alert eyes.

Then he looks away, shifting a stack of papers on the desk, affecting nonchalance. "Anyway, insurance will cover everything. We have receipts, of course. We replaced the locks, and we've taken some additional measures. The young man who was just here is our new head of security."

"We're glad the business is in good hands," Jules says. The tightness around her mouth tells me that she's feeling the weird vibe, too. "We came to thank you for sending meals to our house. Let us know if there's anything we can do to help out."

"Everything is very good, thank you. Except there is the safe." He points to it with his left hand and I see a tattoo on that wrist, too: a snake's head. "Your father didn't share the code with you, did he? From what I know, it's only some cash in there. But it'd be nice to be able to use it."

"I'm afraid we don't know the code," Jules says.

I stand up to go and put out my hand. When he takes it with his, I meet his probing gaze again, and he grips my hand much more tightly than he did a few minutes earlier, mashing my knuckles against each other as he stares into my face. But I have strength of my own; I turn his hand upward and pull it toward me, out of his sleeve a bit, feeling his weight and power as I do.

It's a snake on this wrist, too, the head peeking out of his cuff, the body winding up his wrist, disappearing into his sleeve.

"Interesting tattoo," I say.

Rou looks down at his wrist, and he smiles, but not with his eyes.

"I was born in the Year of the Snake," he says. "That's just something I did when I was young. Like you."

Well, that guy's a sleazefest," says Jules as we pull out of the parking lot. "I hope to God you got what you wanted, because I'd rather mate with a sloth than converse with him again."

"Jules, he could be the killer." I find myself looking at my hands, making fists again. "Or that other guy with the long hair. Did you see *his* tattoo? And now they're sitting there in Dad's office like they own the place, sending us takeout. Fuck!"

My fist bounces off the rubber dashboard. Painful. Useless.

"Victor, chill the fuck out! They *do* own the place, you need to get used to that. And I don't know anything about killers, but a lot of people have tattoos. We can't jump to conclusions here just because a straightforward explanation would make us feel better."

"I know that," I say. "I'm just saying, he wouldn't have acted so defensive with us if he didn't have something to hide."

"Yeah, sure," Jules says. "Or? He knows he's taken over for our dad, and he's insecure about his position here. And you were simply behaving like a couple of alpha dogs, trying to look tough while you sniff each other's buttholes."

I close my eyes for a second, force myself to take a few deep breaths. Sometimes it's hard to understand how Jules and I came from the same parents. I follow simple rules of my own devising, sliding along the deep grooves of my productive habits; she considers every situation from every angle, floundering in the deluge of her hyperactive intellect. I'd like to think we complement each other, one helping the other cover the blind spots, but sometimes it seems like we're just driving each other nuts.

Jules has a tattoo of her own, a Katharine Hepburn quotation in tiny script on her shoulder blade: "The time to make up your mind about people is never."

"So what do you make of Sun?" I say. "Do you think we can trust him?"

"I dunno." Jules frowns into the distance. "Like you said, he's a bit like Dad, all goofy and intense at the same time. But I bet there's something he's concealing beneath that pleasant exterior. I don't think he's telling the whole truth."

I let this stew for a minute along with the fact that Dad never told us about Sun, that he deceived us about his work, his past, and the very foundations of our family. Maybe for our own benefit. Maybe he didn't have much of a choice. But finding out still stings like a slap.

Back at the Quad, we tell Sun everything we saw and heard, pausing now and then to look up Chinese words on Google Translate.

"I know this person, a man named Rou with snake tattoos," Sun says in Mandarin after we finish. "The tattoos are the sign of the Snake Hands Gang. They come from one village in Guangdong where chemical drugs are a cottage industry. They sell the drugs in the streets of Beijing, send home most of the profits, and spend the rest on liquor and prostitutes. Since two years ago, Ouyang has been helping them expand into other businesses. Rou Qiangjun is one of their captains."

"So you think he killed Dad?" I ask.

"This is a possibility, but not the only one. Maybe this new 'head of security' was the killer, or they worked together. We can say definitely Rou was sent by Happy Year from Beijing for some purpose other than helping with the restaurants. But perhaps Ouyang and Zhao are also working with other people in Los Angeles. Zhao also communicates with the attorney, Peng."

Jules and I share a startled look. "Perry Peng? How much does he know?"

Sun knits his brow, scratches his head. "More than we do. We're going to have to break into the restaurant and retrieve your father's documents before we do anything else."

"Wait, what? Break into the restaurant? What the fuck are you talking about?" Jules says, folding her arms across her chest.

Before Sun can respond, Andre comes out of his room in full pregame regalia: fresh sweats, loosely tied AF1s, Jordan duffel, enormous shiny headphones.

"Game time, baby boy," he says to me. "Roll out."

11

You lick my hand?" Sun looks at Eli, incredulous.

"No, dude. You lick your own hand. Like this, and then the salt. There you go. Ready?" He waves his tequila shot and lime wedge in front of Sun's face, as if to say, *Look, it's not so hard.*

We're hovering around the kitchenette counter, the common room too filled with party randos for us to properly teach Sun anything.

"Okay," Sun says hesitantly, like he's not so sure it's okay, and he licks his hand.

We eked out a win against Lafayette, but the victory came at the cost of an injury to a key player, and now there's an unspoken impulse to refill the drinks quickly. I'd subbed in for Howie for a meager four minutes in the first half, four minutes during which Jason Maxwell overpowered me for a handful of buckets at the rim. So Coach Vaughn promptly sent me back to my familiar spot on the bench, opting for bigger, Victor-free lineups, and we maintained a healthy lead right up until Howie drove to the basket with about five minutes left on the clock, landed awkwardly on someone else's foot, and let out a scream that sucked the air out of the arena.

As Andre helped the team trainer carry Howie to the locker room, Vaughn beckoned to me. He told me that Jason Maxwell was only a sixty percent free-throw shooter, and I had four fouls to give.

He told me to play smart, to be realistic. To know when I was beat.

"What do we say again?" asks Andre.

"*Gānbēi,*" says Sun.

"Right. *Gānbēi,*" says Eli, and down they go.

"Unnhhhh," says Juliana. "Why would anyone do that?"

Sun holds out his shot glass and turns it upside down, splashing a few drops of Cuervo onto the counter.

"That is the end of *gānbēi*. Dry cup. No more *báijǐu*."

Just like Jules and me, Sun is lobster red with Asian Glow, and he's getting a little sloppy with the distinction between Chinese and English. He seems to have understood nothing of the basketball game and enjoyed everything. Screaming in the stands next to Eli and shotgunning PBRs in the bathroom with Andre has put him in a pink mood of all-American euphoria.

"During game, why you yelling this word to Andre: *mus-ter*?" he asks me.

"*Mustard.* It's a code," I explain. "When I'm out of his line of sight and I want the ball, I don't yell 'pass,' because the other team could yell the same thing. So I yell 'mustard,' and he knows it's me."

Sun nods approvingly. "This is good idea."

Andre has wandered toward the entryway, and just when I catch a glimpse of Jeanie from the volleyball team looming in his direction, Holly Michaels appears at my elbow.

"Hey, Victor! High five." She throws up a palm, bends at the elbow, makes good contact. Volleyball players: good at high fives. "Y'all played a great game tonight."

"You were there?"

"Yeah. What a thrill ride. And way to hang in there on defense."

"He walked all over me."

Holly shrugs. "I thought you did great."

In my tequila-sharpened vision, her teeth are perfect white wolf teeth, her lips a sunset shade of red that matches the acrylic on her fingernails. She's wearing an SDSU-branded white tank top, a short red skirt, and flip-flops on her tan, calloused feet, where my gaze lingers.

"Hey," she whispers, tiptoeing up into my neck. "D'ya wanna go smoke a joint? Andre said we can go on the roof."

I glance over and see Jules holding Eli and Sun in her thrall: ". . . because anyway the universe has a natural tendency toward complementary binaries: man-woman, yin-yang, Coke-Pepsi, Visa-Mastercard . . ."

"Sure, why not?" I say, and Holly rewards me with a smile.

I know you don't want to lighten up and have fun, Jules said to me half an hour ago. *But it might do you some good.*

Holly takes my hand and leads me out of the triple, and then I show her up the back staircase to the emergency exit door, which is propped open with a plastic pasta sauce jar that Andre cut a wedge out of and brought up here last semester. We walk out into the low, warm sky. The roof is long and flat with no railing. We're only five floors up, but the sandstone buildings of the university around us are wide and dark, and after the hot, loud apartment, I feel high up in the fresh night.

At the far edge stands a towering black silhouette on blue: Andre, bigger than ever when he's standing alone.

"Hey kids," he says, half-turning, half-smiling, as we walk up. He's working his way through one of his long, perfectly rolled Js.

"Whatcha doing there, big fella?" Holly asks.

"Just taking it in." He passes to Holly.

"Wowee, thanks." She takes a dragon-size hit, exhales through her nose, passes to me. We smoke and chat, talk about easy classes, the respective merits of basketball and volleyball as spectator sports, whether Andre should marry Jeanie because she's six-three and makes bomb mac and cheese, and whatever else, until we've killed the joint and my face hurts from laughing.

"Hey, do you hear that?" Holly asks when the laughter lulls and the thumping music from Eli's speakers wafts up from below. "I'm suddenly paranoid that people are dancing on tables or something, and both of you guys are up here with me."

"We live with another guy, too," I say. "He's down there."

"He *is* a moron, though." Andre throws me a meaningful glance and then turns toward the stairs. "Maybe I'll just check up on things."

Without Andre to fuel the conversation, Holly and I stand here quietly, stonedly, looking at the world. She inches up to my side and slips under my arm. I try to think of something to say, but everything I think of sounds stupid in my head. She clears her throat. "Can I—?" She reaches her hands up to my buzzed hair and starts rubbing it. "I love the texture," she murmurs. "When I'm high, I love textures." She giggles and closes her eyes.

This is when you kiss her, I think to myself. Her eyes are closed, her face is inches from mine. I give myself a second to work up the nerve, and then another to savor the anticipation, and then I do it. I totally kiss Holly Michaels. I close my eyes, too, and dwell on the little meetings of our lips, wait for her to end each one, my hand wandering down to the small of her back, her fingertips tickling the base of my skull. It's tender and sweet, and she smiles when our mouths part, and her eyes remain closed, and then we kiss again, sweetly again, like good listeners, and she makes a soft noise, and nuzzles me for a second afterward.

"Hi," she whispers, and I feel fully alive in this moment, open and tickled and trusting, when it starts in my stomach.

"I feel light-headed," I say, opening my eyes.

"Me, too," Holly purrs.

"I mean I'm feeling . . . really dizzy."

Now her eyes are open, so nice and blue and white, and I dive into them, doing flips.

"Are you all right?" she asks.

"Yeah," I say, my hands moving from her back to her shoulders, keeping me upright. "Sometimes when I smoke. After I was already drinking. I get the spins really bad."

"Oh, no."

"Maybe I should go lie down."

"Oh—okay."

She leads me, blinking, toward the door, and somehow we make it back down the stairs to the suite. My stomach is churning, and my sensory experience of life has sharply deteriorated: patchy audio, low frame rate. Amid the throbbing music, everyone seems too absorbed in whatever they're doing to notice us as we stagger through the party. Andre and Eli are teaching the Ghostbusta to Jeanie and some Korean-looking girl.

You see me clubbing, you know I VIP
Blaze it up till we filin' dankruptcy
Drop it low, wave ya hands like a rolla coasta
Bich we do it like this, I'm a ghostbusta

As we pass the kitchenette, I catch a glimpse of Sun, chin in hand, still intently watching the Jules Show.

"—and rot away in a tomb of material possessions, you know?" she's saying to him in Mandarin, gesturing emphatically with her hands. "Everybody else seems to accept it so casually."

We don't walk so much as crash into my tiny room, stumbling over Sun's backpack and collapsing onto the bed. Holly shrieks, sits up, flicks on the bedside lamp, and takes in the scene.

"Yikes," she says.

"I have a guest," I explain from between the forearms draped over my face. I stifle a burp and taste tequila. "Ordinarily I'm quite tidy."

"Here, drink some water," she says. "You know what helps me when I get the spins? I keep one foot on the ground, on the side of the bed. Like this." She moves me around.

"That does help." I close my eyes.

"And keep your eyes open."

"Oh, okay."

"That's better." She nestles in beside me.

"Holly, you know that time?" I try to enunciate. "When I was in your room. I just want to say I'm sorry about that."

"Like, when we were sophomores? Ancient history, Victor. Don't be silly."

"I guess I'm sorry about now, too."

"You had a big day."

"I shouldn't have smoked."

"Maybe so. But hey, you deserve to relax a little." After a pause, Holly knits her eyebrows and says, "I heard about your dad, and I'm really, really sorry, Victor."

I shake my head. "Nothing looks the same to me anymore. People get stabbed to death, and I'm bouncing an inflated leather sphere? I feel like I've been living in a fairy tale my whole life. Everything that's ever happened, I'm replaying it in my mind."

I turn and look at her, my vision lagging a bit behind my head. Our faces are a few inches apart. *She gets it,* I'm telling myself.

She smiles tentatively, traces my jawline with her fingers. "You can let go now. You can rest if you're tired," she says. "I'll stay with you. Here."

She pulls my shoes off, she tries to settle me down, she puts her hands on me in gentle ways until the spins are gone and the high has moved from my stomach to my head, behind my eyes, the base of my skull, and as she draws circles on my chest with her fingertips, sleep overtakes me like a snowstorm.

—

We stared at Mom's coffin, the three of us, the survivors. Linda Eastman Li, Loving Wife and Mother. Someone could go from being a person to being an inanimate object just like that. The organ music had stopped, and the only sound in the church was Jules's quiet sobbing. I caught sight of Reverend Wetherbee coming up the aisle, a book in his hands, his eyes set on Dad.

Wetherbee was quite young back then, just four or five years into his first assignment out of divinity school. Tall and plump, he had recently cultivated a goatee, perhaps in order to offset his baby-facedness. It occurred to me that I should intercept him, stop him from triggering an explosion, because at fourteen I was already adept at reading Dad's moods. Generally, he oscillated between contemplative and cheeseball—he hardly ever lost his temper after Mom got sick. But when he did, he blew big, and beforehand, there was always this tempest in his eyes, this powerful look on his face. A little action around the corners of his mouth. Almost a grin.

The look was no guarantee of an eruption. Far more often—like when Jules or I complained, or argued with each other, or begged for material things—he seemed to shrink from his own anger as much as we did. He would retreat to his office and pretend to bury himself in work, but when I spied on him through the glass panes of the French doors, I discovered him meditating: erect in his chair, eyes half shut, hands resting on knees.

If he was really steaming, he would drive to Santa Monica and stare out at the Pacific, at the shape of the planet, perhaps imagining he could see all the way back to the *hutong* where he grew up. I joined him for that drive once. It was the year before, the day we learned that Mom's tumors had spread—I was thirteen. We spent two hours sitting in the sand and two more on the Santa Monica Freeway. He barely said a word the whole time, but he smiled at me as I buckled my seat belt for the drive home, and he asked me to play one of my favorite CDs.

I saw the look again at Mom's service. He had stood patiently, accepting embraces from a line of parishioners who had hardly ever seen him, a little vein on his neck dancing back and forth. I knew he was hot, and maybe I could have said something, diverted Wetherbee, forestalled the storm. Instead, I shut my eyes, allowed myself to sway a bit on my feet, and tried to imagine what it would feel like to disappear into a void of not-feeling, not-thinking, not-being.

"It belonged to her," Wetherbee said to Dad, offering up the Bible with both hands.

Dad took the book, weighed it in his hands. "It didn't help her much, did it? All that praying."

Wetherbee did not reply. Dad wandered away, gently tossing the book up and down in his hands, glancing around the church, but not at us, not at Mom. Mom's body.

"We had many plans, Linda and I. Dreams that we worked for. Made sacrifices for, both of us," he said, his eyes darting from Jesus to Jesus: figurine, painting, window. "And now she is dead, despite her religion."

Wetherbee eyed Dad warily. He was in his own house. He drew himself tall to defend it, but spoke in soothing tones. "Her faith did not heal her, but it provided her with peace and perspective. Now, her suffering is over."

Dad seemed not to hear him. He looked at the coffin now, then back to the book, then at his surroundings again; he seemed loose, unhinged, like he might keel over. "Many plans," he repeated to himself. "Many sacrifices."

"Dad, don't," Juliana said.

"*Bìzuǐ!*—Shut your mouth!" he barked at her in Mandarin, in a full rage now, naked to his core. The furnace within him that forged my world.

Wetherbee inclined his head to the book in Dad's hands. "Vincent, the Bible tells us that we can only have a limited view of God's will; that we can only take the measure of our lives as if 'through a glass, darkly.' Through scripture, and through prayer, Linda was able to find peace at the end of her time with us. Perhaps the book will offer you consolation as well."

"Consolation." Dad said the word slowly, enunciating each syllable, like it was a foreign word to him. Like he was still learning the language.

He turned back to Reverend Wetherbee. "There will be no consolation for me," he said.

He spun on his heels and hurled the book through the air, past my face, and I turned my head as it crashed through the stained glass window behind me. Saint Dismas, bearing his cross, exploded into ten thousand fragments. They sailed through the air like shrapnel, jagged and sharp, imperfect and unwhole, less than what they had been: a vision, an illusion, a dream.

I wake with a start in a mess of covers in the corner of my bed, and, fucking hell, Holly is gone.

My phone is dead, but the hue of the glow in the window tells me it's something like seven in the morning. I step quietly out into the living room. Juliana, in Andre's comforter, is a snail on the couch; Sun, in my sleeping bag, is a burrito on the floor. Andre's door is open and I can sense that nobody's in there.

In the bathroom I splash some water on my face, look in the mirror, stare at the person there until his face is no longer my face, just some coincidence of shape, light, and color. In the morning light I appear aerodynamic, like some kind of projectile weapon.

Cannonball. Jellyfish. I think a few more things over and decide to flick the glass with my finger instead of punching it with my fist.

"Pathetic," I say to me, shaking my head. I drink some water from the faucet, go to my room, grab my gym stuff, and head out the door.

12

No, you didn't," Eli says plaintively. "Please, tell me you didn't."

I stay focused on the blender. Kale. Frozen strawberries. Coconut water. Almond butter. Dates.

"You college boys," says Jules, perched on the counter, swinging her ankles back and forth. "You're always beating your chests and fluffing your feathers, but when it's time to deliver the goods, it's always two-pump chump or ol' mister whiskey-dick."

"I was too messed up." I pour four smoothies. "I had the spins."

"*Pffft.*" Eli throws his hands up. "It's the same *farkakte* story with you every time. As your loyal friend and suitemate of four years, Victor, I am eagerly anticipating the day that you wake up and realize how much you get in your own way."

Sun has wandered in from the living room. He's wearing another black T-shirt.

I clear my throat. "Sun, you were saying yesterday that we have to break into the restaurant. How are we going to do that? And what are these documents that we need to retrieve from there?"

Sun casts a guarded glance from Eli to Jules, then sets his jaw and slips into his business mode. "To break in is simple. I know the way how. Regarding documents, Old Li only told me, get documents from restaurant safe and show you."

"So you know the code to the safe?" I say.

"Old Li have said he will give it to you."

"No, he didn't," I say, my heart sinking. "Unless it's somewhere at the house."

"Anyway, aren't we ignoring the potential legal consequences of breaking into the restaurant?" Jules says. "It seems pretty risky just in order to get some papers."

"Jules," I say, "the documents could be those yellow legal pads that Detective Lang told me to look for."

"No shit, Victor," Jules says. "But I don't recall him authorizing you to commit burglaries of your own."

"No problem, no problem." Sun waves his hands vigorously. "We can go tonight, into restaurant and out, ten minutes. It's actually easy. But code to the safe, that is, uh, *guānjiàn*."

"Crucial," I say.

"Then I'm glad we don't have it," Jules says.

The subsequent awkward silence is interrupted by Andre strolling through the front door. "Morning, y'all," he says, plucking an apple from his neat row of them on top of the refrigerator. Then he turns to me and asks, "So how'd it go with Holly?"

"Yes, Victor," Eli says vindictively. "Tell the man. Did you show her your girth certificate?"

"I got the spins and we talked for a while," I say. "Then I woke up and she was gone."

Jules pulls open a window, lights a cigarette. "You know, Victor, maybe if you didn't hold so much in when you're sober, you wouldn't spill your guts to whatever random female every time you get shitfaced."

"Too harsh, Jules! Holly is no random female. And Victor's just being Victor," Andre pipes up in my defense, and then turns to me, gesticulating with his half-eaten apple. "So what if you got a little too faded? You're a nice guy. She's a nice girl. Don't be down. Just text her and make a joke about it, piece of cake."

"I don't have her number, and besides—"

Andre pulls out his phone. "I think I've got Jeanie in here somewhere, one sec."

"No, goddammit. Fuck!" I smack a cabinet, hard. Everyone looks at me. My palm stings, and hot little jolts of pain run up my arm, into my shoulder.

"Look, forget about Holly, all right, I already did. And I don't want you to set things up for me anymore! The joint, the roof—I know your little game, okay?"

Andre puts his phone back into the pocket of his sweatshirt and folds his arms across his chest. "Okay," he says. "If that's how you feel, I won't set anything up for you anymore."

His placid tone seems to say, "Whatever you want, you big baby." I pace halfway across the room, then turn back to hurl some more silent accusations at him. *You love being better at everything than me. You knew Vaughn would tell me to foul Jason Maxwell. You think I need you, but I don't. I don't need you.*

The room is silent, and everybody's looking at me like I'm holding a bomb. I storm into my bedroom and lock the door behind me.

Then I snatch the case from under the bed and flip it upside down, emptying the contents onto my unmade bed. The bottom, the inside, the edges of the foam lining—I scrutinize all of it and find nothing. So I start flipping through the cash, examining both sides of each bill and then tossing it aside.

Maybe I'm *not* getting in my own way. Maybe I'm the only one who remembers what's important.

Half an hour later, Jules, Eli, Andre, and Sun are strewn across the common room sofa and floors, streaming a nature documentary off Netflix, when I burst out of my room and tell them that I've found it.

"Twenty-seven, thirteen, seven," I say, waving a pink hundred-yuan note in front of me. "It's got to be the safe code. And there's two addresses on it as well. One in Venice and one in Alhambra."

For a moment, as they exchange looks, the only sound is David Attenborough talking about the dietary habits of the Komodo dragon. Then Andre hits MUTE on the remote control. "I guess we better Google that shit," he says.

"Give it here." A tablet has appeared in Eli's hands. "Looks like they're private residences."

"We've got to check them out, right?" I look from Sun to Jules.

Jules sighs, then smiles weakly, and I can tell she doesn't want to argue. "Okay, fine. If a drive to Alhambra is required for closure, then so be it. Andre, you take Venice."

"We've gotta watch the game film with the coaches at three," Andre says. "But I can drive to the restaurant tonight."

Comprehension dawns on Sun's face. "You don't drive," he says to me.

"He got a DUI. *Kāichē bù hējiǔ!*—Don't drink and drive!" Jules wags a finger in my face. Sun looks at me with surprise.

"That was actually one hundred percent my fault," Andre interjects.

Thinking back to that miserable episode, I feel my face getting hot. "Andre, you've gotta sit it out," I say. "The draft is in six months, and you've got too much at risk. Jules, can you go check out both addresses now while we go to the film session? And then, if you could drive Sun and me to the restaurant tonight, that'd be great."

"So now *I* have to drive to Venice? Are you shitting me? Do you want me to swing by Tijuana, too?"

"Jules," I say, "we have to do this."

Jules addresses Sun in Chinese. "Promise me that my brother won't get hurt," she says. He returns her serious look, holds her gaze, and nods his head.

"Fine, then. I'll fucking drive to motherfucking Venice," she says in English, and snatches the hundred-yuan note off the coffee table. "I'm keeping this for gas money."

"Hey, what about me?" Eli says.

"Shouldn't you be mining Bitcoin?" Jules asks him. "Or whatever it is that you do?"

"You should go with Jules to those houses," I say to Eli. "You can protect her if it's dangerous."

"Oh, I am all over that. I'll go get my camera. Oh, and my sunglasses." Eli bounces up and darts into his room.

Andre bursts out in big, rich peals of laughter as Jules stares at me with her head at an angle and her mouth hanging open.

"You *will* be sodomized," Jules whispers. I turn away from her, hide my smile.

"Let's talk about the restaurant," I say to Sun.

He's gazing pensively past me, into my room, at the pink Maos and green Franklins strewn together on the floor.

When Andre and I return to the Quad after the film session, our triple is quiet and clean. I peek into my room, where Sun has made the bed, stacked the bills back into the briefcase, and planked himself neatly on top of the covers. Andre puts on *SportsCenter* on mute and sits in front of it with a Spanish lit anthology in his lap. We had been sitting together in Spanish class for every semester since the ninth grade, until twelve days ago, when Dad got knifed and I stopped showing up for anything.

"'*¿Quién sabe donde la muerte descansa?*'" I offer. He smiles grimly. Some silence passes. I sit down next to him. "You think I'm an idiot?" I ask quietly.

Andre looks up at *SportsCenter,* squints, thinks. "Your dad passed away. It's not an easy time."

"Yeah." The pain bubble pulses. I study my palms.

Andre shakes his head. "I dunno, man. I know you want to do something, but have you thought about how deep this might go? I like Sun, but hey, you *just* met this guy. And he comes from another world, someplace where they play by different rules."

Andre looks away for a second, wrinkles his brow. I can sense his discomfort in the role of the worrier, which is oddly heartening to me—I feel the love. But then he gives his head a waggle, shakes off any mood unbecoming to the big easy, the captain of relaxin'. "Anyway, we'll hang in there together." He swings a huge arm over my shoulders, pats me on the head with a huge hand. "And we back off before anybody gets dead or pregnant, okay?"

With his hand he nods my head. I smile up at my best friend.

Just then Eli bursts through the door. "What's going on in here? Y'all making some blasian babies?"

"Shhhh. Dude is sleeping," Andre says, tipping his head toward my room.

Jules slumps in past Eli and collapses onto the couch.

"He never shuts up," she hisses at me.

"So? Did you find anything?" I ask.

"Yeah." Eli's head is in the fridge. He comes around to the couch and cracks open a can of energy drink. "Really weird. The address in Venice? Nice house, nobody home. We snuck a look at his mail to get his name: Aron Ancona. LinkedIn says he's a hepatologist at Cedar Sinai."

"Hippopotamus?" Andre says.

"Liver doctor." Jules's voice comes from under a throw pillow.

"And that's all we know, other than that he has a very nice house. But the house in Alhambra, right? Here's where it gets super strange. Big house, probably four, five bedrooms. Toyota minivan parked out front. For a while we sit outside and we don't see much, just a few glimpses of a superpregnant Chinese lady through the windows. Then we realize that it's not the same lady each time. It's multiple Chinese ladies, at least four, maybe more, all just severely pregnant. We sit there for an hour and nobody comes or goes, except right when we're about to leave, another van pulls up and out hops a Chinese guy with two big takeout bags. So we decide to tail the van and he drives back to, drum roll, Alhambra Happy Year."

"Why the hell would Happy Year have a house full of pregnant ladies?" I ask.

"I don't know." Eli shrugs. "We googled 'Chinese pregnant lady house' and all the results were this one adult video."

"Yikes," says Andre.

"Yikes is right." Jules pops up from under her pillow. "We watched a few minutes, but let me tell you, it was not very informative. Or stimulating."

"I wonder if it has something to do with Ice," I say.

"Ice could also be a meth thing," Jules says. "Sun said they're planning to import a volatile commodity, right?"

"They make a lot of meth in North Korea," Eli volunteers.

We all look at him. "Why do you even *know* that, man?" Andre asks.

For a moment we sit there puzzling over the results of our little investigation. *Another world. Different rules.* What was Dad mixed up in, and why did he want me to have this information?

Finally, Eli breaks the silence. "So what happens next?" he asks.

"Let's get this document out of the restaurant safe tonight. Then we'll know more," I say. "Dad left us these clues on purpose. He'll show us what we need to know."

13

Sun kneels outside the back door to the restaurant, takes off his backpack, unzips it. "This is your spot." He indicates the ground next to him with his chin. "Eyes up."

I obey, squatting against the wall and scanning the section of parking lot that's visible from the back of the building. The only car is Jules's hatchback, which she turned around to face the street after dropping us off. From where I am, I can't see the boulevard, but I hear the intermittent sounds of passing cars. In front of me, across the row of staff parking, there's a high wall between us and the video store behind the restaurant. To my left there's a young row of fig trees that Dad planted between us and the adjacent gas station.

We're wearing black clothes and disposable plastic gloves. There are stockings on our heads and shower caps on our shoes, which seems a little backward. It's three in the morning.

Sun takes a small black drill out of his backpack. Even the bit is black. He begins drilling through the dead bolt on the door. The whine of the drill itself is exceptionally quiet, but the metal-on-metal screech shreds my nerves like a cheese grater. After destroying the dead bolt, he drills through the center of the doorknob and slips inside.

I look at our escape vehicle and see that Jules has reclined her seat most of the way. She's lying back with her head turned toward me, watching through the rear window. The night is humid and near.

Long minutes pass and I begin to calm down. Sun and the noise of his weird drill seem like something that happened a couple of hours ago. I squat against the building, hugging my knees, making myself small. Little thoughts about cops and big thoughts about Dad present themselves at the borders of my mind, but I abandon them in favor of an alert, ready watchfulness. I got a lot of practice at this over the past few years, sitting on the bench and waiting to be called into action at a moment's notice. A hair over ten minutes per game for four seasons. Twenty-six box scores with Did Not Play—Coach's Decision next to my name. One barely relevant three-game suspension for violating team alcohol policy. I don't think about it. I feel glad to have a task to focus on, a plan of action, something other than sorrow. I relax, eyes up.

A man pushes a shopping cart along the sidewalk on the other side of the gas station. The cart makes a lot of noise and seems to be sprouting a variety of accessories, which the man stops to adjust, cursing volubly. He tosses off some further profanity at another man walking on the street. The other man, dressed all in white, ignores him; he leaves the sidewalk, cuts through the gas station, and heads toward the row of fig trees.

Now he sees me and breaks into a run in my direction. I see the ponytail. Muscles tense in my forearms, along my spine. I replay Sun's instructions in my head, slip through the door and into the hallway. It is dark except for the faint green glow of the EXIT sign above the door behind me, and adrenaline lights up my body as I will my eyes to adjust, every hair on my arms and neck reaching out into the dark, seeking information like antennae.

The door to the office is closed, and through the glass I see Sun crouched by the safe with a small, bright flashlight in his mouth. I imagine that I see Dad in there, too, searching around for his reading glasses or snacking on some stir-fried noodles in black bean sauce and watching Cirque Du Soleil DVDs on his little flat-screen.

I rap twice on the glass. Then I run down the hall and step halfway through the door to the kitchen.

I wait for Ponytail to appear at the other end of the hallway, giddy with anticipation, my mind full of the stillness of the restaurant. When he reaches the door, he stands there sidewise for a moment. He's holding something in his right hand, low. We stand still, half-facing each other at opposite ends of the hallway, my pulse hammering in my ears, adrenaline crashing around in my blood. Then he steps toward me.

"*Bié dòng!*—Don't move!" he shouts, raising his hands in front of him. I slip into the kitchen. The light of streetlamps coming through the dining room windows spills in above and beneath the saloon doors on the other side of the kitchen, and I can see more. I take a few steps in, turn to face the door, crouch into an athletic stance. My frantic heart feels ready to escape my idiot body and find a hiding place. Then Ponytail bursts through the door, a pistol extended in front of him in both hands.

"Who are you?" he says in Mandarin.

Stall, I tell myself, and I open my mouth, but exactly zero words come out. He lowers the gun a little, takes two slow steps toward me. Then he hears Sun's footsteps behind him and turns—too late. Sun's first kick, a roundhouse right, catches Ponytail's wrists and sends the gun bouncing off a wall and into a sink. His second kick is a swift, powerful left-footed reverse to the chest that throws Ponytail backward into me.

We crash to the ground. I scuttle backward on my hands and heels as Ponytail springs to his feet and throws a punch at Sun's head all in one motion. Sun deflects the blow with his right palm and rolls the next one into his side, but they keep coming: Ponytail is as quick as a welterweight contender, all over Sun in a blur of fists and feet, elbows and knees. Sun steps back, moving like a sheet of silk between Ponytail's limbs, guiding them around the periphery of his body, hollowing out and changing shape with each blow, so that even when he gets tagged, nothing connects with force.

Sun warned me to stay out of any fights unless he asked for help. His defense is deft and fluid, but he's backing up, he's barely fending off the blows, and he doesn't make any attack of his own. As he retreats in a circle around the kitchen, he passes through a shaft of light from the dining room windows, and I see the perfect equanimity in his motions. He's not struggling to evade Ponytail's strikes—he's studying them, picking up the rhythm and the tendencies. Then he catches a punch with a clawlike grip around the inside of Ponytail's wrist. He wrenches the wrist open, turning Ponytail's whole arm, shoulder, and chest upward, and Ponytail cries out in pain. With an explosive exhalation of breath, a *shwuh!* that comes directly from his diaphragm, Sun slams the edge of his right hand into the inside crease of Ponytail's elbow.

"Jesus Christ," I say, as Happy Year's new head of security crumples to the kitchen floor.

Sun snatches the gun out of the sink and releases the magazine, which he slips into the pocket of his black jeans before tossing the rest of it under the saloon doors into the dining room. Ponytail is lying prone, breathing peacefully. Sun hops onto his back, pats him down, and retrieves a flip phone from his pocket. I'm still sitting on the floor, watching this guy handle this criminal shit like he's making the same omelet for the millionth time.

"Let's go," Sun says.

I climb to my feet and give Ponytail a kick in the ribs, eliciting a shallow groan. "Did you kill Vincent Li?" I shout down at him. No response. I kick again, harder. And again. "Who killed

Vincent Li, you shitbag?!" Tears soak into my stocking, making it harder to see.

Sun grabs my arm, hisses into my face, "He's not going to answer you." He drags me out of the kitchen. As we run down the hallway, he snatches up his backpack from the floor in front of the office. He stops at the door, pokes his head out, and then runs out to the car. When Jules sees us coming, she starts the engine and reaches across the passenger seat to open the door for me.

I sprint around the back of the car and jump in next to Jules. Sun swings into the back seat and pulls the stocking off his head.

"Good," he says to Jules, patting her headrest.

I pull the damp stocking off my head and heave a couple of deep breaths, forcing myself back toward detachment, equilibrium. In a moment we are out on the street, back in real life, and it's over.

We come through the door and discover Andre dozing on the couch, waiting up for us like a giant mom. He stirs, rubs his face.

"Success?" he asks.

"Kind of, except Sun had to kung fu the crap out of some guy," I say.

"You kung fu'd the crap out of someone?" Andre drawls, raising his eyebrows, marking the vibe gap between his drowsy calm and me: thoughts racing, body aquiver with recent violence.

"Yes," Sun admits.

"Why the hell didn't you tell us you were a martial arts expert?" Jules demands. "Forget what Dad said for you to tell us. Was that part of your job? Beating people up?"

Sun hesitates, then nods. "Little part," he says.

I turn to Andre. "Can we switch to Chinese?"

Andre narrows his eyes. "Yeah. Sure. Cool with me. I was just about to turn in anyway."

"Good night, Andre," Sun says, and Andre pats him on the head as he ambles to his bedroom.

"First of all," I say in Mandarin, "how'd you knock that guy out so easily?"

Sun points to the inside of his elbow. "It's the fifth point of the lung meridian," he says, matter-of-fact, like I'm supposed to know what the fuck that means. "Qi pools there."

"So what happened to 'delivering packages and sending messages'?" Jules asks, her eyes flashing. "What else have you left out? What is Ice, anyway?"

"I really do not know about Ice," he says, looking at the floor with a pained expression on his face. "You have to understand, my job is like this: I do what Old Li says. If he tells me to beat someone up, I beat someone up. If he tells me to tell you some things, then I tell you what he said to say. And he told me to take you with me and get some things from the restaurant, so that's what I did."

Jules shoots me a frustrated look, and I can tell she's also unsure of how to react to Sun's words. Do we trust him? Can we blame him? Is this the real Sun, the real Dad that we're learning about? Then Sun reaches into his backpack and pulls out a sheaf of paper held together with a binder clip, as well as the small lockbox that Jules and I saw sitting on the safe. My pulse pounds away as he uses his drill to break open the lockbox. There's some cash inside, some receipts, a Chinese passport, and a dozen tiny Ziploc bags of white powder. Sun holds one up to the light, jiggles it a little, squints at it.

"*K-zǎi,*" Sun says. "Ketamine."

"Ketamine?" I stick a finger into one of the bags: the powder is smoother than coke, not as floury. I've never heard of it before, but Jules, who has attended hipper parties, is ready with an explanation.

"People call it Special K. It's also used in hospitals for anesthesia. People say it's like an out-of-body experience. You get totally destroyed, your life fades away, and it feels like you're swimming around. Down the K-hole."

Sun nods. "It started in Hong Kong, but now people sniff it in nightclubs and karaoke rooms in all the big mainland cities. It helps people forget their problems and relax. But after a few years, it destroys your internal organs, starting with your bladder."

"If that's what Ice is, I see why Dad wanted to stay out of it," I say.

"Rou Qiangjun flew into LAX on January twenty-second," Jules mutters. She's holding his passport open to the page with a U.S. visa pasted on it. "He was here a week before Dad died."

"It had to be him—he's the killer!" I say. "What are we gonna do?"

"Tell the cops, obviously," Jules says.

"Have you *met* the cops around here? They couldn't solve a crossword puzzle," I say.

"So what, you're gonna lace up your Nikes and don the mask of Zorro? Victor, have you lost your mind?"

Sun clears his throat delicately. "Lying about when he arrived here does not make Rou the killer. But even if he is, he's only a tool used by others. And if we go after him now, then Zhao and Ouyang will know what we are up to, and then it will be much harder to gather evidence against them."

"Wait, what are you saying?" Jules scowls at Sun. "You're planning to go after Dad's partners?"

Sun tips his chin toward the sheaf of paper. "Not my plan," he says. "He said you have to read this and then you will understand."

I pick up the document that Sun retrieved from the safe: a stack of white paper, printed in Mandarin and clipped to several sheets of yellow legal paper covered in Dad's handwriting. I read the boldface characters printed in the middle of the first page: "*Dài wǒ sǐ le, gěi wǒ de érzi*—For my son, if I am dead."

14

Xiaozhou, your mother always said to me that it would be a good idea to put these matters down on paper, first of all in order to express them and make sense of them. She said in this way perhaps I can face some of my demons. You know I am a worthless heathen, but in my moments of weakness, some of your mother's Christian ideas can seem very persuasive, haha. In fact, I must write this letter now because some things are going to happen soon. I will no longer be able to hide the truth or hide from the truth. Please forgive the quality of my writing, as I did not receive an education like you and Lianying did. Also, I am writing in very simple Chinese because I know you only got a B+ in Business Chinese 202 last semester, haha.

The inspiration for the home that I built for us in San Dimas came from the home I grew up in. My father was a wise, happy man, and also a man of culture, like I never had the chance to be. He was a scholar of the history of Peking opera, and he taught at a university in Beijing. He loved to write and sing. Mother was a former student of Father's. They loved each other very much. These are the grandparents whom you never met. Now they have been dead for many years.

I also had an elder sister like you do. Her name was Ruyu: "like jade." It was an inappropriate name for her because she was a tomboy, just like your elder sister used to be. It was also an unfortunate name for her for other reasons that I will write about later. But first, I will describe for you the times when we were a happy family.

My earliest memories are of a quiet life in the hutongs *of old Beijing, in the center of the city. Do you remember the* hutongs *from when we visited a few years ago? We lived in a courtyard-style home in a winding, cobbled alley. I was born five years after the Communists took over Beijing, but the politics of the time had not penetrated the* hutongs. *We had a simple life. Mother made us breakfasts of fried-dough fritters and warm soy milk. Father rode his bicycle to the university. Ruyu and I would walk to school together. In the afternoons, after school, we played in the streets with our classmates. We played war and shot at each other with sticks that we pretended were guns. Often the other kids made Ruyu and me be the "running-dog Japanese" in the war because they knew we had learned some Japanese words from Father, who had studied in Japan when he was a young man.*

It was not the most fun to have to be Japanese in the war games because after we lost (we always lost) our Communist liberators marched us through the hutongs *with our hands on our heads. However, we got our revenge when it came to fighting crickets. Playing war was a fun game for little kids, but cricket fighting was the real action. Ruyu's crickets almost never lost. Ruyu could sit still for a long time. She was very good at catching the fastest crickets. She taught me how to train them with a split piece of grass and feed them hot chilies to prepare them to fight.*

Ruyu won a lot of candy and allowance from the other kids because of her crickets. One time she even won a blue bicycle from Pan Weiguo, the son of the family who lived on the other side of the courtyard from us, but Father made her give it back. Ruyu was upset, and she did not talk to Father for some days. After dinner, when he would wash the dishes and sing Peking opera for us, she would go into the other room and read a book instead of sitting at the table and drinking chrysanthemum tea with Mother and me like usual. Her protest lasted for about a week. Then Father brought her a box of peanut candies and sang her a song of apology that he had written for her. It was a humorous song, and as he sang it we all laughed until we were crying. Ruyu had a strong sense of justice and fairness, but she also loved Father more than anyone else. I was independent and naughty, and I liked to spend time by myself. Perhaps that is why I survived and Ruyu did not.

In the late fifties and early sixties there was already a lot of political turmoil. People who talked too much about politics or complained about the food rationing often ended up in trouble with the authorities. During the Socialist Education Movement, my second maternal uncle, a midlevel government official, was denounced as a reactionary and sent to the countryside to be reeducated. Mother was very close to her little brother, and she became a more reserved person after he was denounced. One time I saw her crying while reading a letter from him. I remembered my uncle for his excellent calligraphy, but the handwriting in the letter was uneven and ugly. I asked my mother to read the letter to me, but she refused.

Father was good at staying out of trouble. He always attended Party functions and kept his nose clean. He taught the new Revolutionary operas in the same energetic way that he had previously taught The Peach Blossom Fan *and* Sword of the Cosmos. *He always put the family first and never objected to saying what people wanted him to say. Due to his discretion and humility, our family remained unharmed until after Chairman Mao proclaimed the Great Proletarian Cultural Revolution in 1966. At the time, I was ten years old.*

At first we managed to keep up with the political tide. All university classes were canceled, so Father would stay home and play with us during the day. On the night that we heard about the campaign to destroy the Four Olds (Old Customs, Old Culture, Old Habits, Old Ideas), he took all his books of literature and put them into the stove one by one. Rather than get too upset about it, he sang an opera dirge as he did it and then stood up and brushed off his hands and told us that we must all adapt to the times. “Suí jī yìng biàn, suí yù ér ān,” *he liked to say—“Adapt at every opportunity and be at peace with whatever you encounter.” Now you know where I learned the expression that I have repeated to you so many times.*

Father's good attitude could only take him so far. One very hot day in the summer of 1966, a group of Red Guards came through the hutong *looking for Counterrevolutionaries and Bad Elements. These bands of former university students ruled competing territories amid the chaos of the Cultural Revolution. Really they were young people with nothing better to do. Most of them wore their school uniforms with red bands of cloth wrapped around their sleeves. Chairman Mao had given them a great deal of authority and confidence, so they paraded around and sometimes beat people up.*

When they came to our courtyard, they made our family and Pan Weiguo's family stand in a line in the yard while they searched our rooms for signs of the Four Olds. Like most people, we only had good Revolutionary books and portraits of

Chairman Mao on our shelves. They were about to leave for the next house when one young woman recognized my father.

"That man is a university professor," she shouted, pointing at Father. "He knows old operas, and he can speak Japanese!"

The leader of the Red Guards pulled Father forward by his shirt and asked him whether he could speak Japanese.

"It is true that I was a university professor, but I don't really speak Japanese," he said quietly, without looking up.

Some of the Red Guards shouted that he was a liar, a Japanese collaborator, and a Counterrevolutionary, but the leader silenced them with a sharp movement of his hand. He was peering into my father's face. He was a tall and handsome young man. After a few tense moments, he took my father by the arm.

"Come with me," he said. The other Red Guards grabbed Father and took him out of the courtyard, pushing and pulling. They called him a Bad Element and a Capitalist Counterrevolutionary. That day I learned from the handsome leader of the Red Guards that if you listen carefully you can often tell when people are lying. We did not hear anything about Father for five days.

On the sixth day after the Red Guards took Father away, a teenage girl with a red band on her sleeve came to the courtyard and announced to us in quite formal terms that Father's trial would take place the next morning in the sports field at the university where he used to teach.

When we arrived at the sports field the next morning, there were many people there already. It was a hot and dusty morning. Father was fourth in the queue of defendants. The first three trials were difficult to watch. They followed a pattern: The defendants started out proud and defiant, but with the Party cadres, the Red Guards, and the crowd unified against them, they soon wilted and confessed. They hit themselves and pledged loyalty to the Party as the crowd hurled trash and verbal abuse at them. All three were sentenced to reeducation through labor.

When it was Father's turn, a Red Guard brought him in front of the university's Anti-Rightist Revolutionary Committee and made him kneel in the dust. He looked thin. His face was streaked with dirt, and his head had been shaved. He had a bloody bruise on his temple. He stared at the ground.

The Committee Head explained to Father that he had a black background and he was being charged with holding Counterrevolutionary and Bourgeois sentiments. Some former students of his, including the girl who had first accused him of speaking Japanese, came forward to "struggle" against him by denouncing him. They said how he had tainted their minds with his Bourgeois tastes. One young woman said that Father loved opera more than he loved Chairman Mao.

Then Pan Weiguo's father came forward and said they had lived in the courtyard with us for more than twenty years. He said it was true that Father had attended university in Japan. When the Committee Head asked him if he could verify that Father was a Counterrevolutionary who held Bourgeois sentiments, Pan Weiguo's father said yes in a quiet voice. The Committee Head asked him if he could speak up. Pan Weiguo's father did not say anything. The Committee Head asked him again. Finally Pan Weiguo lifted his finger and pointed at Father's face. He spoke in a loud, clear voice so nobody would misunderstand him: "Li Yujun, you are a Counterrevolutionary and a Capitalist, and I struggle against you."

The people in the crowd pointed at Father and shouted the same thing. The Committee Head made a show of quieting the crowd and giving Father a chance to defend himself, but he didn't. He must have known it would be no use. He immediately confessed in a lifeless voice. Ruyu started to shout something, and Mother clapped a hand over her mouth and held my sister against her body in an iron grasp.

I remember feeling like I was watching somebody else's nightmare. Later, I learned that it was very unusual that Father had been detained by the Red Guards and brought back to his university. The relationship between the Red Guards and the Party officials who tried him was unofficial and ambiguous, and perhaps the Red Guards had been deliberately dispatched to collect Father for some other reason, some reason hidden in his Counterrevolutionary background.

But whenever I asked Mother what that reason was, she simply shook her head and said that talking about the past was a waste of time.

The Committee Head told Father that he was a Counterrevolutionary and he would be sent to a labor camp to be reeducated. He said that Father should be ashamed of polluting his family, his neighbors, and his country with his Bourgeois tastes. Father finally looked up.

"I draw a clear line between me and them," he said.

Some people in the crowd laughed derisively. The Committee Head scolded Father for his lack of understanding of Revolution. It works the other way around, he explained to Father. Then he called for Li Yujun's family to come forward. He told Father to kneel facing us, so Father turned in our direction.

We had been standing toward the front of the crowd, but everybody backed away from us in that moment, and suddenly we were alone before the Committee Head as well. Then the man addressed Mother.

He asked her whether she would struggle against the Counterrevolutionary Li Yujun.

Father nodded his head to her. She was crying quite terribly. Through her tears, she told the Committee Head that she would draw a clear line, but he made her say it again directly to Father.

The crowd cheered for her to do it.

"I draw a clear line between us," she said to Father.

My sister was also crying. She wrenched herself free from Mother's grasp and ran to Father. She wrapped her arms around his neck. Father pushed her away from him but she kept trying to embrace him. People in the crowd were shouting. A few people threw garbage and stones at Father and Ruyu. One woman stepped forward with a jar of black ink and splashed it onto their clothes. Then some Red Guards came and pulled Ruyu off of Father. They held her by her arms and forced her to kneel beside Father. The Committee Head told my sister that she had to draw a clear line if she wanted to remain in Beijing with her mother.

Ruyu was still crying. There was black ink on her clothing, and some of Father's blood was smeared on her neck. She pointed at the Committee and then at the crowd. She shouted at them that they were all False Revolutionaries. She said that Father hadn't done anything wrong, and that he was the person who loved her the most. There was more jeering and rock throwing, and then the Red Guards pulled Ruyu away from Father and dragged him away, and I never saw him again.

15

Two years after the Party sent Father to labor reform, Ruyu was sent away to be reeducated herself. I came home one day from playing in the street to find my first maternal uncle standing in a daze in the middle of our living room, his face as white as the crumpled letter that he held in his hand. Millions of educated youths had been deemed out of touch with Revolution, so they would be sent "up to the mountains and down to the villages," where they could "build up and take root" by learning from the "poor and lower-middle peasants"—or so my uncle whispered to me as Mother and Ruyu sobbed in the other room.

"It's a great opportunity for Ruyu," he said, kneeling beside me so our heads were at the same level. "She'll be united with the agricultural class."

Later, on the day before Ruyu was scheduled to leave, I came home to find Mother sitting on top of Ruyu with her knees on Ruyu's arms and slapping her repeatedly in the face.

"Don't fight back," Mother said. "You must endure everything and come back to me when this madness is over."

Ruyu cried and nodded. Mother spat in her face and slapped her again.

"You have a big mouth," Mother hissed at her through her own tears. "They will probably dislike you there. You must promise me that you won't fight back."

"I promise," Ruyu blubbered. "Mom, I promise!"

Mother had her back to me and could not see me. I tiptoed forward and took Ruyu's hand, which was purple from lack of blood flow. She squeezed my fingers with her own.

The next day, after we had seen Ruyu off at the train station, Mother and I moved into the home of my first maternal uncle in a big concrete domicile in the Haiyuncang neighborhood. My first maternal uncle was kind to us. There was not much space in his apartment, so Mother and I slept on a cot in the kitchen. Mother was a delicate woman, and the separation from Father and Ruyu was difficult for her to bear. Despite the clear line she had drawn between herself and Father, she had received a degrading new work assignment: sweeping the streets and cleaning the public toilets. She did not speak much anymore, and she often fell ill.

There was no more school. Mostly I walked around the streets during the day. Everyone in the neighborhood knew that my family had a black background, so it was hard to make friends. People did not trust each other. Nobody wanted to be denounced by association. Eventually I fell in with boys who also had black backgrounds. We stayed together to avoid getting beat up. My closest friends were three boys with the surnames Ai, Ouyang, and Zhao. We called ourselves brothers. We were all twelve or thirteen years old.

The four of us had a lot of fun together. We would play war together, pretending to be spies and guerrillas. There was not much to eat in those days, and sometimes we would work together to steal food from the street stalls. We especially loved to eat hong dou bing*—flaky pancakes filled with sweet red bean paste. Zhao would watch the street stall for hours and then tell us what we had to do. Usually Ouyang would be the one to make a distraction. He would beg for food and throw tantrums in the street. I would steal the* hong dou bing *while the stall manager was dealing with Ouyang. Then I would pass them to Ai. Zhao always said Ai was the best actor, but the truth was, he was simply the most innocent-looking, and his way of speaking was very clean and pleasant. All of us were troublemakers, but Ai did not look the part.*

This was the kind of life I was living when we found out that Ruyu had committed suicide. We knew Ruyu had killed herself because one of Father's cousins, a well-connected Party cadre who had been trying to get Father out of labor reform, sent a letter to my first maternal uncle. He did his best to use language that would not be censored. Ruyu had failed in her reeducation, he wrote to my uncle. She was too stubborn and did not accept the teachings of Mao Zedong Thought. She refused to change her name, Ruyu, which reflected her Bourgeois, intellectual family background. Ultimately, she chose to end her own life despite the endeavors of the patient Revolutionary cadres and poor and lower-middle peasants who tried to help her. There were also a few sentences about how Father was progressing well in his reeducation and learning how to become unified with the working class and studying the lessons of the Revolutionary Martyr Lei Feng. Some other sentences in the letter had been redacted by censors.

The news sank Mother into a depression that lasted for the rest of her life. Being around her reminded me of everything we used to have. Like Ruyu, she failed to adapt to the circumstances and make a new life for herself. I tried to remember Father's voice saying "Suí jī yìng biàn, suí yù ér ān." *I spent little time at home. Because of my black background, I could not join the military or apply for secondary school. I passed the days in the street with the brothers. We stole things and chased girls. Sometimes people beat us, and other times we beat people. Sometimes we were dragged in front of crowds at struggle sessions and denounced, but these exercises were becoming tired and meaningless. Almost everybody had been denounced at some point. Nobody cared that much about making Revolution anymore.*

The brothers and I grew up during those years. We went from stealing treats to eat to stealing rice and cooking oil to sell on the black market. Our biggest customers for stolen goods were government officials and Communist Party cadres. Our dealings with them gave us useful connections. Sometimes our customers asked us to run different kinds of errands for them. Occasionally they asked us to beat someone, but usually they just wanted us to scare someone. We also helped them spy on and blackmail people. I loved the thrill of using the tricks I had learned to avoid detection. I was fast and clever. Maybe if I'd had access to more sources of calcium I would have been quite a good point guard, haha.

There was one customer of ours who gave us the most jobs. He asked us to call him Mr. Dong. We did not know his real identity, but we speculated that he was a senior Party cadre. He paid us well and treated us like humans, which was nice of him. He liked to call us his little monkeys, since we all belonged to that zodiac animal, and we took a certain amount of pride in this nickname. Over the years he cultivated our skills and gave us more and more responsibilities. Eventually he asked us to stop working for other customers. We did what he asked, because he was our biggest client, and also because we were afraid of him.

In '77, Dong asked us to help him with a bigger project: smuggling in goods from Hong Kong. One of us would have to go "upstream" to Hong Kong, and one of us would have to go "midstream" to Luohu. Zhao was the one who maintained contact with Dong, and he said he had no interest in leaving Beijing. The rest of us were dying to escape. We drew lots, and Heaven favored me. I would go to Hong Kong! Ouyang would go to Luohu. Ai and Zhao would stay in Beijing.

Dong arranged all my travel documents for me, including my first passport, and I took most of the cash that he advanced to us. I felt bad about leaving Mother in Beijing, but she urged me to take the opportunity to get ahead. She knew I was breaking the law. She didn't care. After the Party took away her husband and her daughter, she lost all respect for the government.

After I arrived in Hong Kong, I got a room in Chungking Mansions, the cheapest accommodation available. Chungking Mansions was a famous sort of giant slum building filled with hustlers and desperados, and I fit right in. It was an exciting time in my life. I visited stores that had the portable, high-margin products we wanted: Philips VCRs, Zojirushi rice cookers, Casio wristwatches. I cut deals with wholesalers and found boatmen to run the goods across the water to Ouyang in Luohu.

Once the operations were in place, I had lots of time on my hands. In that big international city I did not have a single friend. I spent a lot of time at a bar in Kowloon called the Deep Blue Sea. The bar had a fish tank filled with tropical fish and real coral. I would go there to drink American beer and shoot pool and stare at the fish. Growing up in the hutongs *of Beijing, I never imagined that such splendid creatures existed. I had never seen the ocean at all. But in Hong Kong, I saw the ocean every day, and I liked to think about how grand it was, and how it could be seen from so many different places. And I thought about how there were other people staring at the ocean in all those faraway places, and maybe some of those people had also lost their families, like I had.*

I went to the movies in order to learn Cantonese and English. During the American movies, I slumped low in my seat so that I could not read the subtitles at the bottom of the screen. I saw the same movies over and over again. My favorites were the American musicals, which reminded me of Peking opera. I was awestruck by the rich and carefree lives of the Americans in the movies. Everything looked like so much fun. When Grease *came out in 1978, I began to style my hair like John Travolta. Lucky for you, there are no surviving photographs from those years, haha.*

After Chairman Mao died, China began its period of Reform and Opening-Up under President Deng Xiaoping. It soon became unnecessary for me to remain in Hong Kong. I hired some people to maintain our operations there and moved back to Beijing in '81. I rented a new flat for Mother and me, and although she remained depressed, she told me that she was proud of the success I had achieved. We inquired all over regarding the fate of Father, but nobody had any news for us. Eventually I became resigned to the likelihood that he had died in a labor camp. Mother was still unable to move on. She rarely socialized or left the apartment. It was in this weak state that your mother pounced on her, haha. Linda was a dedicated missionary, and she had learned to speak excellent Chinese. She could stun a crowd of Chinese people just by saying a few sentences. She had a nice way about her, and everyone liked her, even though she talked a lot of nonsense about Jesus Christ. Mother was walking home with two bags of groceries one day when Linda asked if she could share her burden. Pretty soon she was coming around all the time and reading the Bible to Mother in Chinese.

I was glad that Mother had made a friend, even if it was a Jesus-crazed American. Also, I was enthralled by Linda. Her blond bangs and blue eyes reminded me of Olivia Newton-John. When she became my friend, too, I discovered that she was a great listener. I was telling lies to everyone, even though they all knew I was bending the rules. But because she was an outsider, I could tell her everything, and she told me that I could be forgiven. I sang Chinese operas for her and also "Greased Lightning," which she found extremely humorous. She sang hymns and praise songs to me in her beautiful, clear voice. Anyway, you can surmise what happened next.

Mother died shortly after you were born. Lianying was three. At that point the brothers and I were really making a lot of money. In addition to the smuggling, we did a lot of other jobs for Dong and his friends. Ouyang had great business instincts, and Zhao was a natural strategist. Ai was our figurehead: the smooth-talking, handsome one. As for me, well, as you say in basketball, I could execute the play. Together we grew fast, and China's young markets grew with us. Everyone had gotten sick of being Communists, and they really applied themselves to being Capitalists, haha. But my heart was not in it. After Linda gave me the happiness of a family, I felt more fear about working underground. Of course, she did not approve of my line of work, either. Once Mother passed away, we were no longer tied to Beijing. We wanted to move to the United States and start a new life.

Leaving was not simple. The brothers and I had pledged our lives to each other as teenagers. We had tasted each other's blood. I proposed the idea of starting a restaurant in the United States, pointing out that we could use our connections and our capital to create a successful, legitimate business, and I assured them that my protégé, Sun Jianshui, could eventually take my place in Beijing. Ai supported my idea, but Ouyang and Zhao agreed to the move only if I continued to act in the interest of the brotherhood in the United States. And they made me wait a few years until certain affairs were settled and Sun Jianshui had more experience. I did not want to quarrel with them. It seemed like a reasonable compromise at the time.

The only question left was: Where to go? My "in-laws" wanted nothing to do with us, and your mother had no desire to return to Missouri. We thought about places where a Chinese restaurant might succeed. I knew only that I wanted to be close to the ocean. Then one of Linda's missionary friends told us about a trend: many wealthy Taiwanese were relocating to the San Gabriel Valley. Your mother gasped in delight when we looked at a map of the area. San Dimas is Saint Dismas, she said. The repentant thief.

16

My phone is vibrating. I flip it over and look at the screen: it's Darryl, the assistant athletic director. Jules looks up from the page in front of her. We're sitting with two lukewarm cups of coffee, the stack of paper making up Dad's document, and a fat Chinese-English dictionary on the table between us. Jules has been building a little mountain of snot- and tear-filled napkins in front of her. It's 8:30 in the morning.

"Don't answer it. There's like fifty words on this page you need to help me with."

"I have to," I say. "He called me four times yesterday. Hello?"

"Victor! I've been trying to reach you all weekend. Where the hell are you?"

I look around, wondering the same thing.

"IHOP," I say.

"Victor, it's February ninth. You didn't register for classes. The deadline was Friday."

February ninth. Friday. Classes. My foggy brain wrestles with English, with college, with the space-time continuum.

"Things are a little hectic, Darryl."

"I know, Victor, I know. It's really awful about your dad. But you do have to register for classes if you want to play in any more games. There's no wiggle room on this. The online system is already closed. Just pick some classes and go talk to Shellie in the Dean's Office, okay? Today before five. That's all you have to do."

"Okay."

"Okay?"

"Okay. I'll do it." Shellie in the Dean's Office. I feel the onset of a headache scratching at the back of my skull.

"Sorry, Darryl."

"Hey, it's all good, Victor. I'll see you on the court." The phone makes a clicking sound as he hangs up.

Jules has the last three pages in her hand. Over the course of my phone call, her tears have been replaced with a scowl.

"I wasn't supposed to see this," she says.

"What? Why?" I say.

She hands me the pages and folds her arms in front of her.

Xiaozhou, I realize now that it was a mistake to hide these stories from you and Lianying for so long. I wanted us to live in a world without those dark things that I left behind in China. I thought that would be possible here in the United States, but I got it wrong. Those dark things are here, too. I came here looking for a clean and light place, and for some years I thought I had found it. But I learned that there is no such place.

In our first few years in the United States, my brothers back in Beijing did not ask too much. I helped them bring money out of China by setting up dollar-denominated bank accounts and investing in American real estate. Having one foot in the United States also allowed us to get involved in the remittance business. Most Chinese immigrants in the Los Angeles area are not as fortunate as we are. Sending money back to your family in

China isn't easy if you're an "illegal alien" getting paid in cash. Western Union charges high fees, and besides, there may not be a branch in your village in Fujian. Happy Year could take dollars from these people—waiters, fruit pickers, masseuses—and pay their families in yuan, without ever having to exchange the currencies. In this way we could build up our foreign accounts, launder our profits, and help our fellow Chinese Angelenos all at once. Zhao came up with this idea, and I set it up with the help of Mr. Peng, our attorney, who is well connected in the Chinese community.

Handling remittances didn't bother me. Mr. Peng did most of the work, and anyway, everything was going great here in the States for Linda and me. The restaurants were a big success, and you and Jules were growing up like real American kids: playing sports, watching MTV, and disrespecting your parents, haha. But Zhao was not settling down like I was. Instead, as China became more capitalistic and cutthroat, so did he. He didn't have a family of his own, and I think his business ideas were his children. He gave birth to them and watched them grow. But sometimes I had to babysit, and change diapers, haha. Not all his ideas were bad ideas. He hatched a plan to help Chinese parents get American citizenship for their babies. We use our connections to get temporary visas for expectant mothers. Then they come here, and I look after them until they have their babies in an American hospital and become American citizens, just like that. More easy money, and no real victim.

But some of Zhao's ideas were truly terrible. When Zhao came up with Ice, he knew I would fight it, so he asked Ouyang to take charge so he wouldn't be directly involved. For your safety, it's better if you do not know the details of the scheme for now. It's enough to say that it involves smuggling a dangerous product that I knew right away I could never be involved with. Ouyang began to put a lot of pressure on me. "Brother Zhao says that this project is important to Mr. Dong," Ouyang told me. "If we do not help him, Happy Year will be in trouble. And don't think the trouble won't reach you just because you're in America."

As usual, Ai tried to smooth things over. In Beijing, he argued on my behalf, but he also told me that Ouyang and Zhao resented me and didn't think of me as their brother anymore. Nonetheless, I refused to help, and I doubted that they would harm me after all we had been through together.

If I am wrong about that—if our shared history no longer protects me from their destructive ways—then I will accept my fate. Better to go now than to continue living at the whim of such men. They are unrecognizable to me now, and often I regret ever associating with them. But then, perhaps I would have died long ago without their brotherhood. I certainly would not have made it this far. It shames me to admit that there would be no Happy Year restaurants without Zhao and Ouyang. So perhaps they are right about me; perhaps I am the one who has betrayed them. People and circumstances change. I still follow the words of my father: "Suí jī yìng biàn, suí yù ér ān."

If you are reading this letter, then the worst has come to pass. Do not mourn me as a victim, as I have left the world in accordance with my principles. But I also made a backup plan. Zhao and Ouyang may take my life, but if you follow my instructions, then you and Sun can put an end to their depravity.

The plan is not complicated, but you will have to be careful. Sun will be a wanted man in Beijing. Zhao and Ouyang will be on the lookout for him, so everybody else will want to keep their distance. You will have to go to Ai and ask for his assistance. He will feel compelled to say yes because you are my son. Next, you will have to find evidence linking Zhao and Ouyang to Ice. I have found a point of vulnerability in their circle: a Russian dealmaker named Feder Fekhlachev.

Feder is greedy, fearful, and not too loyal. He will not give the information to Sun, but I believe he will sell it to you—he is a bit in awe of Americans. You will have to buy information from him and take it to the Western media. Dong can protect Zhao and Ouyang from the Chinese authorities. But if you expose their dirty laundry to the world, then Dong himself will become an embarrassment to the Party leadership, and they will force him to shut down Happy Year's operations.

When I was your age, I had to fight people all the time. If I were still young, then perhaps I would fight my brothers the old-fashioned way. But I am more mature now, and I know that violence engenders more violence. Instead, I want you to shine a light into the darkness I tried to leave behind in Beijing.

This letter must come as a shock to you, Victor, and I understand you may feel angry with me, but I do not apologize for my choices, because I did what I had to do in order to survive. The life you live has not come free. Now you must help repay that debt.

Also, you must take care of Lianying. You will be the head of the family now. Your sister is sensitive, and you must find the right way to tell her what is happening. Do not tell her before you go to China, because she will try to stop you.

Xiaozhou, I do apologize for deceiving you for so long. The lie has been my life. I never thought I had a choice. You must do as I say so that I can become an honest man, finally, perhaps, after I am already a dead one.

I put down the last page and look up at Jules, who is sitting there with her arms folded, glowering at the table. I can't think of anything to say, either. For a minute I close my eyes, listen to the restaurant sounds. I imagine my new grandfather making bricks in some dusty labor camp in Qinghai, and Dad with a Danny

Zuko ducktail, drinking Bud Light and staring at clown fish in a divey Hong Kong pool hall. I envision Mom patiently pitching the gospel to bemused Beijing grannies in her neat and precise Mandarin. She helps Dad with his English; the two of them huddle together over a map of California. Both dead now.

I picture my future as I thought they intended it: a secure white-collar job; a condo shared with some less-intimidating version of Holly Michaels; pets, children, Brita filter, minivan, timeshare. *PowerPoints about corporate synergies or whatever.* But then I see Sun's foot crashing into Ponytail's chest in the Happy Year kitchen, and, in the dim streetlight leaking in through the saloon doors, I see myself, crouched, alert, and I hear my racing pulse.

"Stop it," Jules says, finally.

I open my eyes. "Stop what?"

"You're thinking about going."

Blinking, I shake my head. "I'm not."

"I want to know what happened, too, I really do. This letter is heartbreaking, and now there so many questions that I want answered. But going to China with Sun and going after these guys, these killers—it's too risky. The side of Dad that's asking you to do this, it's not his good side, okay? I know how much you adored him, but you need to see past that for a minute and recognize how this letter shows that he was completely two-faced and deceitful."

"But Jules, I—"

She doesn't let me finish. She gestures with her hands, her face reddening with some combination of anger and incipient tears. "No, Victor, before you object, please *listen* to me for a second, okay? Did you never wonder why Mom was estranged from her parents? Why you, you bury yourself in basketball to avoid facing the contradictions in your life—just like he always buried himself in his work? He was faking it, Victor, trying to make us look like a normal family, while he was scooting back and forth to Beijing doing God knows what. He doesn't even say! Even in this letter, he's trying to come clean, he's telling us about the immigrants and pregnant ladies he helped, but he doesn't say what this Ice shit is all about."

At some point, she has to breathe, which means I manage to get a word in. "Did we read the same letter just now, Jules? It's not like he was sitting around looking at grad school brochures, and then he decided he'd prefer a life of crime."

I'm furious at her for explaining my life to me, sufficiently enraged to drop in the grad school line just to make it sting.

"Maybe Dad didn't have all the same options that we had, okay? He did some dirty work because he had to, but he gave it up as soon as he could. He married a missionary and moved to the suburbs! If he worked his ass off and lied about his past so that we could have normal lives, don't you think we should be grateful?"

She sets her jaw and glares at me for a moment. "I *am* grateful, but Victor, for once in your life, will you try to see some nuance? You're your own person, not some extension of Dad, and you don't have to buy all this patriarchal 'head-of-the-family' bullshit, all these melodramatic lines about shame and loyalty and debt. If you would spend just two minutes thinking about it rationally, you'd see that he's asking too much. You'd realize that going to China to fight Dad's enemies is a terrible, terrible idea."

Jules: always so great at seeing both sides of the coin. Always so great at coming up with reasons to avoid commitments, reasons to criticize, reasons to separate herself from the pack. I want to say, you don't understand this letter because it's about caring a lot about something. I want to say, you didn't pick up that he was ashamed of us, too, he's asking so much because he made all these sacrifices for a couple of big babies who don't think about anything but ourselves, our basketball season, our dreams, our love lives. We don't care about the past or the future, the vast imbalances in the world that we benefit from. The painful compromises people make just to get a decent job making dinner for people like us. We're blind to that, we're desensitized, we live in a bubble, and he knew it.

He's only asking me to be human, to give a shit, to stand up for what's right. I want to say, you'll notice he didn't bother asking you.

"You're always telling me to think for myself, to be my own person. But in the next breath, you're telling me what to do," I say instead. "You know, I'm so glad you've got everything figured out. You've got Dad figured out, you've got me figured out. Maybe sometime soon you'll have your own life figured out as well."

"Look, Victor, this isn't about me, this is about you." Jules drops her voice low and glares at me across the table. "Dad was good at making you feel special. He manipulated you just like he manipulated Sun. You don't think it's a bit messed up that he pulled Sun off the streets to use him as a mule? That he trained him to become his gang enforcer? That he raised another little one-man fan club for himself in China?"

"That's a typical way for you to see things," I bark back at her. "You don't think even for a minute what Sun's life would be like without Dad, because you take for granted all the love and support you've received. Dad gave Sun a home and taught him to read and write. He taught him to speak English. He gave him a future, even if it's not a perfect future. But you, you want everybody to be perfect just like you are, which is why you've never been happy, and you never will be."

"I wish *you* didn't speak English, you superior little *shit,*" Jules hisses.

Then she glares daggers at my phone, which is vibrating again. I flip it over to look at the screen. Lang.

I take a deep breath before picking up.

"Hello?"

"Victor. Where are you?"

"I'm at IHOP."

"Arrow or Foothill?"

"Um. Arrow."

"Don't move. I'll be there in ten."

"Wait—" But the line's already dead.

I put the phone down, put my elbows on the table, put my face in my hands.

After a minute, Jules says, "Wow, that conversation got nasty really fast. Look, I'm sorry, Victor. I don't want to fight. It's just that you're all the family I've got left, and I don't want you to leave me here by myself. I'm genuinely afraid of what would happen if you went to China, and I'd say I have good reasons to be."

I don't say anything back to her. I just stay there with my hands over my face, waiting for an asteroid to strike the earth.

"So Lang is coming here, now?" she says.

I grunt.

"Why?"

"He didn't say."

"So what do you say, Victor? Do we tell him about the ketamine, and hand off this law-enforcement business to the professionals?"

I take my hands off my face, blink a few times, give my head a shake. "Jules, that would involve confessing to a break-in that we committed, like, six hours ago."

Jules widens her eyes, then rubs them with the heels of her hands. "I'm honestly so fucking exhausted that I forgot that part."

I don't say anything.

"He might even be planning to ask you about that."

"Uh-huh."

We look at the pages strewn around the table, the Chinese-English dictionary, the mountain of snotty napkins.

"Okay. I'll leave and take this stuff with me," she says. "Are you all right to talk with him right now?"

"He's not exactly Sherlock Holmes."

"Fine. But Victor, maybe test the waters a bit, because we might need his help. I'm going to get some sleep, and I suggest you do the same. Let's think things over and talk later. Okay?"

"Sure."

"Promise me you'll call me later."

"Okay," I say. "I promise."

Jules packs the letter and the dictionary into her handbag. She gets up to go. She gives my shoulder a squeeze.

I make the requisite eye contact and nod my head.

Jules lingers for a moment with her hand on my shoulder and then walks away with her head down, her mask of nonchalance left behind on the blue pleather bench of the IHOP booth, her small shoulders sagging beneath the weight of too many sensitivities and indecisions, too much vulnerability and love. Those burdens and also a large calfskin handbag stuffed with the last testament of our father's life.

I'm already feeling terrible for talking to her the way I did. I don't want to fight, either. I have no idea what I want; I wonder if I ever have. All I know is what Dad wants, what Jules wants, what Andre wants, what Coach Fucking Vaughn wants. But now I need everyone else to shut the fuck up and let me think for myself for once.

17

Like a lot of cops, Lang saunters. He takes his time, says, "Hi, folks," to people, strolling around like the patrolmen who break up off-campus parties. Except there's no tan shirt tucked into brown pants. He's still rocking the khakis-and-Hawaiian-shirt look.

I'm watching him make his entrance and head toward my booth, which is now clean. After Jules left, the waitress ran my card and cleared away the crumpled napkins. She also topped up my mug of tepid coffee, but I can't drink any more of it. I don't do caffeine during the season, so I'm already jittery from the two cups I had earlier.

That, no sleep, and a few other factors.

"Hey." He slides in across from me and briefly scans the folded cardboard triangle printed with the breakfast specials. "You eat?"

I shake my head.

"You gonna?"

"No."

"How'd you get here?"

"My sister drove."

"Where'd she go?"

"She had some stuff to do."

"Ah." He digests this, glancing around at the tail end of the breakfast rush. The state of his eyes, hair, and clothes tells me he's been up since before dawn and didn't shower this morning. He strokes his upper lip with his index finger. "So she left you here?"

"She had to go and you called."

"Oh. That's a shame." He grunts. "Well. Let's get down to business and then I can give you a ride."

He pulls out a Korean-made smartphone the size of a small Bible. It's the biggest fucking phone I've ever seen in my life. He squints down at the touch screen and stabs at it with his index finger.

"Just got this thing. Can you believe it's SDSO standard issue now?" he scoffs. "Ah, here we go. You know these people?"

He passes the giant phone to me. The picture was taken through the windshield of Jules's car. It doesn't take long for me to weigh my options. So I tell him.

"Your sister, huh? I thought so," Lang says. "Can you tell me what they're doing in this photo?"

"Jules and I looked through my dad's office for those legal pads. We didn't find them, but we did find this address. She wanted to go check it out."

"Where'd you find it?"

"Just written on some paper."

"Can you show me the paper?"

"I can ask if she still has it." The lies come out nice and easy despite the caffeine jitters. When did I decide to tell them?

Lang is scribbling in his little notebook. "What did she say about the house?"

"She said it was full of pregnant Chinese ladies."

"Any idea why?"

I consider playing dumb, but it occurs to me that revealing some of what I know will make it easier to conceal the rest. *It is true that I was a university professor, but I don't really speak Japanese.*

"Citizenship hustle," I say. "The Chinese babies born here are U.S. citizens."

He raises his eyebrows, purses his lips. "Nice theory. In fact there are five or six operations like this in the San Gabriel Valley. But that's an issue for the folks over at Immigration and Customs Enforcement, not the police. So what's your dad got to do with this house?"

I shrug. "I wish I knew."

Lang gives me a look, then takes the phone back from me and starts punching around on it again.

Rou Qiangjun pops into my mind, his snake tattoos, his affected simplicity, his menacing calm. He probably knows by now that someone broke into the safe at Happy Year. Would he spook and leave town?

"How's it going with the forensics team from Orange County?" I ask Lang. "Do they have the killer's DNA?"

"Crime lab's still backed up," Lang says without looking up from the phone. "They fed us a line about funding cuts. These things take time. Okay, what about this guy?"

He turns the phone to show me a mug shot of Ponytail, looking the worse for wear.

"He works at Happy Year."

"Worked. Illegally, I might add," Lang says. "Someone broke into the restaurant last night and took a couple of things. They also put a beating on this man, who may be charged with illegal possession of a firearm. If he's convicted, his B-1 visa will be revoked, and he'll be deported. Any guesses as to who sponsored his visa?"

"My dad?"

"Actually, his attorney, Perry Peng, who I believe you had a chat with last week."

I sit forward to say something, but Lang raises a finger before I can protest. "I know, I know, of course you had to speak with him about estate stuff. But look, I'm gonna need you and your sister to locate that piece of paper, and if you find anything else that might be helpful to the investigation—" He holds another one of his business cards in my face. "Okay? Are we on the same page?"

"Yeah, I—" *Test the waters a bit.* Would Lang be able to help us? If we confessed, would he "try to see some nuance"? I'm trying to think of some way to prod him, but all I'm coming up with is an overwhelming desire to lie down.

"Yeah." I accept the business card and put it the pocket of my shorts. "Same page."

He smiles and sits back into the booth. "Good. I thought so. Let's get out of here."

Lang takes a peppermint from the basket on the host stand as we walk out. "All right, honey, you have a nice day," the hostess calls out to him, and, without turning his head, he waves the back of his hand over his shoulder. Out in the parking lot, he beeps us into a gold Buick, an incognito cop car which nonetheless has three or four giant antennae mounted on the chassis.

Lang pops the peppermint into his mouth and slips the plastic wrapper into his shirt pocket. Then he starts the car, backs out of his parking spot, and noses the Buick gently out onto Arrow Boulevard. After a minute or two of silence, he punches on the radio, which assaults our ears with a bubblegum pop tune about having both a new car and a new girlfriend at the same time.

It's a song I might have sung in the shower two weeks ago, but now the lighthearted melody strikes a violent contrast with the scene in my head: a faceless woman with a huge belly, biting her lip as she hands her passport to an immigration official. All in order to bring her unborn baby to that clean, light place that she's seen on a movie screen. We drive past Daily Donut, we drive past Vapor

Bliss. We drive past San Dimas Pet Resort and Grooming Spa. And then I decide to shut my eyes.

Cain't nobody hold these niggas down
No doubt
Bringin' bad boys into ya town
Make ya shout
Comin' at ya with the freshest flavas
No doubt
Tell ya aunties tell ya cousins tell ya neighbas
Make ya shout

Sun and Andre are sitting forward on the sofas, elbows on their knees, the remnants of a bagelwich run strewn around the coffee table. Sun's head is cocked to the side as he tries to catch the lyrics to the chorus of one of Regime Change's clubbier tracks.

"Nice sound, but I am not understand too much," Sun admits.

"Makes you want to dance, though, right?" Andre holds his arms out, elbows in, and shimmies his shoulders. Sun laughs shyly. Andre laughs with him and then slumps back into the sofa. "That's the old-school sound. They don't make them like that anymore."

Sun moves the stereo jack from Andre's phone to his own.

"My favorite song is also old-school sound," he says, putting on "Man in Black."

"No way. How do you know about Johnny Cash?"

Sun indicates me with his chin. "His father."

Andre turns around and sees me just inside the door.

"Damn, Victor! How long've you been lurkin' there like a straight-up creeper?"

"I've gotta pick my classes," I say, slipping into my room. I nudge the door closed with my foot and pull my laptop into bed with me.

ECON 301: Fiscal Policy and Sovereign Debt. BPUB 240: International Markets in the Twenty-First Century. EAS 322: Newspaper Chinese. Can I enroll in Marketing 202 if, due to my father's gruesome assassination at the hands of his former blood brothers, I have not yet taken the final for Marketing 201? I guess I'd have to talk to Shellie in the Dean's Office about that. Maybe I should take statistics and finally get that Quantitative Data Analysis requirement out of the way. *I did what I had to do in order to survive.* MATH 105: Business Statistics. Tuesdays and Thursdays at 8:00 A.M. I could still make the first lecture tomorrow morning.

Someone taps on my door. I sit up on the bed, put the laptop aside, and say, "Come in."

Sun pads in in his socks and sits cross-legged on the floor.

"Did you read the letter?" he asks.

"Yes," I say. "Have you?"

"I transcribed it," he says. "Old Li asked me to when he visited Beijing in October. That was the last time I saw him. He told me you could not read handwritten Chinese."

I feel a blush suggest itself around the edges of my face. "Then why didn't you tell me that my sister wasn't supposed to read it?"

Sun cocks his head to one side. "I didn't think anything I could say would stop her from seeing it. Lianying was never supposed to be involved. In October, Old Li did not mention that you couldn't drive."

"The DUI happened in November." The blush deepens. "You two weren't, like, texting about this or anything?"

"No."

We sit like that for a minute or two. Then I say, "It just doesn't make sense to me. Why would he lie about these things for his whole life and then ask me to get involved after he's dead?"

Sun is studying a bruise on his wrist that he must have acquired during the break-in to Happy Year. I notice for the first time how strong and sinewy his arms are.

"I wondered the same thing," he says. "So I asked him. He said to me that you're very capable, you can handle the challenge. He said that I'd be able to keep you safe."

"And you agreed?"

He glances up from his bruise, looks at me.

"Yes, I agreed," Sun says. "But I think he was not willing to admit the main reason he chose you to come with me."

"Which is?"

"Old Li didn't have anybody else he could count on."

I let this sink in for a moment, try to put myself in Dad's shoes: an unbearably lonely proposition. A single father with a double life, running four restaurants, a remittance business, and a citizenship racket. Dad didn't really have close friends, just a few restaurant buddies he played cards with on Monday nights. His life was work and family. Who could he ask to avenge him?

Sun says, "I understand your hesitation. I can't make you go. Maybe if I were you, I wouldn't. And to be honest, I prefer to work alone. But this time I can't."

"Why not? How do I fit into this plan, anyway?"

"You just have to be the face," Sun says. "If I go back to Beijing and start trying to buy information on Ouyang and Zhao, I might be dead within twenty-four hours. But nobody knows who you are. Old Li made sure of that. He never let any of his brothers visit him in the United States. And since you're an American, you can have access where I cannot."

"I never would have thought that revenge would be so important to him," I say.

"I think if Old Li were here," Sun says, "he would say we can make up for past mistakes."

I'm staring out the window at the row of fan palms in the center of the Quad, swaying slightly in the winter wind. *Fiscal Policy and Sovereign Debt. Dad was good at making you feel special.*

"Think it over," Sun says, rising to his feet. He quietly pulls the door shut behind him.

I pull my laptop back into my lap and open a new tab, search for "organized crime in China," and click through to a list of Chinese gangs and Triad societies. The Continentals, the Green Dragons, the Kit Jai. Criminally influenced tongs—what's a tong? I click through more links. The feud between Street Market Wai and Broken Tooth Wan. "The number of people involved in organized crime on the mainland rose from around 100,000 in 1986 to 1.5 million in the year 2000." I look up San Dimas crime statistics on a public database and discover that, on average, there are zero murders here annually. Robberies, petty theft, vagrancy. Detective Richard Lang, firm, calm, and affable, was just the man for the job. Except maybe for this one case.

I do another search and turn up Dr. Aron Ancona's office number at Cedar Sinai. The phone rings seven or eight times, and just when I'm about to give up, a heavy voice comes on the line and says hello.

"Yes, hi, Dr. Ancona. My name is Victor Li? Vincent Li was my father?"

The line is quiet for a while. "Who was your father?" he asks.

"Vincent Li?"

"I'm afraid I don't know anyone by that name."

I grit my teeth, and for some reason Jason Maxwell pops into my head, backing me down, lowering his shoulder.

"So you'd be pretty surprised if I told you that he was murdered and your address was found among his things?"

"My goodness, yes." The heavy voice takes on a troubled, sympathetic tone. "Yes, I'm afraid it would be a complete surprise."

Pinching the phone between my shoulder and my ear, I pull open the drawstring to Sun's backpack. Black T-shirts, black jeans, black socks, little black drill. Envelopes of more U.S. and Chinese cash. Chinese bank cards and credit cards in a black vinyl wallet. *I wear the black in mourning for the lives that could have been.*

Dr. Aron Ancona clears his throat. "If there's something I can help you with—"

"Hey, yeah, right. You didn't know him, you said. So you wouldn't mind if I shared that detail about your address with the police who are investigating his murder?"

There's another long pause, and when the heavy voice comes back, all the concern is gone.

"Look, kid, I don't know what you think you're doing, but you're barking up the wrong tree. Your dad and I were involved in a business deal and he backed out. I found someone else to work with. End of story. Okay? If he got himself killed it's got nothing to do with me, so you can tell the cops whatever the fuck you want."

"What kind of business deal? Was it ketamine? Was it Ice?" I'm asking, but he has already hung up.

"What the fuck kind of business deal?" I say it again to the ceiling, then punch the palm of my right hand hard, twice. I snatch the basketball out of my gym bag, snap it back and forth in my fingertips. I count down two or three shot clocks: pick and pop, high-low, flare off the screen for the jumper. *A Russian dealmaker named Feder Fekhlachev.* Business Statistics, Tuesdays and Thursdays, 8:00–10:00. Practice at 4:30. Another day as an econ major and backup point guard. *You must help repay that debt.* I replay Sun's precise plan at Happy Year: the decoy, the ambush, the flashing kicks. Why did Dad lock the letter in the restaurant safe instead of leaving it at Chateau Happiness with the gun and the passport? *Can you believe it's SDSO standard issue now?* The dearth of certainty roars in my head, unignorable, like a vacuum cleaner.

I put down the ball and dig further into Sun's backpack. In a side pocket, I find a pair of photographs. One is cropped from a team portrait on the SDSU Athletics website: me in my basketball jersey and a toothy grin, the clueless boy Sun crossed the ocean to locate and retrieve. The other is a worn film print at least a dozen years old: Dad in his signature starched white shirt, sleeves cuffed, one long arm draped over Sun's teenage shoulders. They are standing on a beach somewhere in China, flashing grins of their own, the sun casting long shadows on the coarse, seaweed-strewn sand behind them.

Why did Sun show me the monkey figurine and not this?

I should stay. I should enroll in classes. I should never find out the answer to that question.

I put the photographs back and pick up the drill, examine it in my hands. *He was completely two-faced and deceitful.* It's a remarkable piece of engineering, all smooth lines and matte finish. There's no branding or logo on it, only some Japanese writing on the handle. *She will try to stop you.* In my hands the drill is compact and heavy, like a weapon.

PART TWO

PEOPLE'S REPUBLIC OF CHINA

18

I like long plane trips because they restrict your freedom. All your choices of potential actions melt away, and all that's left is time—time to work through the backlog of thoughts and anxieties crowding your mind until nothing's left, and you just tilt your head back and gaze in blissful boredom out at the world floating past. The flight from LAX to Beijing is about twelve hours, which gives me plenty of time to ponder how Jules, Andre, and Coach Vaughn will react to the notes I left for each of them; how long it will take Lang to find out that I've left the country; whether or not I'm a complete fucking idiot; and so on. There isn't anything I can do about any of it on this plane, which is a relief. Actions were taken by a younger Victor, and will soon be taken by an older Victor, but in the air, all this Victor can do is sit here thinking stuff over and eating pretzels.

Sun's story of greed and conspiracy had barely dented the trance I'd been walking around in since Dad's death, but his precise burst of violence at the restaurant woke me up like a glass of ice water to the face. Nothing about his personality led me to expect him to knock out an armed security guard with brutal economy. But then I realized that I'd appraised him through the same biased glasses that our society has leveled at Chinese-Americans from Michael Chang to Jeremy Lin: he's small, he's polite, so he's probably not a badass. It was the sort of superficial judgment that I had to defy every time I stepped on the basketball court.

Dad had never minded being misjudged in this way. He probably saw it as an advantage: a benign disguise that helped him conceal his backdoor dealings, past and present. But now that I had an idea of what was going on, I wouldn't be satisfied with skating along the surface anymore. I couldn't send Sun back to China and go back to basketball practice like nothing had happened, knowing my world only *through a glass, darkly.* Ice: the frozen form of the source of all life, a shelf in the Antarctic, a volatile commodity, a smuggling operation that had cost Dad his life. Glass: both a liquid and a solid, *two opposed ideas at the same time.* Perfectly hard, ostensibly clear, yet it can be stained, soiled, distorted. And one good scratch could destroy its integrity; one well-thrown Bible could shatter the barrier between two realms, previously compartmentalized.

I attempted to reconstruct Dad's letter a few times on the plane, tried to organize my thoughts around all the new information. Dad had started a new life by leaving China and opening the restaurants, but Zhao and Ouyang insisted that he help them from his position in the States. When he fought back against their plan to import ketamine, they sent Rou Qiangjun to take over the U.S. operations. And Dad, like the clever crook I guess he always was, had anticipated all of it with a contingency plan: Sun would come collect me from San Dimas, and the two of us would travel to Beijing to shut down Happy Year for good.

But was Rou the killer, or just the replacement? And what about that first break-in at the restaurant that he mentioned—was that just a disgruntled employee making a cash grab? Then there were Aron Ancona and the lawyer, Peng—I have no idea where they fit in. When I think back to my brief, testy phone conversation with Ancona, my jaw clenches until my crowned molar starts aching. I'm sick of people patronizing me and hiding behind lies. Maybe Dad didn't have much of a choice. But I'm not going with Sun just because Dad wanted me to. I took Jules's advice, thought about it rationally, made my own decision. I need some answers to the questions that are pinching my brain like clothespins.

And then a moment comes when we fly over a break in the sea of marshmallow fluff and I glimpse the vastness of the Pacific Ocean toiling away below, the biggest damn thing on the planet, and it strikes me how absurd it is for me to be hurtling over it in a metal tube—when did traversing an ocean become such a casual thing?—and even though I haven't felt like breathing in a week, I wonder whether the hard part is just beginning.

Speaking with Sun so much over the past few days, my Mandarin has gotten a lot smoother. My tones have always been good, but now I don't have to focus on them—I can just talk like I'm talking, without expending so much energy listening to myself to ensure all the dips, sings, and chops are in the right places. It's whenever a rising second tone follows a scooping third tone, like in the words for "originally" or "American dollar," that I get tripped up the most, often mispronouncing the two syllables in one of the more common double rising patterns for two second tones in a row, or two third tones, or a second tone followed by a third tone. A third tone to second tone word is like an unbroken two-syllable journey from the bottom of my voice to the top: *běnlái, měiyuán*. Then there are the ringing, level first tones and the sharp, dropping fourth tones—I mix those up sometimes, too, especially when I'm speaking quickly. In order to get it all right, I have to remember to talk at my own speed instead of trying to match the rapid-fire pace of native speakers.

I'm keeping all that in mind as I stand in line to pass through immigration, ready to break out the answers that Sun drilled into me, but the poky, bored-looking guy in the booth doesn't even glance up at me as he stamps my passport.

"*Kàn zhèli*—Look here," he says, tapping a little camera with his index finger. I look there, he clicks his mouse, and there I go into the system.

"Next."

We step into the immense main concourse, the strange light of Beijing streaming through endless rows of plateglass windows. The air is a dense gray, hanging around too closely to be clouds, the sun low and crimson, an unfamiliar star lent an insidious tint by the exhaust pipes of five million cars, the smokestacks of ten thousand factories, the dust storms blowing in from the Gobi Desert. The airport is a fortress of organization and filtered air; the city stretches beyond it, ocean-like in its scale, a place to conquer or vanish.

"The air has gotten a little better," I say, dumbly.

"Yes, it has," Sun says without glancing up from his phone. Sun has grown more tight-lipped and serious now that we've arrived in Beijing, probably nervous about popping up on Ouyang or Zhao's radar. As soon as we passed customs, he slipped into the bathroom to change into his disguise: gray drawstring joggers, a smart yellow messenger jacket, and a trucker hat pulled low over his eyes. He blends in well with the hordes of suave millennial Chinese. When we came to visit as a family more than a decade ago, this massive terminal hadn't been built yet. The old one was filled with novice travelers listing around in a daze, squinting at signage, lugging giant plaid duffel bags made of cheap vinyl. Now the air is slightly clearer and the yuppies have cleaned up nicely. Their suitcases have four wheels; their sunglasses say Givenchy; they order without glancing at the menu at Burger King, at Yoshinoya, at Jackie Chan's Cafe.

Sun leads me out into the frigid afternoon and over to a black German luxury sedan with tinted windows and a tall guy leaning his hips against the passenger door. The guy looks around my age.

He is muscly, with a shaved head and a big jaw, and he seems to be smiling at his cigarette until he looks up and sees us coming.

"Motherfucker! Fucking shit!" he exclaims, beaming, in a thick Beijing accent. "So you brought us Old Li's son, huh? Fuck! You look pretty fucking Chinese for a mixed-blood kid."

He kind of hugs me and punches me in the stomach at the same time.

"My name is Ye, but everyone calls me 'Biceps,'" he says, flexing his arms to make sure I understand why.

"Uh, hi," I say, but he's already dancing around Sun and slapping the top of his head.

"The cat is back! You are so motherfucked! I shouldn't even be here," he says, laughing.

"I knew you'd do whatever I said," Sun says, ducking his head and gamely fending Biceps off with a push to the chest. "Can you take us to see Old Ai?"

"Of course. Where else could I take you? Oh man, he's going to be steamed. Don't get me in any more trouble, okay?" says Biceps.

"I thought Ai was on our side," I hiss to Sun as we put our bags in the trunk.

He purses his lips and nods thoughtfully. "He will be when he sees you."

We sit in the back of the car, which is immaculate except for several empty cans of Chinese Red Bull on the floor in front of the passenger seat. Biceps navigates the airport expressway with manic enthusiasm, swiping through traffic, slamming on the pedals, and keeping me awake by compelling me to hang on to the grab handle. I am vaguely reminded of the time Eli rented a Camaro for a day and we put two hundred miles on it without leaving Los Angeles County. But these Beijing drivers put L.A.'s best daredevils to shame. Throughout the journey, Biceps uses his horn to express a variety of sentiments, from "Here I fucking come!" and "Fucking thank you!" to "I hope your children are born without assholes, you cow twat!," which he occasionally supplements with verbal versions for extra emphasis. In between these interjections, he catches Sun up on a number of topics that are difficult for me to follow because of his accent and vocabulary.

The gist is that the national soccer team once again fucking humiliated itself in a loss to fucking Iran; he has a new favorite karaoke spot with *sānpéi* girls from Anhui Province who are way hotter than the *sānpéi* girls from Henan Province at his old favorite karaoke spot; he personally witnessed an actual fucking Ferrari explode at the Thirty Seconds Club; various people are extremely fucking angry for all sorts of reasons; et cetera. I divide my attention between his spirited monologue and the forest of bland office and apartment towers that float deep into the sooty haze in every direction, the farthest mere ghosts of the nearest. The toxic particulate matter suspended in the air intercepts the yellow of the sun's light, casting everything bluer, lending the endless concrete—roads, bridges, walking bridges over roads, tunnels—a purplish tint. And in this lavender surreality, people are compacted into not tiny spaces but enormous ones, hulking edifices built to accommodate thousands. Godzilla might go to Tokyo for a light dinner, but he'd hit Beijing for the Thanksgiving buffet.

As I listen to Biceps's casual patter about the seedy side of Beijing, my worries about everyone back in San Dimas fade into mental background noise, and I recall that I have a purpose here, a goal to accomplish. Ai, Feder Fekhlachev, and Dad's killers are lurking somewhere in this sea of smoggy concrete, and it is up to me to persuade, bribe, and expose them, respectively. Sitting in the back of the sedan reminds me of a long bus ride to an away game, the giddy calm before the storm—except this time, the action will have consequences beyond next week's Coaches Poll.

"What's a *sānpéi* girl?" I whisper to Sun when Biceps takes a break from talking to light a fresh cigarette.

"*Sānpéi* is three 'withs.' Girls who work in clubs. They will drink with you, sing with you, and dance with you."

"And that's it?"

"Sometimes," he says.

Up front, Biceps cackles. Apparently, he has excellent hearing.

"Old Ouyang controls several bars and karaoke salons in the Finance Street area," Sun says. "He has the *sānpéi* girls there selling ketamine."

Biceps clucks in disgust. "Those motherfucking bitches are hitting up every single customer for one hundred yuan per line! That's why I can't go there anymore. The sluts get all disappointed if you don't want to score drugs from them and then lie there staring at the ceiling."

"So what's the Thirty Seconds Club?" I ask louder.

"Street racing on the ring roads," Biceps says. "Rich brats who like losing their money. They race their Ferraris against the mechanic kids and their homemade Japanese rice rockets."

"And they lose?"

"Usually. The rich kids aren't afraid to lose the money, but they're afraid of losing their pathetic lives, so they don't dare drive all-out. The mechanics don't value their pathetic lives, and they don't even have the money." He cackles again.

"So what happens if the mechanics lose and can't pay?"

"Oh, usually they'll just set up some bullshit installment plan and everyone saves face. But sometimes some silly cunt is so high and puffed up that he demands the cash, and then someone has to send him home, know what I mean?" Biceps cracks his knuckles, which are enormous, and frowns. His mood seems to be downcycling as we get deeper into the city. "It just increases the appeal for those bored fuckheads," he mutters.

He grows increasingly subdued as we traverse the Third and Second Ring Roads and enter the narrow, winding *hutongs* in the heart of old Beijing. His driving slows and gentles as well, and I have almost dozed off, my head lolling back against the headrest, when we come to a stop.

"You go on in," he says. "I'm going to stay out here and take a nap. Don't want to watch Old Ai break your heads." He manages a final guffaw.

Sun pats him on the neck and hops out with his usual contained grace. He doesn't seem worried about getting his head broken. I go around to the trunk, but he waves me off.

"He'll bring the suitcases later. First, we say hello and have tea."

The entrance to Ai's *hutong* compound is a plain iron door in the long cinder-block wall that runs along the alleyway. Sun presses an intercom buzzer, and after a minute, a low and sweet female voice answers. Sun mutters something unintelligible, and the door beeps open more smoothly than I might have expected. We step into an outdoor perimeter space, basically a path around another wall, with weeds pushing up through the cobblestones. Across this path stands a big set of wooden double doors, painted red and studded with thimble-shaped mounds painted gold. These doors are unlocked, and we push through them into what is without question the sickest, most pimped-out dwelling I have ever laid eyes on.

19

Ai's combination house and nerve center off Orange Blossom Hutong appears at first glance to be an ordinary *siheyuan*-style courtyard surrounded by four buildings. The courtyard itself features a cobblestone floor, some plain wooden and stone furniture, and a gnarled mulberry tree, casting pleasing dappled patterns of shadow that fluctuate in the Beijing breeze. The buildings are a reverent recreation of *hutong* style: ornate wooden screens and furniture, brocade silk cushions and quilts in reds, yellows, and teals, hanging scrolls of calligraphy and ink painting—all very Qing Dynasty except for the modern kitchen ruled by Ai's live-in chef, Master Lin. Anyone dropping by would notice nothing more than a tastefully renovated *siheyuan* with remarkably good plumbing for one of the oldest neighborhoods in Beijing.

But then there is the basement.

Tucked behind a false wall in the kitchen, hidden down a steep, narrow stairway, Ai's underground lair is a dark, sleek refuge, a union of chic hotel lobby and modish bachelor pad, all shades of gray, stainless steel surfaces, and mood lighting. There is a soundproof conference room and a pair of facing L-shaped desk setups with flat-screen displays. The lounge-y area has a nice TV, a pool table, and a wet bar displaying a small fortune in cognac. There's a cutting-edge sound system with little chrome satellite speakers mounted into the ceiling wherever the walls meet. The furniture is the kind of beautiful high-end stuff that looks uncomfortable but isn't. There are no windows, and the temperature is perfect. There isn't a speck of dust on anything.

I take all this in as Sun and I stand on the inside of the vault-style door at the base of the stairs, waiting for Ai to acknowledge us. Ai's standing with his hands behind his back, bent forward at the waist, squinting into a floor-to-ceiling tropical aquarium in the middle of the main room. A barrel-chested man of average height, he has a handsome face and the Chinese equivalent of Kennedy hair. His expensive-looking sport coat fits him perfectly. His look is debonair to the point of talk-show host or news anchor, except more matte, more classy, more money. If ignoring us is an intimidation play, it's working. I want to grab Sun and scurry out of there, find another place to stay that doesn't reek of money and secrets. But I wouldn't mind taking a few pics for my Snapchat story first.

When Ai finally speaks, his voice is deep and gravelly, a voice that commands respect. "Your father gave them to me." he says, turning to face us. The left side of his face is lit blue by the undulating aquarium light. "The tank and the fishes. 'A piece of the ocean for you,' he said. He gave me very specific instructions on how often to feed them."

He walks toward us and stops right in front of me. He is running a big silver coin over and under the fingers of his right hand. "Recently, I've been looking at them a lot."

Then he hugs me. It is a long, strong, superawkward hug. He more or less pins my arms to my sides, so I gingerly reach up with my wrists and pat his ribs. Just when I begin to worry that the two of us might spend all day like this, he releases me, wrings my hand in a viselike grip, and says, "I am Ai Yongping. Your father was my close friend."

"Thank you. He was my dad, but also my close friend."

Ai raises his thick eyebrows, and a wide smile spreads across his face. He turns to Sun. "Well, Young Sun, what about you?"

Sun shrugs and smiles without showing his teeth.

"Ha! Ha ha ha! Ha ha!" Ai laughs. He actually laughs like that. "I knew it. He was your close friend, too. What a friendly son of a bitch. Ha ha ha ha! Here, come look at this stuff. You want a drink?"

Within a few minutes we are all perched on a futuristic sofa, looking at an old photo album and sucking down VSOPs. I have no idea what Biceps was talking about—Ai has no intention of breaking anybody's head. He is clearly the hands-down nicest guy in the world.

"That's when I visited your dad in Hong Kong back in seventy-nine. Ha! Ha ha! You see what a dump he lived in." In the photo Ai points to, he and Dad are perched on a single unmade bed in a narrow room with dirty white walls. *Chungking Mansions.* Dad has sideburns, a mustache, a cowboy shirt, and a deep tan. Ai wears a boxy suit and has his hair slicked back. They are grinning. Ai turns the page.

"Ah, there he is with Bairui when she was pregnant with your big sister," Ai says, using Mom's Chinese name. Dad had adopted a more clean-cut look by then, and Mom wore a prim denim dress, but her rosy cheeks and unselfconscious smile strike me. She looks like a person—instead of, you know, *Mom.* I notice a picture on the facing page of Dad and Ai with two other men: a stout, fleshy guy and a lean man with an intense face and rimless glasses. The four men are standing shoulder to shoulder, their hands clasped behind their backs, by the railing of a bridge or vista point, the Forbidden City stretched out in the background. *Brother Ouyang, Brother Zhao.*

I lean closer, learning their faces, silently asking them what kind of betrayal they have inside them.

Then someone breezes into the room from somewhere deeper in the lair and passes behind the couch to the kitchenette area with a perfumed *whoosh,* bringing me into the now on a knife's edge and flipping all my systems into freak-out mode.

"*Dàgē, nǐ huílái le*—Big brother, you've come back," she says to Sun as she crosses the room. The low voice from the door buzzer, a voice that sounds the way strawberries taste. Her tone is pleasantly nonchalant, a perfect fit with the little smile that occupies the southern real estate of a face so beautiful that I can't fully process it. I can see all the symmetry and clarity even across the room, despite partial obstruction by the bangs portion of her shampoo-commercial hair. She's wearing black patent-leather pumps and a sleeveless wool dress the color of charcoal. She glances up at me, red lips and white-gold skin, the little smile lingering.

"You also brought a friend," she says. "I'll make a pot of tea."

"Oh, too good. Xiaozhou, this is Wei Songqin. She is, ah, my executive vice president, ha! Young Wei, come over here," Ai says, throwing his arm over the back of the sofa and craning his neck in her direction.

"No rush, no rush," she mutters without looking up from the silvery green needles that she's scooping from a little glass jar into an earthenware pot. "The water hasn't boiled yet."

Ai gives me a knowing look, as if to say, *Females! What a disobedient gender.*

I swallow and stare at my knees, mesmerized by not just her beauty but also the way she navigates the room, her slender frame shifting through the light in a relaxed gait that says everything. She doesn't need words—she sets a tone with her movements, her glances, her dissemblance, showing us that she's friendly and curious, but laconically so; cool, but just so cool. Now she's behind us, assembling the tea things on a tray, but despite Ai's insinuation of control, I feel her presence dominating the room. As we flip through the old photographs, Ai speaks in a voice that seems deliberately pitched at a volume to include her, or more quietly, to exclude her, if it's some trifling remark that she doesn't need to hear. As for me, I'm having trouble focusing on what he has to say. It takes all my willpower to keep from turning my head to watch her make tea.

Wei comes over with the tray and sets it on the low table in front of us. She sits erectly on the edge of the sofa opposite me, tosses her hair behind her shoulders, and smiles the secret smile again.

"Like he said, I am Wei Songqin." She holds her hand out to me.

I stand partway, lean across the space between us, and shake it. "I am Li Xiaozhou."

Her eyes widen and she looks to Ai, who curtly lowers his head a few millimeters. She turns away, rolling her lips into her mouth and blinking rapidly.

"Excuse me," she says. "I am so sorry."

Her emotions catch me off guard and threaten to uncork mine. My face goes hot as the unqualifiable fact of Dad's death rushes back to me. I feel especially mad at myself for neglecting my grief.

Ai gives a stern *huff,* then reaches forward to pour the tea from the earthenware pot into four little porcelain cups.

"You can see how much your father was loved here," he says, and he pats Wei's knee with his hand. "Young Wei, we will be masters of our emotions like Brother Li always was, and drink to his memory with tea instead of wine. Come."

With two hands we raise our cups to our lips. The tea is astringent, clear, and slightly bitter, and it sharpens my senses. I shake off the daze of our arrival here and the jolt of Wei's appearance, and sit up a little straighter.

Wei produces a tissue from her clutch and dabs at her eyes. "Have you two eaten already?" The standard Chinese greeting.

"Yes, we've eaten." Sun gives the standard reply, even though our meal on the plane feels like a month ago.

"Certainly you must be quite sleepy," she says. When I lift my eyes to meet hers, I find them inquiring about much more than jet lag. Her gaze is curious and attentive to an extreme—am I being invited or invaded?

"A bit sleepy," I say, glancing away.

Wei turns to Ai. "I'll go get two rooms ready," she says.

He grunts in approval. Wei stands and smooths her dress. The tiny smile is back in its place again as she glides back out the way she came in.

After she leaves, Ai flips through a few more pages of the photo album, but all the air seems to have gone out of him. After a minute or so he sets it aside with a sigh.

"It's a sad thing," he says to his lap. "I always wanted to go see him in the United States, but—as you know . . ." He trails off, and a confused senior-moment look passes across his eyes.

Wei is standing in the doorway.

I glance at Sun, who looks a little pained himself, and then I say, "Mr. Ai, can you tell me about Ice?"

He snaps out of his reverie and looks at me keenly. "Ice? Hmm. I don't know much about Ice. But I will tell you what I do know. We will speak of such things later. And please, call me Uncle Ai, or Old Ai. Ha! Ha! Even your father called me that. Even though I am only a few months older than him, he always called me Old Ai, never Brother Ai. Well!" he says, slapping his thighs and sitting forward. "You are tired. Young Wei can show you to your room."

I wake up with a parched throat after a heavy nap of God knows how long. I blink, disoriented, struggling to reattach myself to reality, a specific time and place. Looking around the room doesn't offer much help, because I had barely glanced at my surroundings before collapsing onto the bed. I'm in a compact, windowless cell with decor consistent with the rest of the place: slate-gray walls, angular furniture, and recessed lighting. Like a cabin on a futuristic submarine, Ai's lair is sensory experience once removed. There's nothing natural in the whole environment, no plants, no daylight, just the fish confined to their curated environment, a simulacrum of ocean. I feel like I'm in a magazine advertisement for an airport lounge, or in an airport lounge, flipping through a magazine.

The events of the day flood back. The grief tugs at me as I recognize the reflections of Dad visible in everyone I've met here: Ai, Wei, even Biceps. I had begun to think of him as duplicitous, but he was evidently the same person in both parts of his life: the loving, charismatic guy everybody liked to be around. Filling in the blanks, I see him in a new way, and I feel like I know him better than before, more thoroughly. So the hurt is deeper, too. But I haven't chosen the path of moving on.

There is a simple iron dead bolt on the wrong side of the door. It isn't locked. I pad out of the room in my socks, hoping for a glass of water. Across the hallway I find a bathroom that matches my cell: small, sleek, and functional. I'm about to turn toward the central room when a strip of light leaking under a closed door at the end of the hallway catches my eye. As I walk toward the door, I hear the faint thrumming of large quantities of electronics. Pulling it open, I discover another one immediately behind it, this one with no handle facing me. Like doors between adjacent hotel rooms. Pressing my ear against the second door, I discern a whiff of cigarette smoke. I hear nothing but the deep hum and a distant, sedate conversation in some regional dialect I don't know.

I remember my thirst and head back down the hallway toward the main room, but I pause when I get to the doorway. The door is about a foot open, and I can hear Ai talking in a tense tone.

"—your expectations? That I would condone a plan that would destroy the brotherhood? What you've proposed is dangerous for all of us. And we don't know with certainty that Brother Ouyang or Brother Zhao is responsible."

He is pacing in and out of my field of vision, gesturing animatedly with a glass of golden liquor. I can also see Sun, who is sitting upright in a chair by the dining table, his eyes down, his hands in his lap.

"Who else could it be?" Wei Songqin protests from somewhere I can't see. "Do you think he was randomly killed just as he was quarrelling with them about Ice?"

"Of course it's not random," Ai snaps. "But it could have been the Big Circle Boys or the L.A. Fuk Ching. Or the lawyer, Peng. I never trusted that slippery prick."

Ai glares at his fish tank. The register of his Chinese has changed now that he isn't speaking with me; he talks with a local accent, and crude slang has replaced some of his eloquent flourishes. Wei Songqin's voice is less sweet, more plain; Sun sounds like the same old Sun, measured, calm, neutral.

"Someone from the Snake Hands Gang has taken over the restaurants," Sun says, speaking without lifting his gaze from his lap. "A captain named Rou Qiangjun. He arrived in Los Angeles a week before Old Li died. I'm sure you haven't forgotten that it was Ouyang who got Snake Hands involved in Ice."

Ai takes a slug of his cognac and rubs his eyelids with the heel of his hand. "Sure, I'm not blind to the facts. But don't forget: if it *was* Ouyang who planned Brother Li's death, then just the fact that his son is in my house would be a declaration of war between us. Don't you see the risk I am taking by allowing him to stay here?"

"So what, we throw Xiaozhou out? After Old Li sent him here to ask for your help?" Wei lowers her voice. "If they ordered the hit, they already destroyed the brotherhood. How can you defend those two bastards when you know what they're up to?"

Ai stops his pacing and wheels around in the direction of Wei's voice.

"You don't know what you're talking about. Fuck!" He hurls the glass to the ground at his feet, where it smashes and scatters in shimmering fragments. "You want to see me dead?"

He stands there a moment, glowering, and nobody speaks. Then he turns to Sun. "You can stay here and use what you need. I will help you get a visa for that Russian slime. But that's all. And nobody can know. Nobody! Don't let yourself be seen coming and going. And don't tell me anything. You have three days."

I hear a door slam as he storms out of the room. I look to see Sun's reaction and find that he is looking right back at me.

20

In between sets of push-ups on the floor of my little room in Ai's underground lair, I sit on the side of the bed and replay the events of the last twenty-four hours—the last-minute arrangements in San Dimas, the flight, the rude awakening to the reality of our situation in Beijing—and think about how I might regain a modicum of control over my life.

I do push-ups on my fingertips. I cross one ankle over the other, then switch. I bring my hands together beneath my chest for a set, then plant them wide for another. I step my feet up onto my bed for a different angle. I plank on my forearms.

Someone taps on my door. I silence the music on my phone and say, "Come in." Sun pokes his head through the door.

"You're exercising," he says.

"Just a little. Helps me think."

He sets a plastic shopping bag on the ground and sits down on the bed. "How many can you do? In a row?"

"I don't know. I never max out anymore. But when I was a kid, Dad used to make me do fifty straight before dinner. Every night."

"Me, too." We share a smile at this shared history, then sit a moment in silence as the weirdness of the thing settles in.

"Actually," Sun says, "he made me do one hundred."

I wonder if Dad was more worried about Sun getting killed in some alleyway than me getting overpowered on defense. "You said my dad hired you off the streets. How did that happen?" I ask.

Sun hunches forward, rests his elbows on his knees. "Old Li saw me begging near a lamb skewer place where he liked to eat lunch, kowtowing on the sidewalk with a tin can in front of me. He came up to me and said, 'Are you busy or can you take a break?' He was smiling, of course. It was a few years after he had returned to Beijing from Hong Kong, and he was in his early thirties, the prime of his life. I said, 'What do you want?' He said, 'I'm going to eat over there. I'll treat you.' So we ate lamb skewers together and some hand-cut noodles as well. He didn't say anything to me the whole time. Then he paid and said to me, 'If you're here at the same time tomorrow, I'll treat you again.' I was eight years old."

I want to ask how he ended up begging on the street, but it seems like an impolite question. So I say, "What happened after that?"

"We continued like that for a while. Each day he would ask me one question after we ordered, while we waited for the skewers and noodles to be prepared. Sometimes it was a question like 'Where is your hometown?' or 'Where do you sleep?' and sometimes it was a question like 'Tell me about that man; what's he thinking?' Then we would eat in silence. After having lunch like that every day for a few weeks, he asked me if I wanted to work for him. At that time, I had nothing. I didn't think about it too hard. I just said, 'Okay.' Actually, it was the best day of my life. Right after lunch he took me to the Happy Year office in Chaoyang. Back then, all four of them worked from the same place. There was already a cot set up against the wall. That was my home for eight years.

"Every morning I woke up there and made congee for myself.

Then I had two hours of martial arts lessons and two hours with a tutor, learning how to read and write. In the afternoon I would do errands for him: delivering messages, picking up lunch, that sort of thing. When there was nothing to do I would hang around the office, do homework, and practice handwriting. He trained me to copy his handwriting perfectly, and then he trained me to copy other people's handwriting as well. He brought me simple clothing when I needed it, and I could eat at a few different restaurants in the neighborhood on his credit. He sparred with me and taught me sleight-of-hand tricks. He taught me to pick pockets, but he made me promise not to do any stealing that wasn't part of the job. Trust and loyalty were very important to him. He liked to repeat that proverb, '*Zhōngchéng lǎoshí chuán jiā yuǎn*—The families of the loyal and honest will thrive'"—

I finish it for him: "—'*lángxīn gǒufèi bù jiǔ cháng*—and the betrayers with hearts of wolves and lungs of dogs will perish.'"

Sun shakes his head ruefully. "You know, he was always singing around the office. I didn't know any kids my age, but everyone in the office was nice to me, and I could stay up late watching TV if I wanted to. I didn't ask any questions. My whole world was Happy Year.

"On my sixteenth birthday, your father told me I would start getting paid. I would have enough to rent a room for myself and buy my own clothes. It wasn't much, he said, but it would go up ten percent every year. I would have more responsibilities, too. I was very excited to hear this news. But then he told me I would still be his assistant, but Ai would supervise my work. He was moving to the United States. He would be back a few times every year."

Sun pauses for a moment, studying his hands, smilingly slightly.

"He didn't see or didn't want to see that I was sad. I didn't know what it meant to have a family, but he was my best friend. I just said thank you, but then that night I followed him home. That was the first time I saw his wife and children. I sat in a tree and watched through a window as he cooked the same dishes he had taught me to cook for myself. I watched all through dinner and after, when he read you and Lianying stories before you went to sleep. Finally, when all the lights were turned off, I climbed down from the tree and went back to the office."

Sun falls silent after this. He looks a little flushed with emotion, matching the heat of exercise on my body. I'm not good at these moments, so I think about Andre, who is, and then I reach out tentatively and put a hand on his shoulder.

"I'm sorry," I say.

He looks up into my face with a curious light in his eyes, and in that moment I see all the boons and burdens that Dad gave him, the traits we have in common, the fire and the cool, the rock and now the pain, too. There are those things and the differences, too, the edge that is already sharp inside of him, the harsh lessons I am only beginning to learn.

Sun breaks eye contact, manages one of his ducky little nods. "I owed him a lot. He owed me a lot. It's something that gives me complicated emotions."

"Yeah." I cut my eyes away to the floor and we both stare at our feet for a minute or two.

"So, Wei Songqin is Ai's assistant like you were Dad's?" I ask, breaking the silence.

Sun nods.

"And she has ninja training, too?" I ask, trying to be light.

"In fact, she can fight a little. Ai asked me to train her in self-defense." Sun says. "But she has other capabilities."

"Other capabilities?"

"You didn't notice anything about her that stands out? Something that she could use to her advantage?"

"Oh," I say, frowning. "Jeez. I bet she's good at it."

"She is an expert at using other people's emotions and disguising her own," he says. "But—she is our friend."

"And what about Ai? Is he our friend?"

Sun thinks, then nods. "We have put him in a dangerous position by coming here. He can't refuse you, because you are Old Li's son. But he doesn't want to go to war with Ouyang and Zhao, and he fears that if we expose them, he will be exposed as well."

"What's up with that coin he was fidgeting with?"

"It's a silver tael from the Qing Dynasty. Ai had the blackest background: his family were aristocrats in the Qing. So he suffered the most during the Cultural Revolution. Both his parents were sent to labor camps."

"I can't figure out if he's supposed to be one of the good guys or the bad guys."

"I'm not sure there's such a thing as good guys and bad guys," Sun says. "But we should be grateful for the help he's giving us."

"Uh-huh."

"So, are you ready?"

I look up at him, a little startled. Clearly, sentimental Sun is done and all-business Sun is back.

"Ready for what? It's almost midnight."

"Yes, the timing is perfect. Here, I have some clothes for you."

He holds out the plastic shopping bag. Inside it I find a rayon black button-down, some slim-fit black jeans, and a black-on-white pair of box-fresh Chuck Taylors.

"What's with the clothes?" I ask.

"Nice enough for the dress code, but also good for running. You have the gun?"

"I haven't even checked." I look in the bottom of my bag. Back in San Dimas, Sun had written some kind of code on an envelope, stuffed it full of cash, and taped it to the PPQ. Now the gun is here and the envelope is gone.

"I can't believe that works."

"Only works for one at a time," Sun says absentmindedly. He has produced a box of bullets from his pocket and popped out the empty magazine, and now he's loading it with mechanical efficiency. Fifteen rounds. "Very hard to get these into China. For larger quantities, you have to go overland from Myanmar. How about the rest of the cash? We will have to promise most of it to Feder."

"It's all there," I say, nodding to the orange shoebox I had slid partway under the bed. "Did you say something about a dress code? Where are we going?"

"Velvet," he says. "It's a nightclub."

21

Velvet is in the basement of Alien Street Market, a shopping center in the Russian neighborhood of Beijing, close to Sun Temple Park. In our taxi on the way there, a screen embedded in the passenger headrest plays an advertisement for "Korean movie star eyelid surgery" on a loop. Though it's the middle of the night, we pass trucks, motorcycles, bicycles, ambulances, three-wheeled gleaner carts loaded with uncountable bags of plastic bottles. The city streets remain alight with signage: Sichuan cuisine, Hunan cuisine, Guizhou cuisine, Peking Duck, or, as it's known locally, Duck. Party World Karaoke—the size of a large hotel. In the side street behind it, stalls selling skewers and noodle soups, stacks of flimsy plastic stools, pool tables under awnings made of tarps.

Sun tells me that he started researching Feder Fekhlachev after Dad pinpointed him as a weak link who could potentially provide dirt on Zhao and Ouyang. He found out that Feder had been posted to Beijing by the KGB more than thirty years ago, at the beginning of China's Reform and Opening-Up era. After the Berlin Wall fell, Feder's extended family emigrated en masse from

Moscow to Brooklyn. But Feder's background in Russian intelligence meant he couldn't get into the States. He decided to stay in Beijing and try his hand at capitalism in its latest hotbed. He leveraged his connections in the intelligence world, as well as his fluency in Mandarin, to ingratiate himself with the city's powerful Russian community. Nowadays, any time a Russian mobster or oligarch shows up in Beijing, Feder is there to show him a good time and arrange meetings with the relevant local scumbags. As a result, Feder has a thumb in almost every pie in town, despite the fact that he never lifts a finger himself—unless it's wrapped around a vodka shot.

The more Sun tells me, the less I like our plan. "Former KGB? This guy sounds like a badass."

Sun has amped up his disguise for the nightlife with an asymmetrical pleather jacket and a dyed-look blond wig that sweeps down over his face. It seems a bit much to me, but he certainly looks nothing like his austere normal self. When he shakes his head, his yellowish bangs flop back and forth.

"Feder's not that tough," Sun says. "If he were really a good businessman, he'd be retired by now. He drinks too much. Plus, we have something he wants."

"Why are you so sure that forty grand is enough to make him cross Happy Year?"

"Forty grand and a visa. Remember, Feder can't get past Immigration, so he has never visited his family in America. Old Ai can fix that."

"Yeah, but why would he trust us? We're coming out of nowhere."

Sun does his microshrug. "Feder is a survivor. He does business with Happy Year but owes them no particular loyalty. You have to convince him that the Happy Year ship is sinking. Then you offer him a life preserver. Just remember, you are representing 'a major American interest.' He'll assume you're with a powerful conglomerate or crime syndicate. Or better, the government."

"A major American interest. Right. And what is it that we're asking for? Didn't Dad say that Dong can protect Ouyang and Zhao from the authorities?"

"We need photographs, tapes, emails—something that links Ouyang and Zhao to Ice. Maybe Dong, too—although he's very discreet. It's true that domestic law enforcement won't touch any of them. But if we take the story to the foreign press, it becomes a source of embarrassment, and then the Party has to clean house."

"Oh." I restlessly finger Dad's old Nokia candy-bar phone, which Sun gave me to use. To keep things simple, Sun only saved the numbers for himself, Ai, Wei, Biceps, and Feder, and forbade me to answer calls from anyone else. Someone might think it was him answering, when everyone assumed he was overseas for his own safety. Or worse, someone might figure out it was me.

Me. In Beijing. With Dad's phone. Going after his killers instead of registering for classes. Trying to implicate a senior Chinese official in the international drug trade. Was I really about to use a bag of cash and a U.S. visa to buy information from a Russian ex-spy? I feel my armpits going damp despite the frigid winter weather. The pistol, tucked into the back of my waistband, is pressing into the vinyl taxi seat and pinching the skin on my tailbone.

"You know I don't know how to use this thing, right?"

"That you will have to is highly unlikely," Sun says. "It's just the last line of protection. In the worst-case scenario, you pull it out and wave it around a bit. Like I said, guns are hard to get here. Chinese thugs mostly carry knives. If they see it in your hand, they'll go running."

"Christ almighty," I mutter, mentally preparing myself for that worst-case scenario—just wave it around. Do not shoot someone. I roll my shoulders out a few times and decide to emulate Sun's calm confidence in Dad's plan. It's like a close game and I've got to make the right plays. Maybe I'll chop someone in the fifth point of the lung meridian.

The cab pulls to a stop in front of Alien Street Market. I glance around at the English signage: APPAREL & SWEATER TECHNICAL SERVICE CENTER, EMAIL FASHION, a shoe store hopelessly named BerFeelny. Inside the shopping center, all the lights are off except for the atrium area, which has a down escalator in the middle of it lined with flashing yellow, green, and magenta LEDs. At the bottom of the escalator is a refrigerator-shaped Russian bouncer, who collects our thirty-yuan cover, and a swarthy little person with a black mohawk, who listlessly hauls open one of the giant, medieval-looking double doors for us.

"The doorman is a Chinese dwarf? Really?" I whisper to Sun.

He shakes his head. "Mongolian dwarf."

"Ah."

The interior of Velvet is no less bizarre: a cavern of round red booths rising in a scalloped pattern from a parquet stage in the middle. A ring of massive murals depicting a litter of bears engaged in various activities—drinking, wrestling, playing chess—covers the walls above the top row of booths. The crowd is a UN Security Council of debauchery: suited Chinese businessmen downing pony glasses of *baijiu;* wasted American expats and exchange students making out by the bathrooms; unshaven Russian patriarchs hunkered around bottles of Stoli. A Central Asian girl with an excellent midriff and a python draped over her shoulders is gyrating around the stage to Arabic music playing over a scratchy speaker system. Her pants and skimpy top are gold, sequined, tasseled.

"Woof," I say.

"There he is. Follow me," Sun says.

The booth Sun indicates with his chin is a big and conspicuous one close to the stage. The closer we get to it, the more it looks like everyone from the first ten pages of *Vogue* sitting in a pouty circle.

"You didn't say he runs a modeling agency."

Sun nods curtly. "It's one of his various enterprises."

Now we're close enough to see the man, who I assume is Feder, sitting at the center of this ring of teenage Slavic beauty. He's one of those aging guys who's managed to remain handsome, despite a balding pate and a softening middle, by paying the mysterious price of becoming extremely shiny—is it some sort of expensive, youth-preserving skin oil? His white oxford shirt is tucked into his tan slacks, rolled up at the cuffs, and insufficiently buttoned, revealing a gold chain in a rumpus of chest hair, as well as a pair of thick wrists and an expensive watch.

Somewhere in my head, Jules wrinkles her nose and says, "Vomfest."

Feder is engaged in a close conversation with one of the girls, a leggy brunette in a blue dress with an angular, androgynous bone structure, and now he brings his finger up into her face and says something that makes the tendons in both of their necks stand out. The girl whirls up and stalks past us with a stormy look on her chiseled face.

"Do it now," Sun says.

I press a button on the Nokia candy-bar.

"Hey!" Feder calls after the girl. Then he pats his pockets and pulls out a phone. "Allo?"

"Feder Fekhlachev?" I say.

"Vincent? Is that you?" Feder says.

"Vincent's dead."

Feder looks up at the sound of my nonphone voice. We're standing in front of his table. I end the call and put the phone back in my pocket.

"And you are?" he asks me in a neutral tone.

"May we sit down?"

Feder looks us over thoughtfully, then mutters something in Russian to the two languid toothpicks sitting to his right before returning his nonchalant gaze to my face. The toothpicks obediently stand and we slide in, Sun first, then me.

"So. Vincent Li is dead. What happened? And you are who,

who tells me this?" Feder's English is thick and accented. He reeks of cologne, and his eyes are cloudy. I wonder how far into the Stoli he's gotten so far tonight.

"My name is Vaughn. And this is my colleague, Teddy," I say, using the American-sounding pseudonyms I chose for us, both of which also happen to belong to SDSU basketball coaches. "We represent a major American interest."

I glance around the table, but nobody seems interested in our conversation. The girls are busy pouring drinks, chatting idly, and taking selfies, which seems to be the only time they smile.

"Perhaps I can ask what is the major American interest of which we are speaking?"

I frown, dig, compose. Bullshit time.

"I can't tell you that, but I can tell you that it doesn't matter. All you need to know is that we had a good relationship with Vincent, and now he's dead. We know his former associates are responsible. I'm talking about Mr. Ouyang and Mr. Zhao. These men have caused problems for powerful people in the United States. We also know that you know them. What we'd like to know is this: Do you have any information about Ice?"

Feder brings his palms together in front of him on the table. "And if I do?" he asks me.

"We'd like to know what you know. Everything. If you can give us what we want, there is a stipend in U.S. dollars"—close to the table between us, I do a four with my hand, followed by four zeroes, raising my eyebrows at him, making sure he understands. I glance at Sun, who nods. "We can also assist you with certain consular privileges—say, for example, a visa for the United States."

Feder rubs the bridge of his nose. He sips Stoli from a tall shot glass. He gazes at the dancer with the snake. I can almost hear the booze-lubricated gears turning in his head.

"And if I don't?" he says at length, lingering a little on the final consonant.

Sun leans in close to my ear. "Ouyang is here. We have to leave soon," he whispers.

I look across the club and see a hostess leading a small party in our direction. There's a lot of slinky black leather and tattoos; they look less like a crew of gangsters and more like a shitty band or the cast of a Chinese punk porno. It's obvious which one is Ouyang, since he's by far the oldest. He's also bald, hugely fat, and dressed like Chinese John Daly: pleated khakis, loafers, and a polo shirt that fits him like a poncho. He's walking at the back of the group and talking to a tall, well-built guy who's apparently wearing nothing but black leather overalls. The tall guy leans over him to listen.

"He looks like a complete fucking moron," I whisper back to Sun.

Sun nods slowly. "Despite his appearance, he's quite capable."

Capable of what? I grimace. The idea that this Jabba-the-Hutt-looking motherfucker had Dad killed—that this gross clown was ever even his friend and associate—brings my blood to a simmer. Feder seems unimpressed with our act, but I remember what Sun said in the cab and decide to double down. I lean in a little bit, hunt inside for the can of festering fury, and pop it open.

"Ouyang and Zhao made a dangerous miscalculation when they took out Vincent Li," I hiss in a voice I don't recognize. "They are going down hard, no matter what. That doesn't mean we can't be friends. But if you're not on the right side of this, you could end up on the wrong side. Do you understand me?"

Feder looks at me again, furrows his brow, and then looks down into his shot glass for a moment. Then he purses his lips and nods his head.

"I understand you. Yes, I understand you." He glances around warily. Ouyang and his entourage have reached their table a few tiers up. The girl with the python has left the stage, replaced by a shirtless strongman who's a dead ringer for Zangief from *Street Fighter*. He's juggling kettle bells and wearing a Viking helmet that appears to be on fire.

"There is a place we can talk," Feder says. "Come, follow me."

I stifle a sigh of relief by clearing my throat as Feder leads us toward the back of the club, away from where Ouyang is sitting. As we walk, I catch a glimpse of the girl, now snakeless, performing what looks like a lap dance for a table of Russian gentlemen. Someone has changed the music to bad Top 40 techno remixes, and near the stage, a smoke machine has been cranked to eleven. For some reason, Holly Michaels pops into my head—what's she up to right now? Sunning herself on the Quad, probably, or assembling a stir-fry bowl in the dining hall.

We come up to a filthy staff door manned by two stocky men wearing too-tight V-necks and slouchily drawing on unfiltered cigarettes. Feder confers with them in hushed tones, then pushes the door open and looks back at us expectantly. I look at my blond-banged companion, and inevitably, barely, he shrugs. Fine. We walk in after Feder and the door swings shut—then it swings open again and the goons fall in behind us.

We walk down a dingy hallway with a tile floor that looks like it has never met a mop. Some of the closed doors we pass on either side have stickers with Cyrillic writing on them; on others, blocky letters are written directly on the door in marker. Others aren't marked at all. Eventually we reach an emergency exit. Feder pushes through. No alarm sounds. We push through and find ourselves outside in the chilly Beijing night, surrounded by overflowing dumpsters. The other two push through after us, and then the bigger one, the one with stripes on his muscle shirt, looms in front of me, and a switchblade materializes in his hand.

"Oh, shit," I say, and back up into a dumpster. Then a rush hits my system like the real Vaughn just told me to check in to the game. I put some flex in my knees and try to evaluate the situation. In my peripheral vision I see the other goon is similarly armed and standing in front of Sun, who appears to be stretching his hamstrings.

Feder storms toward me and aims a heavy hook at my head. I throw up both arms against it, but the force of his swing sends me crashing down to the asphalt.

"So who the fuck you are, huh? You think I am so easy to push around?" He leans over me and grabs a fistful of my collar, his neck all bulgy.

"So who are you?" Feder repeats, giving me a shake. My eyes track his wide fist, cocked back and aimed at my face. My mind flips through answers so quickly I can't make sense of them.

"I, I"—I start to stammer something, but an unruly shriek of pain interrupts me. Feder stiffens up and turns around, unceremoniously dropping me onto the pavement. I look past his legs and see Sun's goon rolling on the ground, clutching his knee. Sun is standing loose with the guy's knife in his lowered hands, a frown on his face.

The other goon turns away from us and dutifully inches toward Sun, his hands wide like a fencer's. Feder watches Sun with a knit brow, scratching his chin. I sneak my right hand behind my back, grip the handle of the pistol. Swallowing hard, I close my eyes for a moment and imagine a shot clock counting down from five, four, three—I psych myself up to draw.

Then Feder barks something in Russian, and the goon backs off with a relieved look on his face.

"Wait, wait, wait wait wait," says Feder. A bemused smile dances across his face, then vanishes. "So you are the deadly fighter, huh?" he says to Sun, who stares back at him blankly.

"And you"—turning to me—"you speak the fancy English and like to make threats. What a skill set between you two! What a perfect combination."

He claps his hands a few times, slowly, and then throws his head back and laughs like Russian Santa. Slowly, slowly, I loosen my grip on the gun.

"Yes! Oh, hoho, yes, I will help you funny boys. I can give you what you want. But first, before I help you, you must help me."

Rather than going back through the club after we've made our deal with Feder, we walk through the alley into a wide parking lot in front of two newer, sleeker nightclubs with glowing yellow and purple signs that light up the dense gray sky. The adrenaline is still humming in my veins.

"That was so impressive. You really handled that guy. I mean I looked away, and then I looked back, and you were just, hey—"

Sun plants his hand in my chest, steering me to one side.

"Be careful," he whispers, and looking around I see that I was about to walk into a crowd of people behind a club called Coco Flaire. No, not a crowd—a row of guys around my age, on their knees on the asphalt. They are uniformly dressed in black pants, button-ups, and vests, some well fitted, others not so much. There's a man in a suit pacing up and down in front of them, yelling in their faces, and another man and a woman standing by with clipboards.

"Don't watch," Sun hisses as he pulls me past, giving them a wide berth. "Don't draw attention to yourself. Pretend it's not happening."

"What's going on?"

"I don't know. I guess they work at the club. Maybe something went missing, or maybe they are just having a bad night."

We're closing in on the taxi stand out front, where slender girls in party dresses are standing barefoot in an orderly line, holding designer heels and clutches in their hands, leaning on pimply young dudes with Korean boy band haircuts.

I sneak one more glance over my shoulder just in time to catch the man in the suit kick one of his employees in the head.

22

Victor, you MONSTROUS ASSHOLE, YOU NEED TO GET BACK HERE IMMEDIATELY. Buy a ticket, get back here. You PROMISED to call me, you broke a promise to your last surviving family member and chose instead to wing off to a foreign autocracy to FIGHT THUGS, you unspeakable ass-candle! You are being so fucking reckless with your life right now, and it's not just your life, Victor, it's mine, too. Because I'm here sick worrying about you, handling all this other shit and staying in this terrible house on my own, and meanwhile bullshitting on your behalf every ten minutes.

Lang called the house to say that he paid a visit to the crime lab at Cal State L.A. to ask for more resources on Dad's case. And he's coming over here tomorrow to take Dad's computer. This nice professional crime solver is trying to help us, and you're only making it harder for him. I was *this close* to telling him everything. I would have if you hadn't roped me into driving you to break into the restaurant and made me an accessory to your asinine escapades. So thanks a lot for making me lie to the cops, shitlicker!

Victor, Dad is not coming back. What this "family" needs is you here, now, to deal with his death the grown-up, responsible way, by signing a bunch of papers and figuring out how to work the lawnmower and not dropping out of college.

If I don't hear from you within twenty-four hours, I'm going to call up Lang and the Beijing embassy and tell them everything I know.

I'm sitting in the kitchen of Ai's *hutong* lair, scrolling through emails on my laptop and polishing off two dozen of the most delicious pork-and-scallion steamed dumplings to ever bless my taste buds. I reply to Jules, letting her know that I'm with Sun, and I'm okay, and I'll get back to her again soon. As I skim through a legion of messages from various SDSU Athletic Department personnel, a chat message from Andre pops up on my screen.

AndreAllDay: sup rice??

AndreAllDay: you in beijing?? everything ok??

Victory121592: Yo Dre! Yeah I'm here. Everything is ok.

AndreAllDay: u straight up ghosted on us. people are stressin.

Victory121592: I know. Im sorry man. had to do this. Hopefully it will all make sense later. but Sun is Master Chef. He cooks up the dishes and I just have to eat.

AndreAllDay: yeah? sick. srsly sick.

AndreAllDay: but, r u sure this is the right call? youre under a lot of stress right now. maybe u feel obliged to be there, maybe part of it is, its exciting. but you left your whole life behind here

Victory121592: yeah, look . . .

AndreAllDay: student athletics is freaking out but you can still enroll and play if u want. team needs u bad. howies out for the season. u and me, going to the tourney together. march madness baby!

AndreAllDay: maybe u recall that was our dream for a long time

I stare at these words for a minute, swallowing a little dryness. I know that Andre thinks of me as obsessed with basketball and that maybe the allure of playing on the big stage with him is the best way to entice me onto a plane back to SoCal. But the idea that Howie's knee injury has any influence over my decision to fulfill Dad's dying wishes strikes me as ridiculous, betrays the bleed between his genuine concern for me and his desire to have it his way.

So maybe I should feel guilty and stupid instead of irritated. Or maybe I feel irritated because Andre wants me to feel guilty and stupid.

Victory121592: I know I'm letting some people down and causing some chaos, but I have to do this.
Victory121592: I'm really sorry.

Long seconds pass in which I feel Andre's face move a few millimeters away from the screen, see the powerful muscles around his jaw tighten and flex. I sense his enormous uniqueness, his enormous cool, his enormous need—for a point guard, for a confidante, for an audience—all grow a bit more enormous.

AndreAllDay: hey im chill! hakuna matata.
AndreAllDay: just want to make sure ur ok.

I blink a bit and put my fingers back on the keys, but somehow I know that nothing I can write will bridge the distance between us.

And now I hear footsteps on the stairs.

Victory121592: Hey man, I gtg.
Victory121592: I'll be back as soon as I can, I promise.
AndreAllDay: aiight man, big love. fyi jules is straight trippin, u gotta talk to her. and be safe.
Victory121592: I will.

I'm sighing to myself and shutting the lid of the computer when Wei walks in.

"Your friends are worried about you?"

"How did you know that?"

She doesn't answer, just smiles her secret smile as she fills the kettle. She's got a thin, tan, drapey wool sweater on, along with a dark gray pencil skirt, red lipstick, and dark nylons. The effect is electric.

"Sun told me that you have nice friends in America. They are kind to you, and you have lots of fun together."

"That was nice of him to say."

"We don't really have any friends. Would you like to drink tea?"

"Yes, thank you." I toss my empty Styrofoam dumpling container into the trash and wipe some renegade soy-vinegar dipping sauce up from the surface of the table.

"Did you get what you wanted last night?" she asks as she pours wulong into two small porcelain cups. Her motions are collected and reserved, like there's something she's holding in.

"I don't know. You know this guy Feder Fekhlachev?"

"Mmhmm."

I copy the way she drinks the tea, lifting the cup to my mouth with both hands and sipping loudly, sucking in air to cool the piping hot liquid as it enters my mouth. It has a clean, bracing flavor, arugula bitter with a floral aftertaste. We stand opposite each other, leaning our butts on facing kitchen counters.

"He wants us to harass some French journalist for him, and then he says he'll give us the information we want."

"Hmm." She refills my cup, then her own. "And what does he want from the journalist?"

"He didn't tell us. He said, 'You don't need to know. You just need to persuade.'"

"I see."

"Would you trust him?"

She laughs quietly. "If I were you, I wouldn't trust anyone here."

"Not even Sun?"

"I trust Sun more than anyone. More than Ai, more than your dad even."

"And you? Can I trust you?" I allow a hint of humor, a teaspoon of flirt to enter my tone.

She stands up abruptly from the counter.

"What do you think?" she says, frowning.

"I—I don't know," I stammer.

"Well? You asked Sun about me, right?"

"How did you know that?"

"You asked about me, so you know what I do. You know I know all the games. You know you can't trust me. Right? Look. Right at this moment, you're feeling a little frightened of me. And also?"

She raises her eyebrows and shifts her weight onto one hip, letting a sassy curve fall into her posture. She tips her head back and parts her lips. "A little excited?"

I swallow dry air. "And you? What are you feeling?"

The posture disappears and she un-becomes a vamp, re-becomes a person. She gives me a somber, full-on look and shakes her head very slightly. "I'm feeling like not working on my day off."

Whups, I murmur as she clops lightly out of the room on her three-inch heels. Her dissection of my attempt to be cute calls to mind my painful debriefing with Dad after I got my DUI, when I tried to deceive him and he saw right through me. *You're out of your depth,* I remind myself. *A tuna swimming with the sharks.*

Sun walks in, turning his head toward Wei as she passes, then giving me a quizzical look.

"I said the wrong thing," I say. "It's one of my hobbies."

He nods. "She is a sensitive person," he says in his particular way of making such comments devoid of appraisal—not a compliment or an insult, just a little truth.

"She said she trusts you more than Ai or Dad."

"Mmm." Sun looks like he's doing long division in his head. He arrives at the quotient and leans in to mutter in my ear, "Just remember that she is vocationally good at getting what she wants."

"What are you saying? Watch out for the 'no-games' game? Really?" I throw up my hands.

Sun smiles his tight-lipped smile. "Something like that. Are you ready for our coffee date?"

Café Zehra is a well-lit, pleasant place filled with solo expats and their MacBook Airs. I had thought a French journalist would stand out in any crowd in Beijing, but almost everyone here fits the bizarrely vague description Feder had given us: "Thin. Pale. Expensive glasses. You know, a tight-pants kid." We are in the Drum Tower neighborhood of north Beijing, but it could be Echo Park. I'm on the verge of loudly asking, "Who's Gregoire Babineaux?" when a youngish man sitting at the only four-top waves us over. He has a mop of unkempt brown hair and a finely featured face that strikes me as somehow familiar.

"Gregoire?" I ask.

"*C'est moi*—that's me." He smiles and puts out his hand.

"I'm Vaughn."

"I am Teddy—wait. You!" Sun, mid-handshake, points into Gregoire's face with a look of shocked delight.

Gregoire cocks his head to the side and puts out his hands, as if to say, *Who else?*

"You know each other?" I ask.

"You don't remember? Last night?" Sun elbows me in the ribs. Gregoire bats his eyelashes at me coquettishly, and they both burst into laughter.

"I am so confused," I say.

"He had the makeup. And blue dress."

Blue dress, blue dress—my eyes go wide as comprehension dawns. "You're the brunette Feder was arguing with last night."

"Yes, yes. A brilliant idea, concocted by a puerile mind. I do it purely out of professional necessity, but I admit I enjoy it much more than I expected."

"Professional necessity?"

"It's a clever story, and I'll tell it to you later, perhaps, but first: Who the fuck is Vaughn and Teddy, and what the fuck are we here to talk about?"

Gregoire says all this with a little smirk on his face. He's charming, and knows it—expansive, witty, a little unhinged, an adventurer, the kind of guy who could delight and entertain you for a whole weekend of booze and cigarettes, but God, you wouldn't want him for a roommate. His accent is a fountain of delight all by itself; when he says *fuck,* it sounds like "facque."

"Feder wants us to persuade you to do something," I say. "He said you'd know what."

"Ah. And if I don't agree, you will . . . eh?" He makes a slapstick gesture.

Sun nods solemnly, but a giggle dances around the corners of his mouth.

"*Terrifique!* Wow. Okay. Well, we can't do that here, can we? My flat is not far; you will come with me there, please. We can talk some more."

We wait outside the café while Gregoire settles his check.

"I don't want to actually beat him up," I say, a little shocked to hear the words coming out of my mouth—how did that even become a topic? I've never beaten anyone up in my life. Sun nods glumly. Gregoire comes out the glass doors, pauses for a deep, zesty breath, and then steps past us to a bicycle rack. He fishes around in his satchel for his key then takes the lock off a handsome Taiwanese ten-speed with fenders and disc brakes.

"Sweet bike," I say.

"Merci. This way, please, gentlemen. Yes, you are new in Beijing, no, Vaughn? I can always tell. So I will educate you. The nice people at the Public Security Bureau, they make sure that the foreign journalist, he is never lonely! Gray bomber jacket, buzz cut, seven o'clock, about thirty yards back and across the street—don't look now! You already saw him, Teddy; you are a clever one."

"They keep track of your whereabouts?" I say, scratching an eyebrow in order to surreptitiously glance behind us.

"Oh yes, oh yes. They are very nosy boys. On foot, in a taxi—no, I can't get away from them. But the bicycle, it drives them batty. Haha. The dress is the same."

We turn onto a more crowded road, weaving through panhandlers, bootleg DVD stalls, and weird phone booths of sculpted orange plastic in the shape of giant, bulbous mushrooms. The black T-shirt of a Uighur kid selling walnut cakes catches my eye: it's printed with three English words, SEX DOGGIE STYLE. The driver of a black, tinted-out Mercedes honks relentlessly at a donkey cart driven by an elderly hunchback in a hot pink T-shirt. Gregoire, clearly at home on the streets of Beijing, hardly looks where he is going as he leads his bike with one hand and gesticulates with the other. Sun glides like a ghost.

"How exactly does that work?" I ask.

"You'll see! Here we are, here we are. Oh, she will be so amused to see you," Gregoire sniggers. He leads us into a massive complex of eight or ten identical apartment towers ringing a manicured garden.

"What? Who?" We walk into a lobby, wait for an elevator. He ignores my question, but, having come to a stop, suddenly peers into my face with renewed interest.

"You don't work for Feder," he says.

I look down, almost embarrassed, until I realize that I'm glad he's right. "No, I don't. He has something we want, so he asked us to talk to you. If you help him, he'll help us."

Gregoire clasps his hands together and heaves a gratified sigh. "It's just too perfect."

We get off the elevator on the eighteenth floor. Gregoire walks us down the hall, fits his key into a dead bolt, and pauses. He looks back at us with a conspiratorial half smile, and then pushes the door open.

"Finally!" A girlish voice with a thick Russian accent. "Did you bring *baozi*?" Then a scream. We're halfway through the doorway; a tall, naked girl just on the skinny side of perfection moves through the room like a dervish, collecting garments and cursing violently in Russian before disappearing into a bathroom with a room-shaking slam of the door.

"Sorry, my darling," Gregoire calls after her. He winks at us. "Shall we have a drink?"

I glance at Dad's Casio: it's not quite noon.

"Ah, Vaughn, don't be such a good boy. Trust me, you're going to need one." He busies himself setting three plastic tumblers, a bottle of *baijiu,* and a hammer on the table.

The bathroom door flies back open. The girl, now wearing a familiar blue dress, marches up to Gregoire and strikes him across the cheek with a resounding slap. He reaches his fingertips up to his face, where a smarting red mark and a look of surprised glee quickly bloom.

"*Ublyudok!* What the matter with you? Do not I have enough humiliations every day without you bringing your pervert criminal associate friend to come see free show before breakfast? Fack! Hello!"

She wheels on her heels and turns to us.

"How do you do?" she intones with exaggerated politesse, bows, and points to her nose. "I am Yulia Three. Agency have five Yulia, right now, only two in Beijing: Yulia Three and Yulia Five. Yulia Two is in Milano. Yulia Four is in Bangkok. Yulia One got too fat. Ha! Maybe you are not criminal, but anybody who know this ffffackhat is pervert by association."

With that, she storms out of the apartment, slamming the front door even harder than she slammed the bathroom door.

"Fuckhat?" I raise my eyebrows.

Gregoire spreads his palms as if to say, *Beats me*. "Yulia has learned many new things here in Beijing. When she first showed up, she would hardly look a man in the face. Now she chats a lot of bullshit to me because she can get away with it. In Russia she's nothing but an anorexic punching bag for her degenerate pimp of a boyfriend."

Seeing something tense in my face as he tosses off this casual remark about domestic violence, Gregoire makes a patronizing expression and says, "Hey, welcome to the Jing, Mr. Vaughn."

"Wait—so she's your alibi," I say. "Feder sends her here, then you put on her clothes and some makeup and go to meet him, and she waits around here. And your government minders just think your girlfriend stopped in. But why?"

"Very good, Vaughn. Now, please, remove the batteries from your mobiles before you bless us with more of your insights," says Gregoire without looking up from pouring the *baijiu*.

We pull our phones out of our pockets and I see that I have two missed calls from a number ending in 8998. I tip the screen toward Sun, who glances at it and shakes his head.

Then I flip the thing over and pull out the battery. Gregoire nods in approval.

"Yes, thank you. Feder is slipping me dirt for investigative reports that I publish in my magazine in France. It's really good information, stuff that could get him into a lot of trouble. Right now, nobody knows where I'm getting it. People are watching him and watching me, and not just Public Security. Normally we meet at his agency—that's more discreet. But last night we had the urgent thing to discuss. To meet at Velvet is a risk, even with the disguise. If certain people saw us together? Bad news for everyone."

He demonstratively grinds his fist into his hand. Then he pulls a silver cookie tin off the top of the refrigerator, pops off the top, and plucks out a jar with a brown marble of goo in it.

"Smoke hash?" he offers.

"Uh, no, thanks. Back to the investigative reports—what's in it for Feder?"

"He's doing his job. When I write a report, someone ends up looking bad. And maybe that someone has a rival who benefits from the report, and maybe that rival is a little poorer and Feder is a little richer than he was last week. Win-win-win, until two months ago? My magazine won a major prize for a report I did on the Beijing operations of the *yamaguchi-gumi*. Eight thousand words!"

As he talks, Gregoire rolls a Zhongnanhai cigarette between his fingers, sprinkling tobacco into a king-size Rizla. He pinches off a bit of the goo, rolls it into a smaller marble, and sticks it onto the end of a chopstick. He toasts the marble with a lighter, crumbles it with his fingers into the Rizla, and skins the whole thing up into a neat, narrow cone.

"*Yamaguchi-gumi?*" I ask.

"Yakuza," Sun says quietly.

"Ah. So the prize you got—that was a problem?"

"The *attention* that came with the prize was the problem. Some *putain* media watchdog in Paris began criticizing me for relying on anonymous sources. No accountability, ethics abuses, mouthpiece for special interests, la la la. Those imbeciles have no idea how things are done in this place." Gregoire rolls his eyes and exhales sticky-sweet hash smoke from his nose. Then he leans in, opens his eyes wide, and lowers his voice. "So I am quiet as a mouse until last week, when Feder come to me with the most juicy one yet. Some developer gets a big loan from a state-run bank to build a research megaplex for a major German engineering firm. So?

How would you like to see a photograph of three men receiving foot massage, eh?"

Without rising from his chair, Gregoire reaches over his shoulder and snags a folder off the kitchen counter. He pulls out an eight-by-ten print and sends it spinning onto the table in front of me with a flick of his wrist. In it, two Asian-looking men and a white guy, all dressed in robes, sit deep in side-by-side recliners. Three ponytailed someones kneel between the men's legs, their heads in front of the men's crotches. Behind each someone, a rattan footbath waits patiently.

"The developer. The managing director of the state-run bank." He taps the men in the photo one by one with a longish fingernail, smoke rising in snakes off the joint held in his fingers. "And? Voilà! The VP of Asian Operations for the German firm. It's just too beautiful."

"How did Feder get this?"

Gregoire tips his head back, blows a smoke ring, and then leans across the table toward me with a smile in his eyes. "A lot of times, Feder's clients will get the stuff themselves and then pay him to find a channel for exposure. But this time? Feder pulled double duty! You see, for his modeling agency, Absolute Fashion? Feder flies in these Yulias from Russia on his own ruble and collects their passports when they arrive. Usually, one or two of them clean up big-time on the best jobs: catalogs and campaigns. Those are the good bets. Most of the others break even on runway crap, car shows, or my personal favorite: the phony beauty pageants out in the provinces. Have you ever seen such a thing? The noble but uneducated proletariat think they're buying a ticket to the Miss World competition, but ninety percent of the girls are Russian, heh. Yulia Three? She's been Miss Argentina three times and Miss Canada twice!"

Gregoire smirks again, evidently pleased with his particular association with a three-time fake Miss Argentina. "Anyway. The bad bets, well. Those are the ones who don't break even. They have to pay him back for their tickets home, don't they? So, they do what they have to do." He taps the ponytails in the photograph.

My head spins as a world I didn't know about adds itself to the solar system. "Jesus," I mutter.

Gregoire pats my shoulder. "He's not listening, *mon frère,*" he says.

"Who ask Feder to do this?" Sun interjects.

"He says it's better if I don't know," Gregoire shrugs. "And I'm certain he's right! But now my editor won't run my story. He say we have to have sources we can name, or no go. And you think Feder wants his name in the French papers? So we have our little argument last night, and here you are! To solve the problem! So, please. Do it fast."

He abruptly slugs the rest of his *baijiu,* sets the joint to rest in an ashtray, and pushes the hammer toward me. He spreads out his left hand on the table and squeezes his eyes shut. I look to Sun, but he looks just as perplexed as I am.

"Gregoire? I don't get it."

He opens a quizzical eye at me.

"You already want to run the article, but you can't. So why would I smash your hand?"

Gregoire opens his other eye and gives Sun a bewildered look that says, *Can you believe this guy?*

"Merde, it's true what they say about you Americans, huh? Did you go to Yale with George Bouche or something? Look, if I'm being tortured—*if my life is in danger*—these media watchdogs can't criticize me for protecting my sources. When they find out what you did to my hand, my critics back in France will look like callous fools, and I will be a hero. I might win the Londres Prize! So for fuck's sake, just smash my hand! I get my story, Feder get his pat on the head, and you get your whatever it is that vodka-bucket is keeping from you. Win-win-win once again. You see now?"

Everything he said makes perfect sense, although I don't know why Gregoire thinks something that twisted would be so obvious to me. I shut my eyes and give my head a shake.

"Okay. I get it. I—how bad should I do it? How many times?"

Gregoire heaves an exasperated sigh. "I don't know. A bunch of times. It has to look bad and show up nice in photos, okay? But I'd still like to be able to fingerblast your mother someday. No, no, I didn't mean it. Just, please, have mercy and do it fast, before I lose my nerve. Remember, you have the easy part, right? But you are doing me a favor. So thank you, Vaughn." He gives me a look of sincerity with these last words, then squeezes his eyes shut again and squares up his shoulders. "Please."

I take the hammer in my hand, which has a tremor in it. I look at Sun, who looks a little tired.

"You want me to do it?" he asks in Chinese.

I shake my head, put the hammer down, and grab the *baijiu* instead. Clear sorghum liquor, 114 proof. It's the local brand: Red Star Double Still, about two bucks a bottle at current exchange rates. I pour a good three fingers into my tumbler.

"Gregoire, just so you know—my name isn't Vaughn. It's Victor."

"Okay." He nods his head and swallows. "Victor."

I toss back the *baijiu*. My eyes and my sinuses burn as I get up out of my chair and stand above Gregoire's arm with my legs wide and bent. I grip his wrist with my right hand and lean on it. He inhales sharply as I pick up the hammer in my left.

"*Yǒu shíhòu nǐ xuǎnzé shǒuduàn, yǒushíhòu shǒuduàn xuǎn nǐ*—Sometimes you choose the means, sometimes the means choose you," Dad would say. I raise the hammer above my head. Gregoire was right. I do have the easy part.

23

After I smashed Gregoire's hand, we finished the joint and most of the *baijiu* together. Filled with relief and elated on adrenaline, we laughed like hyenas. Gregoire regaled us with some choice stories from his days and nights in Yulia Three's clothing. We also gave him a short version of what we were up to in Beijing. Gregoire said he didn't know much about Ouyang, but he'd heard a story about Zhao: that he'd planted a mole in an American tech joint venture and sold proprietary algorithms to a Chinese competitor. This theft of intellectual property had lent Zhao a mythical status, and now foreign companies were constantly on the lookout for his spies.

Once Gregoire's hand had turned purple and swollen up nicely, we helped him take some photos with his SLR. Then we split a cab and dropped him off at the hospital on our way back to the *hutong*. By that time he had declared us all brothers for life. He also promised to publish whatever we dug up on Ouyang and Zhao.

I wake up from another groggy, jet-lagged nap to the sound of the Nokia vibrating and dancing across the little table beside my bed. Another call from the same number ending in 8998—I refuse it and put the phone back on silent. Then I shower in the bathroom across the hall, running the water cold for a few minutes at the end to clear the *baijiu* and hashish haze from my head. Arms crossed, head bowed forward, I let the frigid torrent pound the muscles between my spine and scapulae, cool the tension held there. Back at SDSU I had a habit of spending an hour or two each week at the Athletic Center, where even benchwarmers like me were treated like blue-ribbon ponies. One of the work-study premeds would hook a TENS machine up to my left shoulder, which has a history of popping out, while another would massage my calves and ply me for details about Andre's love life.

I wonder what sort of injuries Sun has accrued during his service to Happy Year and what sort of treatment he got for them, what perils he faced in China while Dad and I were in the States, pretending my next game was the most important thing in the world. *As for me, well, as you say in basketball, I could execute the play.* Violence, that's what Dad meant, and not the play kind. Until today, I had been led through the violence by Sun, spending most of my time crouched on the ground while he put on his hard hat and went to work. But Gregoire had slid the hammer to me—Vaughn, Victor, the guy speaking English with him. I could've let Sun do it, but I didn't, and not just because Sun had done his share. There was more to it: an exhilaration. Before it was over I heard myself screaming—matching Gregoire's shrieks of pain, but also releasing something from my insides, something ugly. And now that it's out, I feel better. I feel almost good. But I also feel insane.

Ai has pretty good water pressure down here.

I'm sitting with a towel wrapped around my waist, making a frame with my forearms around a glass of water on the kitchen table, when Wei comes down the stairs and through the vault-like door.

"Hello," she says in English. She's dressed differently from this morning: black zip-up hoodie, black cargo pants, black boots. With the exception of some uncooperative bangs, her hair is gathered in a messy bun. She lowers herself into a chair across from me.

"Sun is running some errands." She switches back to Mandarin. "You two will meet Feder at one tonight. At Velvet. He told me to tell you that Feder will give you what you want."

"Thanks. What's Old Ai up to?"

"He's at a charity auction."

For the first time I notice a second pair of eyes looking at me. "My God, what is that?"

"You mean Xiaofang?" Wei reaches up with both hands and gingerly lifts the tiny white and brown creature out of the hood of her sweatshirt. "He is a lazy monkey."

"A what?"

Xiaofang has bandy limbs, stubby little round ears, and oversize, weirdly human hands. He looks like the fruit of a union between a lemur and a Furby. The teardrop shape of the brown fur around his enormous round eyes gives him a look of perpetual surprise and vulnerability. He's holding his arms straight out in front of him, like a zombie or a slow-dancing schoolgirl, and his mouth seems to be frozen into a gleeful grin. He's staring at me.

"I think in English you say 'slow loris.' Ai gave him to me. He buys them from poachers in Indonesia. They're worth quite a bit on the black market."

"Because they're insanely cute?"

"He is, isn't he?" She sets Xiaofang on the table on his little butt and tickles him under one of his outstretched arms. He tilts his head up and beams at her. "Partially because they're cute, but mainly because they're believed to have all sorts of magical powers. Like they can see ghosts. And the meat is an aphrodisiac."

"That's awful."

"I know. They're going to go extinct."

"What else does Ai buy from poachers?"

"Everything. The worst things you can imagine. Ivory. Rhinoceros horn. They grind it up and snort it. Do you want to feed him a lychee?" She steps into the kitchen to find a lychee while Xiaofang takes my fingers into his hands one by one and smells them. When I hold out the lychee to him, he accepts it with both mitts and tries to put the whole thing in his mouth at once. Once he's done working his way through it with his hands, tongue, and tiny teeth, he stretches his arms out again and looks up at me with an even huger smile than before.

"I think he likes you," says Wei.

"I think I'd take a bullet for him," I say, and the three of us laugh a little. Then I say, "Hey, also, I apologize. For flirting. This morning."

She looks down at the table, traces a drop of water around with a fingertip. "Reading people is part of my job. I spend most of my time with people who work with Old Ai. Everyone I meet has an agenda, a game, a secret. So when I first saw you last night, I was struck by how sincere you seemed, how innocent. I can look through most people, but not you. Because it's all right there."

She smiles the little smile to herself.

"Sun is pretty frank," I say.

She rolls her eyes. "He is, but for him, that's just another advantage. With you, it's obvious right away that you come from another world. So I was chiding you for treating me how everyone else does. But I'm the one who should apologize. I wasn't angry at you. Really I was upset about something else."

She looks down, away.

"A work thing?"

She nods. "It wasn't actually my day off."

The implication of this statement fills the silence for a moment.

"It's not like this all the time." She tonelessly addresses the table. "Many days I'm more like Ai's assistant, doing administrative tasks or what have you."

"But not today," I say.

She looks up at me with a different smile, a sad one. She lifts her shoulders up to her ears and lets them drop, and I'm certain that she is indeed the most beautiful person to walk the earth. Xiaofang has curled up into a ball on the table and appears to be sleeping.

"I'm sorry," I say.

She lets out a stream of breath, buzzing her lips and floating her bangs into the air.

"There was this man I had to see. He was disgusting," she says. "On the outside and on the inside. Especially on the inside."

"Why did you have to do it?"

"I'm not sure. Sometimes I'm supposed to extract some specific information. In those cases I know a little bit more. But a lot of times it's just to make a video. You know, for insurance or blackmail. This guy was government. Maybe Ai needs his permission to do something."

"So you have a hidden camera?"

"I have a few."

"Ah." Silence settles in again. I imagine things, then realize that she knows I'm imagining things, then hate that feeling.

"Can't you quit? Find some other job?"

"You don't understand. Ai found me in a horrible place. And if it weren't for him, I would have died in that place. I was very young. He gave me a safe home, an education, a living. I owe everything to him."

"But for how long? If he really cared about you, he would want you to have your own life."

"He does care about me. I asked him before. He becomes upset because he knows I am unhappy. And he says, 'Not now, Young Wei. Soon, but not now.' The same thing your dad said to Sun for years. Ai worshipped Old Li, he learned everything from him. He's a good boss, too. He takes care of me. I doubt I could do much better on the job market. You don't know about China. People are not protected from their bosses here. And all the bosses are men. A pretty girl from a poor background—well, maybe she isn't looking for sex, but sex will find her."

"America isn't so different."

"I don't know. Men here are used to treating women a certain way."

"But Ai never?"

"Now, never."

"Oh."

"At the beginning, he did. When he first took me, I thought he wanted me to be his wife or his mistress. But he already had both. When he slept with me, it was only to teach me certain things. It turns out his wife and mistress are *very* knowledgeable women," she says.

"It's not right to talk about it like this. You talk about all this stuff like it's completely normal."

"Xiaozhou, it *is* completely normal," she says, looking up from the table and meeting my gaze frankly. Her face is devoid of expression and I see her young age in it, the life she's learned, the walls she's built inside herself in order to survive.

"How do you do it?" I ask her.

She does a hapless shrug I'm sure she picked up from Sun, or the other way around.

"We all have our burdens," she says pointedly. Then she switches to English. "Isn't it so, Victor?"

I look away, feeling my eyes moisten and my face get hot. "I'm fine," I mutter.

"Anyone could tell you're not fine," she says. "It's okay to feel awful when your father dies."

"It's not that." I look back into her open face, then down at my hands. "I mean, sure I feel awful. But this last week—finding out all these things about him—it's like all along I was living in a world I didn't know anything about. It was all built on this rotten foundation. But I didn't know—how could I have known, right? Well, fuck that. Now I want to know everything."

As I say these things, I feel the pain grow and throb, and a void within me howls with great arctic winds of disillusionment. I push away from the table and retreat to Ai's tropical fish tank. *A piece of the ocean.* Angelfish. Clown fish. Tiger prawn. I try to put myself in Dad's shoes back at the Deep Blue Sea in Hong Kong. I see my past as his dream of the future: *a clean and light place,* one he had never seen except on the silver screen. A place made out of car washes, golf courses, Starbuckses. What would I do in order to get there: Draw a clear line? Extinguish a few endangered species? Adopt an orphan and mold him into a weapon? *I learned that no such place existed.* But Dad had passed his fish-tank vision to Ai, along with his father-savior-master routine.

I squeeze my eyes shut and imagine how much fun it would be to free the tropical fish from their perfect little prison by smashing it with a hammer.

"Xiaozhou?" Wei puts a hand on my arm. "I was going to go someplace. Do you want to come with me?"

"Now?"

"Yes."

"Where?"

"It doesn't matter."

I open my eyes; I look at her. The secret smile is back on her face.

"Just say yes."

"Okay, yes."

She returns to Mandarin.

"Put your clothes on. Hurry; we have to be back in time for your other date."

An overnight frost has begun to dust the tops of the cinder-block walls that line the *hutongs,* and I'm fighting shivers in my SDSU Athletics pullover. Wei's got the hood of her sweatshirt pulled down over her forehead, the partial concealment lending yet more allure to the exquisite hint of her face that remains visible. Rusted bicycles, laundry lines, and piles of anonymous detritus skirt the narrow alleyways. There's an occasional parked car, too, the nicer ones with squares of plywood leaned against the wheel wells to protect the hubcaps from errant traffic. Everything is gray except for Wei's face and lips, which catch the ambient light reflecting down off the gray sky and shine porcelain and ruby.

She speaks without looking at me, her breath escaping into the icy night in plumes of vapor. "I don't know what Sun's told you," she says. "But you might be better off leaving these people alone. Ouyang—he's a brute; he doesn't care who he hurts. And Zhao—he'd relish hurting you. He hated your father, and he hates Ai, too."

She tells me about Zhao's sense of inferiority to Dad and Ai, how he envied their ease with people and resented their willingness to be led by him. As Zhao saw it, he made all the hard decisions while they tagged along, reaping the benefits. He particularly took exception to their attempts to slip into the appearance of decency. Zhao saw them as treasonous posers, particularly Dad, who had crossed sides in more ways than one. In contrast, Zhao began to justify his own criminality as patriotic.

"He's nothing more than a crook, but he likes to pretend he's some kind of great servant to China," Wei says in her matter-of-fact voice. "You see, Ouyang didn't care to become respectable, but I think Zhao would have liked to. He's intelligent, but everybody despises him, even Dong, and he knows it. So he decided that Ai and Li were hypocrites, playing the saint at his expense. Probably nothing would please him more than to harm you, because you are the embodiment of Old Li's escape from his world."

She turns to me and smiles the secret smile again.

"You are still innocent," she says. "If you can stay that way, and stay alive in the United States, out of his reach, perhaps that would spite your father's enemies more than anything you can accomplish here."

Innocent? I don't feel innocent, but perhaps an innocent person wouldn't. Images flash through my mind: Gregoire's purple hand, Ouyang's thugs ambling through Velvet, Dad pinching fish food into his tank back in San Dimas.

"Are you telling me this because Ai told you to encourage me to leave?" I ask.

Wei turns forward again, her eyes tracing the red tile roofs of the buildings along the *hutongs*. We pass a squat, foul-smelling brick structure with a sign in English: PUDLIC TOILET. Briefly, I wonder if my grandmother ever cleaned it.

"He doesn't have to tell me what he wants. I just know," she says. "But I wouldn't say it if I didn't believe it. So if Ai happens to agree with me, and your best interest coincides with his, does that make me wrong?"

Trying to make sense of that makes my brain hurt. I doubt Wei thinks that I'd flee back to the States after following Dad's trail this far. So why bother to warn me, if not because Ai has obliged her to?

"Maybe you agree with him too often," I say.

She doesn't respond, keeps walking a pace or two ahead of me, her gaze now tilted down at the lane, and I worry that I've crossed another hidden line, tripped another defense mechanism.

"Tell me again where we're going," I say, just to break the silence. The nonsensical name of the place has an antiquated sound to it, so I ask what it means.

"*Yúgōngyíshān*—The Foolish Old Man Moves the Mountains," Wei says. "It's an ancient parable about a house with two mountains in front of it. The foolish old man who lives in the house decides to move the mountains somewhere else so people can come and go from his house more easily. He and his son and grandson pick up their shovels and get to work.

"A wise old man comes along and tells them that the mountains are far too large to move. He says that the foolish old man is so old and weak that he couldn't even destroy a blade of grass on the mountain, let alone move the whole thing."

"The wise old man sounds like a jerk," I say.

Wei continues without acknowledging my commentary. "The foolish old man replies that he has a son and a grandson, and they will have sons and grandsons of their own. 'My descendants go on and on without end,' he says, 'and the mountains are not growing any taller. So why should I worry about not being able to move them?'

"The old man and his family continued to shovel away at the mountains day after day. The lord of the heavens took notice of the foolish old man and was moved by his zeal. So he sent two immortal giants to carry away the mountains on their backs."

"So the moral of the story is what?" I ask. "Dream an impossible dream and God will take your side?"

"I think it's more like: people are not always the way they seem. Or maybe: being foolish can be better than being wise." Wei shrugs. "It's just a story."

"And this bar is named after it?"

"Yes. Yugongyishan. It's not a bar so much as a place to see live music."

We come to the end of a *hutong* and arrive T-boned to a real street, one with sidewalks and lanes. Yugongyishan, just around the corner, has a traditional stone facade framed by a big red gateway and two massive stone lions, but after we pay our thirty yuan each to get in, it reveals itself to be like underground music venues the world over: bad light, bad noise, no real decor, and a smattering of smoky hipsters skulking around in clumps. Some of them, lurching around the dance floor like zombies, are clearly wasted on more than *baijiu*. I glance around, wondering who's selling *K-zăi*. How did Jules describe it? *You get totally destroyed, your life fades away*. I could get behind that right now.

Wei disappears for a minute and then reappears with two bottles of Yanjing beer. She puts one in my hand.

"You like this music?" I ask.

She shakes her head and smiles: *I can't hear you*. There are three skinny-jeaned Chinese punk boys mauling two guitars and a drum kit on the stage. I lean in close to her and repeat my question in a whisper-shout.

"Not really!" she shouts back.

"But you like this place."

"Uh-huh. Follow me." She takes me by the hand and leads me along the side wall to where it meets the stage. Then she turns around to face me and scoots herself backward onto the stage. She sits hugging her knees there in a little nook between the wall and the stack of massive speakers between her and the band. The speakers are angled out so nobody can see her. She inclines her chin at me, and I join her.

We lose a lot of the high end sitting beside the speakers, but the bass is so huge and near that it feels like the barriers between my organs are dissolving and they're all blending together into one superorgan. It's far too loud to talk, too loud even to think, and all I'm left with is emotions and sound. We're in a waterfall, we're in a jet engine.

Wei has her hood pulled down over her face, but after a minute she tips her head up to look at me. I meet her gaze. I try to say nothing at all with my face, just listen, but I find that she is doing the same. I watch as she looks from one of my eyes to the other and back again. Then she leans her head back against the wall behind us and closes her eyes. I do as she does and it all washes over me, washes through me. We are alone together and it washes over us.

Even Dad's fish could hide within their tanks, take refuge in a concealed pinch amid the coral. We both lived within boundaries, although Wei was aware of her prison, whereas I had been drugged into obliviousness, raised on a steady drip of attenuated reality, filtered and packaged, tailored to my little fish-brain. And even so I also feel that we are brilliant beings, our splendor unmistakable, undeniable, even while we huddle behind the speakers, as dense and nuanced as the plumage of the caged bird, the prismatic scales of the tropical fish in the tank. And our fetters as distinctively human as a wire cage or a glass box—no, *more* human, subtle and insidious: they intertwine us with the fate of men and of nations. Men and women. Nations and empires.

The four tones cannot be sung, which means that it's hard for me to understand Chinese songs, and we're so close to the speakers that the band's droning lyrics sound more like shapes than words. But I can clearly make out the words when they switch to simple English for the refrain:

We don't wanna play, we don't wanna try
We don't wanna hope, we don't wanna lie
We're gonna fly clear yeah yeah
We're gonna fly clear

We don't wanna click, we don't wanna drive
We don't wanna fight, we don't wanna thrive
We're gonna disappear yeah yeah
We're gonna disappear

24

Did you remember to put the battery back into your phone?" Sun says. He had been sitting at the kitchen table, losing a staring contest to Xiaofang, when Wei and I returned from Yugong-yishan. We went to my room together and stuffed forty grand into his backpack. Now we're in a taxi on our way back to Velvet to meet Feder. It's pouring rain.

"Yeah. And I got two more calls from that same number ending in 8998. Someone's being really persistent."

"Can I have a look?"

I pull out the Nokia candy-bar to show him.

"Hmm. It's a landline. You can tell from the number of digits. And it's a good one. But I have no idea who."

"What do you mean, 'a good one'?"

Sun explains that people pay extra to have eights and nines in their phone numbers because *bā* (eight) rhymes with the first part of the word for "get rich" (*fācâi),* and *jiŭ* (nine) sounds like *chángjiŭ*—"long life." "So this number ending in eight-nine-nine-eight probably belongs to someone with good connections."

"I'm learning all kinds of things on this little trip."

"Maybe we are almost finished. Maybe you can go home after this." Sun smiles without showing his teeth and pats me awkwardly on the back of the neck.

"I hope so. My sister is pretty upset."

Sun nods. "You did not have to come here, but I'm glad you did."

"Thank you. I guess I'm glad, too."

"Because you got to play the no-games game?"

"Ha. Sure, a tiny bit for that reason. But also, I had to learn the truth about my dad and what happened. I'm not happy about all this stuff, but I feel like it's better to know than not."

"I understand what you mean," Sun says. "But there are many things I wish I did not know."

There's a weary note in Sun's voice that catches my attention. In the thirty-six short hours since we arrived in Beijing, I've learned how foreign reporters dodge police tails and media watchdogs. I've seen how pretty Russian girls and Mongolian dwarves earn their keep in the shiny new Chinese economy. I've discovered how debonair gangsters like Ai pose as socialites while sending their assistants out on hidden-camera sexcapades. It's a new world to me, revolting but also titillating.

But for Sun, it's just another couple of days at the office. Dad's office. Which he had never been allowed to leave.

"Maybe you feel that way because you didn't have a choice," I say.

Sun knits his brow, weighing the idea in his head. "Perhaps you are right."

The taxi pulls up in front of Coco Flaire. We pay the driver and then jog-walk through the rainy parking lot to the back alley where Feder took us last night. Now that Sun has mentioned it, the idea of going home fills my head and lightens my step, even as the icy rainwater soaks my clothes. Reporting back to Andre, Jules, and Eli—mission complete, Dad avenged, time for tacos—sounds unbelievably fantastic. The mess of my enrollment status and the basketball team don't seem so daunting now that I've smashed someone's hand with a hammer. Blue skies and second chances. I want to go to the beach.

When we come around the corner to Velvet's back door, Feder is alone there, smoking a clove cigarette under the back-door awning. He sees us and smiles.

"My boys! You did your errand, eh?" He throws his arms wide as if he wants a hug, but Sun doesn't move and neither do I.

"Yes, we did. Gregoire said he'll do what you want."

"*Konechno, konechno,*" Feder mutters, glancing around. A hint of dread presents itself in my stomach. I follow his eyes and turn around to see Ouyang's leather overalls dude leading half a dozen guys toward us from the direction we came. They're soaked, too, and walking slowly. He's carrying a machete.

My eyes flutter wide, the hairs on my forearms stand up. I dart around Feder and try the door into the club, but it's locked. When I turn back around, Ouyang's guys have fanned out. I recognize another one of them from Ouyang's posse, a shorter, muscly guy with a gelled fohawk and a black tangle of indecipherable neck ink. The other guys all look pretty rough, too. Everyone's got a knife, a sap, brass knuckles. The rain shower fattens into a downpour.

"*Mā de, nǐ zhège piànzi*—You're a fucking liar." Sun spits the words at Feder, the first time I ever hear him curse. Then he turns toward me—or rather, toward the dumpster next to me. He takes three quick steps, vaults up onto it, and then begins scaling a drainage pipe up the side of the building. He's on the roof before Overalls has even reached the dumpster. I'm tempted to laugh at how easily he escaped until it occurs to me that I, Victor, have not. Wait, why didn't Sun lay out some of his kung fu skills this time? Shouldn't we have talked about what happens if people with machetes show up? I'm squinting up into the rain, hoping to catch a glimpse of him, doggedly refusing to look back down at the reality that awaits me. The dread metastasizes to my guts, my lungs, my spine.

"I knew it!" Feder says to Overalls. "It *is* Sun Jianshui."

"You set us up," I hiss at Feder in English. He shrugs and gives me a look that says, *What's a guy supposed to do?*

"You can come with me," Overalls says to me in Mandarin. His machete is wet, rusty, nicked. My eyes crawl up the blade to the handle, the hand, and the wrist, which sports a winding snake just like Rou Qiangjun's. Another member of the Snake Hands Gang.

"I think there's been a misunderstanding," I say. Sour rainwater runs down my face, into my mouth.

The grin on Overalls's face is the last thing I see before someone pulls a cloth sack down over my head. Two more someones grab my arms and start pulling me forward at a jog. Deprived of my vision, I trip and fall, and as I fall they let go of my arms and I scrape my palms on the asphalt, earning me a chorus of laughter and taunts.

Lying on the ground, I rip the bag off my head only to find Overalls towering above me with a syringe in his hand. I try to roll away, but a boot catches me on the back of the skull. I cry Sun's name at the rooftops, crawling with one hand, clutching my head with the other. All I want is to be left alone, to curl into a fetal position behind a dumpster. But then the boot presses into my back, pinning me to the ground, and I feel a pinch in my neck, and then everything goes red, and then everything goes black.

"Okay, explain," Dad said. "This had better be good."

I was sitting backward in a kitchen chair, my upper body draped over the back of it. I wasn't really drunk anymore, but I was exhausted, my mind scattered by fear and adrenaline. My clothes were wet from standing in the rain on the highway shoulder. Dad was pacing back and forth in front of me, his jaw working double time. It was the Saturday after Thanksgiving, and he had just collected me from the San Dimas Police Station.

"Go on," Dad said. "I'm all ears."

It was still pouring rain outside.

I started at the beginning, with the facts: A week ago, at an off-campus kegger, Andre had got the number of some girl on the Occidental dance team. Ashley. Then he called her to set up what he called a grown-up-style double date, basically a favor to me, Victor, the shy guy. We met Ashley and her friend, Tiana, for cocktails at a speakeasy-style bar in Eagle Rock. So far so good, right? But Tiana didn't seem even remotely interested in me, and besides, none of the four of us really knew how to make conversation in such a polite setting.

Dad gave a derisive snort. I was giving too much detail, loading him up with truth in order to slide in a lie. I didn't really think it was working, but I had no Plan B, so I just kept on paddling my idiot canoe.

We were used to standing around kegs, playing flip cup and quarters, that sort of thing. So we bought drinks to try and grease the gears a bit. Maybe we bought too many drinks. It seemed to work great on Ashley, who before long was speaking to Andre in a too-loud voice about her favorite Pixar movies while more or less pressing her body into his hands. But Andre wasn't too busy with her to notice that Tiana was hunkered over her phone, exploring the bowels of Snapchat, while I hiccuped down into my ice cubes in solitude. So he got up and made some excuse about a team workout in the morning, and we left.

I heard myself building Andre up in my story, showing Dad how considerate he was of me. Like I wanted to set him up for the truth, because I already knew he'd see through the bullshit.

"Anyway, I wasn't speeding at all. One of my taillights was out. Did the police tell you that? That's why I got pulled over. Then the cop smelled alcohol, so he made me blow in the Breathalyzer. My driving was fine."

Dad stopped pacing and turned to face me. "Your taillight was out?"

I held his gaze, I nodded blankly. "I had no idea. Anyway, that's usually just a warning from the cops. And I was just barely over the limit for blood alcohol content. It was just bad luck, Dad. Really bad luck."

Dad squatted in front of my chair so that our faces were close together, almost level. "Why would you lie to me?" he said. He sounded genuinely curious, but also like he was asking himself, not me. "It's not like you at all."

"I'm not lying." The plaintive sound of my voice filled me with self-loathing. "It happened just like I told you."

Dad gave me a long look.

"Okay, I was speeding a little. I was going five or ten over. But so was everyone else on the two-ten, Dad! It's true what I said about the taillight. The officer didn't give me a speeding ticket, did he?"

"No, just a DUI," Dad scoffed. Then he stood back up and resumed his pacing. "But that doesn't matter. There's more. Just tell me truth."

"I did," I said. "I told you the truth."

He smacks the back of his hand, then his forehead. "Of course! You're protecting your friend. It's the only reason you'd lie to me. So what did Andre do?"

I sighed. I'd doubted I'd be able to fool him, but I hadn't expected him to get to the heart of the matter right away. He was still riled up, but his anger had taken a back seat to something else. He seemed to be enjoying himself.

"Well, he didn't do anything, Dad, it's just that—you see, I—"

He squatted on his haunches again and watched me intently, his lively gaze fixed on me like a spotlight. "*Lái, shuō ba*—C'mon, out with it," he said. "I'm not going to spank you."

I flushed. "Andre was driving, not me. I told him I felt a little tipsy when we left the bar, and he said he was fine and took the keys. When we got pulled over, we swapped seats. It wasn't his idea, it was mine. I knew that if he got a DUI, it might be on ESPN by now. It might really hurt his draft position."

Dad stared at me in amazement. "You swapped seats? How on earth did you swap seats?"

I explained how I figured that the heavy rain and the dark tint Andre had added to his windows would prevent the cop from seeing us. Before we even came to a complete stop, I pointed out the greater risk that Andre was facing and suggested that we swap. I was already diving into the back seat as I talked him into it. As the cop was running my license plates, Andre managed to hoist himself into the passenger seat, and I scrambled forward into the driver's seat.

"It took less than a minute," I said.

That's when Dad burst into laughter. "Quite the little criminal, you are. Jumping into the driver's seat to take the heat for Andre. And this maneuver, it was your idea, not his?"

"One hundred percent."

It was true, and I was proud of it. Even though it meant I had volunteered for three months in an alcohol-treatment program, six months with no driver's license, and more than a thousand bucks in fines.

Dad was still pacing around, and I watched as the rueful smile faded from his face, replaced by a vexed expression of deep contemplation. Finally, he stopped his pacing, pulled up another chair, and sat down in front of me.

"Well, you're old enough to live with the consequences of your decisions," Dad said. "And I'm impressed by your devotion to your friend, and your cleverness—I really am. But Andre set up this date, right?"

"Yeah," I said. "It was something he wanted to do for me."

"But not necessarily something you wanted for yourself. And then, when the cops pulled you over, he let you take the fall?"

"I told you, it was *my* idea, Dad." I looked down. "I knew you wouldn't understand. That's why I lied about it."

That was when the phone started ringing in Dad's office. It was well past midnight, but that wasn't unusual. Dad often got calls from China at that hour—it was already tomorrow afternoon in Beijing. He glanced at the French doors to his office, hesitated for a moment, and then returned his attention to me.

"No, I understand. I really do," he said. "You have a pure heart, Victor. I'm just saying, in the future, there's something you must remember: the people closest to you are the ones with the greatest capacity to hold you back. And they don't always do it on purpose."

The phone had stopped ringing. Dad rubbed the bridge of his nose with his fingers and exhaled slowly. Then the conversation took a weird turn. For some reason, he brought up this thing we hadn't talked about for a long time: my choice of college. He reiterated his opinion that maybe it would've been a good idea for me to go to Berkeley, a better academic option, where I had also been accepted.

We'd been over it a hundred times. I reminded him that I didn't choose SDSU because of Andre. Berkeley hadn't offered me a basketball scholarship. He knew how much I wanted to keep playing basketball. And if I had gone to Berkeley, it would've cost a lot more, and I'd have been a lot farther from home.

The phone started ringing a second time, and again, Dad stared into his office. Without looking back at me, he said quietly, "Maybe it would have been better for you to be farther from home. To start on your own path, away from San Dimas, from Andre, from me."

I knew he'd be angry about the DUI. I was prepared for anger. I wasn't prepared for regret. For rejection. Tightness spread across my forehead, and unwelcome tears sprang into my eyes. I looked away to hide them from him, but I couldn't keep the hurt out of my voice as I asked him: Was that really what he wanted?

The phone stopped ringing as the answering machine kicked in again. Dad sat still, alert, waiting to see if the caller would leave a message, but instead the machine beeped twice to indicate that the caller had hung up. Dad looked back to me, draped despondently over the chair back in my damp clothes, and sighed.

"You can't understand now, Xiaozhou, and that's fine. You have lived life without the sort of difficulties that teach people to be wary of reliance on others. It's a good thing. But my life hasn't been like that, so let me tell you something that you may understand later, even if you don't right now."

The phone started ringing for a third time. This time, Dad didn't even glance at the doors to his office. He stayed fixated on me, his eyes filled with ferocity.

"Just remember this, Xiaozhou. *Yǒu shíhòu, qiān nǐ shǒu de rén yě shì zhàqǔ nǐ xuè de rén,*" he said. "Sometimes the hand that leads you is also the hand that bleeds you."

25

I wiggle my fingers, wiggle my toes, will blood into the frigid appendages of my body. I heave deep breaths to jump-start my lungs and diaphragm. *Where am I?* Wherever I am, it stinks of urine. I winch an eye open for a fraction of a second, then quickly give up on that idea. The white light above my head is too bright, the space is too tight, and I can't change the position of my body. My clothes are still damp from the rain, so I must not have been unconscious for that long.

Why did Sun ditch out on me? Am I past the point at which I can avoid getting cut to pieces? For a desperate moment, pure fear gives me an icy blue stare, and I breathe very fast, and my heart pounds in my ears, and I squeeze my eyes shut as hard as I possibly can. And then I send the fear away, and here we are again back where we were.

Where I am seems at first to be in a casket, long enough to fit me with my arms stretched out above my head. I poke around with my feet and find walls above and beside me, so close that I can't roll over onto my back. It's not a casket, though, because the wall above me doesn't have any play, like a lid might, and it's definitely metal. The wall to my right is the same material, but the wall to my left isn't really a wall at all, just an arrangement of scrap metal and wood packed in here to make me more unhappy.

Then there's the light. I squint my eyes open long enough to determine that it's coming from a single white bulb up in front of me. I slither forward on my ribs until my hands hit a dusty metal grate. The spaces in the grate are big enough for my fingers to fit through and grip it, but it's screwed tight. I open my eyes again, one at a time away from the light, and give them a minute to adjust. Then I sneak my gaze forward and see that the light is coming from a flashlight—a big rectangular one with a handle, sitting on the other side of the grate. The floor out there is reflective, maybe tile or linoleum.

And that's it. I nudge the junk to my left around with my elbow, but it doesn't have anything to tell me. The urge to urinate begins a slow conquest of my headspace. I focus on listening, detect some unsurprising building sounds: a drippy faucet, the snap and buzz of a failing fluorescent light, the groan of a refrigerator. I close my eyes again and think about all the things I want to think about before moving on to the things I don't want to think about. How long until hypothermia sets in? What am I even *doing* here? Dad should have planned better. And what if Sun—abruptly the cell phone pops into my head. I try again to squeeze an arm down my side, but it isn't happening—the space isn't tall or wide enough. I rock left and right on my thighs, but I can't feel it there in my pockets.

I run through plays in my head—flex plays, motion plays, inbound plays, pick-and-rolls. My arms are aching and so is my crowned molar. At some point I decide that peeing is a better plan than not peeing, so I do that, the warmth of my urine a momentary reprieve from the cold. I croak out a bellyful of hoarse sobs. This is the worst jam I've ever been in by a fat margin, and I have nobody but my own dumb ass to blame. I may be dead in half an hour, and all I can think of are some stupid fucking basketball plays? What a useless sack of shit.

I came to Beijing thinking I'd fulfill Dad's wishes and figure out who he really was. He'd sent Sun to look after me, so I didn't even have to leave my comfort zone, the role of second fiddle. But all I'd learned about Dad was that he'd been lying to Sun, too. He'd been telling him that he'd have a life of his own, but even after his death, Dad was still making Sun do his dirty work. And Sun had really learned from the pro. We get in a jam and off he goes up the drainpipe to the roof, leaving me in the tattooed hands of a gang of drug-crazed street thugs.

So here I am, the trusting fool, lying in a puddle of pee and waiting around for someone to drag me out and cut my ear off. And the person I was a fool for trusting was the person I loved most.

I'm pottering down this path of self-disgust when someone kicks the grate.

"*Xǐngle ma?* Did you wake up?" A deep, throaty voice with a southern Chinese accent.

"Yes," I mumble, opening my eyes in the same careful fashion as before.

"It's not very comfortable, is it?"

I don't respond, so the deep voice repeats the question.

"No, it's not very comfortable."

The voice chortles merrily. I hear screws turning, and then the light and the grate are both gone. Strong hands grab my wrists and drag me out of the tiny enclosure fast enough for my forehead and chin to scrape the metal frame where the grate was. The strong hands drop my arms and back away. I bend my elbows, bend my wrists, crawl up onto all fours and flex my joints around, which is painful but incredibly relieving. I look in front of me and my eyes travel upward: black boots, tight black jeans, and a black tank top. It's the muscly dude with the fohawk. He's got the snake tattoo on his right forearm and a cyborg geisha on his left.

I stagger to my feet. We're in a dingy industrial kitchen—lots of giant steel racks, huge refrigerator and freezer units. Most of the fluorescent tubes hanging in the ceiling fixture are dead. The drippy faucet is here, too, plinking into a deep rectangular sink with a heap of bloody towels piled in it.

"You pissed yourself," Fohawk observes.

"You're not wrong," I say.

"Fight?" he smiles suggestively, points his toes toward me, and tentatively raises his hands.

I lower my eyes and shake my head. He makes a clucking noise, pulls a zip tie out of his pocket, and binds my wrists behind my back. "Down the hall, to the right."

His smile grows bigger as I turn my head to keep my eyes on him as I pass. The corridor is dark, wide, and worn. There's a medical smell, something antiseptic, and under that the greasy odor of old machines. No windows or even hints of windows anywhere. Overalls is standing in the middle of the hallway, arms crossed and stance wide, in front of an open set of double doors with more stark light spilling out of it. Without changing his stoic-dipshit facial expression, he points me inward with his chin.

He and Fohawk follow me into a cavernous room. It must have been a factory floor: shafts and belts suspended from high ceilings stretch away into darkness. Long tables with machines wilting on them line the floor in regular rows, except for the area immediately around us, where a number of the tables have been pushed into a vague semicircle around the double doors.

There's one table left in the middle, with a little laptop sitting on it, as well as my Nokia, disassembled, and Dad's PPQ. Ouyang is standing behind the table, or rather leaning onto it, his chubby fingers splayed, his bald head sweaty, even though it's pretty cold in here, too. In addition to Overalls and Fohawk, who are standing a few feet away on either side of me, two more members of the Ouyang punk posse lounge on one of the peripheral tables: one a lanky boy with three parallel lines shaved into the clipped hair above his temple; the other a snide-looking girl cleaning her nails with a hunting knife.

Ouyang gives me a nice long glare. Then he gives the table a shove, finds himself upright, and waddles around it.

"You're Old Li's son, aren't you?" he says, in a tight, congested voice, like his larynx is fat, too.

I say nothing. I expel fear from my face, look at the wall, devote my attention to the greenish-white hazmat suits hanging from a row of pegs there.

"It's okay, don't say anything. That's a dead giveaway! I'd recognize that superior air anywhere."

He comes to a stop a few inches away from me and bugs his eyes up into my face.

"Think you're better than us? Of course you do, you and your daddy. Living a nice life in the big clean USA. Retired. *Retired.*" He says the word twice, "*Tuìxiū le. Tuìxiū le,*" lingering on the singsong tone of the second syllable, soaking it with irony and bitterness. Then he barks a laugh and wheels away from me.

"You like breathing that clean American air, don't you?" He paces around, firing his questions loosely toward his lackeys, winning jeers and snorts.

"Eat a little *steak*. Play a little *baseball*. Screw the tall-nosed, white-skinned *cunts* with double eyelids." The peanut gallery howls at that one, though I'm not exactly sure what he's talking about. Ouyang wheels back toward me, closes the distance between us in three heavy steps, and clubs me on the temple with the side of his fist.

Pebbles explode behind my eyes, and I reel backward, sideways, trying to blink my head clear of the sting.

"He still came to see us once or twice a year, acting all cheerful and handing out cartons of Marlboros like it was still the eighties or something." Ouyang sneers. He holds out his hand without taking his eyes off me. Fohawk hands him a rag, which Ouyang uses to mop the sweat from his forehead.

"But he never wanted to have any *real fun* anymore—your fault, probably. You and your righteous white mama."

He wraps the rag around his right hand. He squints at me.

"How old are you now—let's see, you turned twenty-two in December, right?"

He pops a jab at my left eye, does a little bob-and-weave to the further entertainment of the crowd, and then pops me another one as I attempt to roll away from his huge fist. Groaning, mumbling curses, I attempt friendship with the pain, treat it like a workout. Consider ways to steer myself toward unconsciousness or a quick death.

"When we were your age, we used to fuck Manchurian whores together in the alleyway behind our favorite bar. Did your daddy ever tell you about that?"

Just when I thought I was having a bad day. I glare up at Ouyang. *He never mentioned it, but thanks for filling me in, bro. I really needed to hear that right now.*

"No, he didn't, did he. You see?" He turns and addresses Overalls, who is in his signature impassive-asshole stance, his hands folded behind him. "Old Li liked to keep everything nice and separate for his little prince and princess."

Then he turns back to me and screams into my face: "So why the fuck are you here?" I keep my eyes down and don't say anything. The others are quiet now, leaning in toward the six tense inches between his face and mine.

"You don't want to chat with me?" He hits me in the stomach this time, doubling me over and erasing my mind of anything except agony. "You want to go back into your little hole?"

Left ear, right ear, stomach again, and then a kick in the shin.

I look up at his blurry shape with what I hope is defiance in my eyes.

"You're pretty tough," I say. "Why don't we try it with my hands free."

"Ha! That would be very fair, wouldn't it?" Ouyang cackles with genuine amusement. "What a great American idea. Okay, cowboy! A nice fair fight. Playing by the rules. It's a great idea, especially if you wrote the rules. Ha!"

He laughs again and takes a step back. Then he lunges forward and smashes his forehead into my face.

I go all the way down, my head a swollen balloon of blood and nerves, threatening to pop. He puts his hands on his knees and grunts his way down into a squat.

"You know he never loved her, right?" He says in a conversational tone. "She was just his ticket out of this country. Sure, he did a good job of pretending. That was his specialty. He hated it so much, here among the *liúmáng,* the thugs he was born with, his so-called brothers. He hated us enough to pretend to love that stupid Christian slut."

I spit teary, bloody phlegm onto the cold concrete and tell him that I hope his children are born without assholes.

Ouyang sighs, dabs at his brow with his sleeve, and then grabs an awful lot of my neck in his paw.

"It's that motherfucker Flat Head Chen who put you after me, isn't it?" he growls, pressing his thumb into my throat.

"Who's Flat Head Chen?" I manage to wheeze. It comes out of my mouth before I think twice. Ouyang recoils from me, and his caterpillar eyebrows pile toward each other.

Then I hear an airy whine and a thunk, and his face goes blank as a narrow piece of wood pops out of his left eye—a knife handle. Ouyang reaches his hands up to the sides of his face. He wavers, then falls forward onto his knees, and I roll out of the way as he crashes to the floor.

"*Lǎodà?!*—Boss?!" Overalls rushes to Ouyang's side, but it's too late: the fat bastard is dead. Just as Overalls cranes his head around in the direction the knife must have come from, I hear another whine and catch a flash of glinting metal in the air, and then there's a handle sticking out of his face, too.

"Fuck!" Fohawk exclaims generally. Halfway to Ouyang, he cuts for the table instead, dives underneath it, then reaches up and snatches the pistol just before a third throwing knife clatters off the tabletop.

Nothing happens for a moment. Overalls is rocking back and forth on his back, taking shallow, wet breaths. The knife handle is sticking out of his cheek, close to his nose. As soon as he was hit, the two lackey punks dove under the table they were sitting on, and now they're watching Fohawk for cues. I cozy up beside Ouyang so his massive body is between me and Fohawk, roll into a ball, and wriggle my bound hands past my butt and feet so that they're in front of me.

"Don't move!" Fohawk shifts his eyes and the barrel of the PPQ to me. Then he hollers back into the network of hanging machines, "Sun Jianshui, you motherfucker! Give up now or I'll shoot your foreigner!"

"You're making a mistake."

Now Sun's voice comes from the opposite direction of the knives, and Fohawk whips the gun around.

"Don't fuck with me, little cat. I'll blow his head off and yours, too! Throw down your weapons, and we'll let you go."

"Maybe we can talk about it," says the disembodied voice.

Lying on my back, I reach over to Ouyang's face and tug the knife out of his eye socket with my thumb and forefinger, unplugging a rivulet of blood that burbles down his temple and starts to pool around his head. I spin the little knife around and, squeezing the handle between my thumbs, saw on the zip tie until it breaks apart.

Overalls starts to cry between his wheezy breaths. He reaches up to touch the knife handle, then pulls his hand away, screaming in pain.

"Get out here where I can see your hands," Fohawk calls into the darkness.

"I'm not sure that's a good idea."

Peeking over Ouyang's body toward Fohawk, who's still squinting over the gun in the general direction of Sun's voice, I catch a movement in the shadows behind him. Then Sun pounces, flattening himself onto Fohawk's back and knocking him to the floor. With one forearm braced against the back of his neck, he smashes Fohawk's hand against the cement floor until the PPQ clatters away.

The two others rush over as Sun wraps Fohawk up into a choke hold. The girl punk with the hunting knife doesn't see me until I'm driving my shoulder into her ribs, knocking her into the boy, and all three of us go sprawling onto the ground. As she's clambering to her feet with the knife in her fist, I lunge forward on my belly and thrust the throwing knife into her ribs. She screams, rolling onto her back and looking down in horror. I pop up onto my feet and kick the hunting knife out of her hand.

"Don't move! Don't move! I'll shoot you."

It's the boy—he's clutching the PPQ in his outstretched hands. Fohawk is out cold, and Sun is crouched over him, watching the boy attentively.

"Stand over there. Put your hands up." He looks about nineteen years old, and his chin is trembling to match his hands. Out of the corner of my eye I see the girl punk pull the throwing knife out of her side, groaning with effort as she does it.

"Safety on," Sun mutters to me in English.

"What?"

"Shut up!" the boy shouts. The girl climbs to her feet with Sun's throwing knife, dripping with her blood and Ouyang's, clenched in one fist.

"Safety on. Gun won't work," Sun hisses between his teeth.

"Ah."

"I told you to shut up!" the boy screams, and, squeezing his eyes shut, he pulls the trigger. His eyes pop back open when nothing happens, just in time to watch Sun whirl around and toe-kick the girl in the stomach so hard that my whole body winces. Two more kicks relieve her of her knife and her verticality. I turn back to the boy, who is frantically fiddling with the gun, close the distance in two quick strides, and tackle him to the ground. We hit the concrete and the gun skitters out of his hand.

"Don't kill me," he sobs into my chest, making fists in front of his body, beneath my shoulders. "Don't kill me, I beg you."

It's over—the only sounds are his sobs and Overalls's shallow wheezing. He is warm and trembling beneath my body. I crawl off of him and puke expansively.

26

"Are you injured?" Sun says, squatting on his haunches beside me and holding out a bottle of water.

"No," I croak.

He turns his head to survey the carnage, then looks at me with his eyebrows raised in some blend of wonder and concern.

"You were fast," he says. "Your actions were effective. It could've been a lot worse."

I rinse my mouth with water and spit it out onto the floor. Sun nods grimly, then kneels over the sobbing boy and speaks to him in gentle tones.

"I'm not going to hurt you. Would you please roll over?" He fishes around in his little black backpack and pulls out some first aid supplies and more zip ties—am I the only one not carrying zip ties around? I sit there, watching as if from a great distance, as he does a neat little bandage job on the girl punk's stab wound. Then he hauls Overalls out of the fetal position, unceremoniously yanks the throwing knife out of his face, and rolls him onto his belly, eliciting a series of aggrieved gagging sounds.

"There's blood in your sinuses," Sun says without emotion as he pulls a zip tie tight across Overall's wrists. "Try not to choke on it."

When he's done with them, he goes back into the backpack, pulls out two small digital cameras, and turns his attention back to me.

"We have to move quickly. I'm guessing that Ouyang was working on Ice in this factory. You take video, I'll take stills," he says, tossing me one of the cameras.

"Wait." I squeeze my eyes closed for a moment, seeking words. "I need to ask you something."

"I'll explain as soon as we get out of here, I promise. A car is waiting for us outside," he calls over his shoulder as he walks into the dark mess of machines outside the ring of tables. He comes back in a moment, shoving something into the backpack.

"What was that?"

"This?" He pulls his hand back out of the bag, revealing a small black cube with two buttons on one side and a little grill on the other. "It's a Bluetooth speaker. You see."

He pulls out his phone and punches around on the touchscreen, and then his voice comes out of the cube: "You're making a mistake."

He presses another button.

"I'm not sure that's a good idea," the black cube says.

I shake my head. "So simple."

"Come on, let's go."

I follow him out into the hallway and watch vaguely as he tries a few doors. My body's not much up to the task of resisting gravity, and first I'm leaning against the wall, then sliding down to the cold floor. I sit on my ass and sip water out of the bottle Sun gave me. My neck is sore from whatever Overalls injected me with, and my whole head feels like a bruise, thanks to Ouyang's big mitts.

Ouyang. Half an hour ago I expected him to kill me. Instead, he's the one lying dead on the cold factory floor, warm blood still leaking out of his face, and I am alive in a blurry new universe, my mind slowing to the trickle of the moment, my thoughts failing to discern familiar patterns or comforting landmarks. I close my eyes, squeezing teardrops out onto my cheeks, and in my mind I see the knife hit Ouyang again and again. I see his face go from vexed to blank as the blade reaches his brain, and it feels like it's me who's been hit by the knife, and I take some quick shallow breaths and cry some more.

I'd never met a fucker who I thought deserved it more. I just never expected to watch it happen. *I shouldn't be here. I should never have come here.* The words keep repeating in my head.

"Xiaozhou! Over here."

I look up to see Sun wave at me from a doorway down the hall, then slip out of sight. I rally myself upright, careen over to the doorway, and find Sun taking photos in a room that used to be some kind of office. There's a dead guy lying naked on top of a big desk that has been pushed to the middle of the floor.

I stare at him, blinking, until Sun snaps his fingers at me and gestures impatiently at the camera in my hand.

I flick on the camera and start a video. Sitting on a stool next to the desk, there's a tray of scalpels and forceps and such. And a little baggie of white powder next to a beaker and a syringe. I dip a finger into the powder and stir it around. More ketamine.

"He was prisoner—probably labor reform," says Sun, pointing to a ring-shaped mark, presumably from a manacle, on the man's ankle. I start there and drag the camera's eye up his body: wiry leg hair, hairy crotch, waxy belly with a long incision down the side, farmer's tan on the arms, blank eyes, shaved head. The smell is bad but not so bad—maybe he hasn't been dead for long.

Waxy belly with a long incision down the side. *It's also used in hospitals for anesthesia.* I lower the camera and close my eyes. Aron Ancona, hepatologist at Cedar Sinai. *Importing a volatile commodity.*

"No, no, no fucking way." The haze lifts from my mind. The fatigue vanishes from my body. *Ice.*

I run out of the room and back down the hallway to the kitchen where I woke up half an hour ago. It might as well have been a lifetime ago. I throw open the door to the industrial freezer and there they are—half a dozen grapefruit-size hunks of pink meat suspended in steel-lidded jars of bluish fluid. Little wisps of crimson emanating from them like solar flares.

Sun is beside me, scratching his chin. He raises his camera. "Take a video of this, too."

27

It's a new technology. Before, you could only freeze an organ for a few hours. Then some researchers built a machine that can revive a frozen liver before it's implanted in the patient. It's not approved yet, but Dr. Ancona has a prototype."

We're sitting in the back of Biceps's sedan, heading back toward Beijing. Ouyang's goons had driven me a couple of hours outside the city, to an industrial area in Hebei Province, which surrounds the capital.

"What was wrong with the normal way of getting a liver transplant?"

"To be eligible for a transplant, you can't drink. But a lot of people who need a new liver are alcoholics. And some of them are very rich alcoholics. So there is a black market."

"So, what—Ouyang was gonna send one of his tattooed teenagers to the U.S. with a suitcase full of livers and dry ice?"

"That's why they needed Old Li. His restaurants were already flying refrigerated containers of foodstuffs across the Pacific. Now that Old Li is gone, Rou Qiangjun can receive the livers and get them to Dr. Ancona."

"And Ancona will do what? Revive the livers and perform transplant surgeries in his garage?"

"Something like that."

"I don't believe it. It's just so sick."

My left eye is swollen almost shut, and my head feels like someone ran it in a clothes drier for a few hours; the Chinese Advil Sun gave me hasn't done a damn thing. Figuring I might be hungry after my period of captivity, he also brought me a bag of shrimp-flavored corn snacks, and I'm munching on these as I try again to work my way through the last hour. After we finished up our little photo project, we stuffed Ouyang's laptop into Sun's backpack and called the cops from the punk girl's phone, placing it on the cement next to her face on speakerphone. "Sorry," I muttered to her in a stupid moment before we climbed through a smashed skylight and rappelled down the side of the building to where Biceps was waiting for us.

"So you knew about this all along? And you let me think that Ice was about importing ketamine, when they were only using it for anesthesia?"

Sun nods. "Old Li told me not to tell you unless I had to. He thought you would refuse to come to China if you knew the truth."

"And I suppose you knew that Snake Hands would be waiting for us at Velvet, too?"

"No, no." He shakes his head. "I hoped Feder would give us the information. But I had to prepare for every contingency."

"So you put a tracking device on me and used me as bait," I say, fingering the ladybug-size sticky black tag that Sun had shown me on the inside of my collar and thinking back to that awkward pat on the neck he gave me on the way to Velvet.

"Yes. I am sorry."

"What if they had killed me?" I say, louder, blood rushing to my face.

"It's highly improbable. These people, they are businessmen, not psychopaths. They only kill when they really have to."

"Highly improbable? Not psychopaths?" I shake my head. "That's bullshit, Sun. Those guys were Grade A psychopaths. They just carved out some guy's liver."

I catch Biceps watching me in his rearview mirror.

"What the fuck are you looking at? Keep your eyes on the road," I snap at him in English.

"Xiaozhou, you ought to calm down," Sun says.

"Calm down? After that?" I say. "I'm sick of being dragged around with a blindfold on. That's the second time you used me as bait—no, wait, the third. You know what? You and Dad are just right for each other. A pair of expert bullshit artists keeping me in the dark as long as possible. Well, it's gone on long enough."

I don't know if I'm expecting Sun to argue back or what, but he just sits there, looking at his lap, as rain pounds down on the roof of the car. We sit like that a long while, plowing down this wet highway in the middle of nowhere. I glare out the window as we pass through an anonymous county-seat town the size of Seattle. There are the iconic Chinese white characters on the red background of a propaganda banner: RESOLUTELY STRIKE DOWN LAND SPECULATION. Then a gargantuan billboard featuring the garbled English slogan of a new residential development: DYNAMIC CRYSTAL'S FACILITIES ARE OF YUPPY STYLE UNIQUE AND IN HARMONY OF EAST-WEST CULTURE.

Nothing feels normal in my body, nothing feels familiar. My flesh is the wrong temperature, my blood is like cold gasoline, I taste it in my mouth with each bite of shrimp-flavored corn snack. Blood—I am aware of it everywhere, those nine pints coursing through my veins, how easily it can drain away, end up on a cold concrete floor, and who am I without it? Dad's blood, on the floor of his office; my own blood, in my mouth, now; the pinkish fluid seeping from the incision on the liverless man in Ouyang's slaughterhouse; the blood of Ouyang himself, running in a stream down the side of his face, spreading across the floor, spreading across my mind.

Blood that Sun spilled. He looks up from his lap and talks to the back of Biceps's headrest. "Old Ai used to be the bait. He and your dad came up with the idea together," he says. "The fist and the face. Your dad was the fist. Whenever Happy Year had a problem with a partner or a competitor, he was responsible for resolving the problem. By the time I came along, he didn't want to be the fist anymore. That's why he invested so much in training me. So he could be the one to wear a nice suit and charm our competitors. He proposed alliances to them. He negotiated poorly, on purpose. They would swell with confidence. Then they would not notice the development of a vulnerable situation. So what happens to them? The fist. Me. The face opens the door and the fist comes through."

"Cool, man. So that's how you killed people together."

If Sun detects the sarcasm, he doesn't show it. "Killing was rarely necessary. We renegotiated from a more advantageous position. Sometimes I didn't know why I was beating someone up. Sometimes I knew and I wished I didn't know."

Then he turns toward me, and the look on his face is pure icicles. "For years he promised me that I could be my own person. 'Soon, soon,' he would say. 'When my children are older I will come back to China and settle my affairs. And you can do what you want.' Then your mother got cancer. He had to take care of her. Then he had to take care of you because she passed away. And I was handling his dirty business in China the whole time. Do you think I liked it any more than you do?"

Now it's my turn to stare into my lap. I was furious at Sun for bringing me into this game, but Dad had made him play for years. Dad was the one who had led me straight into Ouyang's hands. Sun had kept me alive.

"You could've walked away after he died," I say after a while. "Nobody would have known if you didn't do this last thing for him."

"The idea occurred to me. I was ready to move on from Happy Year. But I thought, *Why quit now with only one task left to repay my debt to Old Li?* We agreed that stopping Ice was a good idea."

I think about Ice, and the circumstances that make it possible and profitable—the same circumstances that bring thousand-dollar handbags from sweatshops in Anhui to malls in Orange County. There's a lot of money in the States, and there're a lot of poor people in China, able people with time, with ambitions, with—well, with livers. Still, something about it doesn't add up.

"If you're a senior government official like Dong, or some high-powered gangster like Ouyang or Zhao, why would you get into such a dangerous business when it can't be scaled up? I mean, how many livers are you realistically going to move across the Pacific? The whole thing couldn't be worth more than one or two million per year, split among Ouyang, Zhao, Dong, Ancona, and all the goons down the line. With tons of risk at every step along the way. And they were willing to kill Dad just for that? Aren't these guys already loaded?"

"You're right," Sun says. "Maybe that's the saddest part. It's not a good business. The problem was the supply: once you have it, it's hard to make it go away. Dong had been using Ouyang and the Snake Hands Gang to provide organs from prisons and labor camps to government hospitals for years. But then some American reporter exposed the whole operation and the Party was embarrassed. The regime is so sensitive, they care more about the front page of the *New York Times* than anything in a Chinese newspaper. So the Party tightened the regulations at the hospitals, and Dong lost a source of revenue. But the real problem for him was the surgeons, the prison guards, all the people who had depended on him for extra income. People who knew secrets. He had this whole organ-stealing infrastructure that ground to a halt. So Zhao came up with the idea of selling the livers on the American market. Just like Ouyang, he resented Old Li for leaving Beijing. They both thought that Old Li felt he was better than them. So Zhao said, 'What a great way to bring him back to earth.'"

"Yeah, well. Zhao was right about Dad," I say. "Bullshit was his number-one hobby. I'm starting to feel like they deserved each other."

"You shouldn't see it that way. Old Zhao, he is a special kind of bad person. He has no interest in being good, and he is not weak and indulgent, like Ouyang. Old Zhao doesn't spend his money. He likes the power it gives him."

"Uh-huh." I pound another fistful of Chinese Bugles and contemplate all the special kinds of bad person I'm learning about. "So can we get to him?"

"You haven't had enough yet? I thought you'd be ready to go home by now. We can't link Zhao to Ice, not with these photos." He sighs. "But there is a chance we can find something in here"—he taps the laptop resting on the seat between us. We already tried to access the hard drive, but surprise surprise, it's protected by security software.

"If not, well, Old Li did not leave any further instructions," Sun says. "Ouyang is dead, and we can give the photos of the Ice body to Gregoire to publish. I think then you can go home and I can retire. *Tuìxiū*." He says it in the same singsong tone as Ouyang did, with a little tip of his shoulders from side to side.

"I suppose so." I touch something on my ear that hurts, find more blood on my fingers. "I mean, on the one hand, Dad was right: if you had told me the truth about Ice back in San Dimas, I wouldn't've agreed to come with you. But on the other hand, it's hard for me to say I'd rather be studying for my next midterm or whatever. Using my time to practice basketball and chase girls, after what I know now—it just seems ridiculous."

Sun thinks it over. "I think if you can go back and be carefree like you were before, that's better. The way you are feeling about visiting Beijing is the same way I felt about visiting San Dimas: like I saw another world. Watching basketball and doing tequila shots. I didn't know what it means to be carefree until then. I like your life, your friends—they are so relaxed, so funny. I never knew anything like that before."

I spend a minute thinking about this, about Sun and Wei and what it'd be like to see them playing beer pong or doodling in a notebook during an econ lecture.

"I don't know if I'll ever feel carefree again. I mean, I was only able to mess around playing basketball because Dad had conned you into doing his dirty work for him. It's not right to be carefree if someone else is paying the price."

"Right and wrong—it's rarely so simple. I say, if you can be free, you should. I wanted to stop Ice"—Sun looks away with a scowl—"to make amends for things I have done. But to say these violent acts are a good thing, I think that's arrogant. You know what I learned from my martial arts training? *Wúwéi.* The principle of nonaction. Do nothing, and nothing is left undone. Because maybe Ouyang will be replaced by someone even worse. It's like the old man who lost his horse—who's to say it's not a blessing?"

"The old man who lost his horse?"

"Old Li never said that to you? It's an ancient story. The old man lives with his son close to the border and raises horses. One day his finest horse goes missing and his whole household is upset. But the old man says to them, 'Who's to say it's not a blessing?' And sure enough, a few weeks later the horse comes back leading another fine horse.

"Everyone congratulates the old man, but he says, 'Who's to say it will not bring us misfortune?' He was right, because soon afterward his son was riding the new fine horse, and he fell off the horse, broke his leg, and became permanently crippled. Everybody came to console the old man, but he was not upset at all. He said it again: 'Who's to say it's not a blessing?' The next year, a neighboring state invaded the old man's country. All the able men were conscripted to join the war, and most of them died in battle—but not the old man's son."

"Huh."

We sit in silence, looking forward, until Sun says, "You still think what we did is something called 'right'?"

I crumple up the empty bag of Chinese Bugles and lean my swollen cheek against the cool of the tinted window, gazing out at the sea of skyscrapers as it begins to take shape in the predawn haze.

"I don't know. This whole thing is the worst shit that's ever happened to me, and tonight was the worst part. But it's not all about me. These things would still be happening if I weren't here, you know what I mean? Ouyang was a straight-up evil bastard and he had it coming. And if he gets replaced by someone worse, maybe another good person like you will take out that guy, too."

"Good person?" Sun weighs this for a moment, then does a tiny shake of his head. "We can talk about good and bad, but perhaps it is simply because you prefer excitement to leisure."

I give a surprised snort. "So? You prefer leisure?"

Sun closes his eyes and leans back into the headrest. "I'd be willing to give it a try."

28

What is this place? A top-secret Internet café?" I whisper to Wei.

After Biceps dropped us off at Orange Blossom Hutong with an explicit promise to rearrange our faces if Ai got wind that he'd chauffeured us around Hebei, Sun and I woke up Wei and showed her the laptop. She led us to the thrumming door at the end of the hallway by my bedroom. She opened the first door and then rapped a beat on the second—*one, two and three, four*—and after a minute, a blinking teenager in sweats pulled it open from the other side.

Now Sun and the kid are huddled together, fooling around with the laptop. The room is long and narrow, with rows of classroom tables lining the two walls and another closed door at the opposite end. At identical workstations along the tables, other geeks tap away, about a dozen of them altogether, oblivious to the presence of two variously lethal retainers and a bruised half-breed from the land of opportunity. Under the tables, aside from a minifridge filled with squat orange cans of Chinese Red Bull and a large round trash can overflowing with junk-food packaging, there's enough server hardware to drain the power grid of a small country.

But we're not in a small country.

"They are Ai's army," Wei whispers in my ear. "These soldiers post on social media, manipulating people's reputations and that sort of thing. The sergeants like Young Zhang here do espionage and sabotage."

At the sound of his name, Zhang shoots a puppy glance up at Wei, who is as mesmerizing as ever in blue silk pajamas and no makeup. When we roused her from her chambers in another wing of the compound, she touched my puffy face with her fingertips and looked into my eyes with an expression of tender concern, and for a moment I was glad Ouyang had gotten in a few good punches.

"Sergeant? He looks about eighteen years old. What kind of hours are they working?"

I use my toe to nudge an empty bag of chips under the table. It's not yet eight in the morning.

"There are three shifts. Fresh troops come in at nine."

"I was able to circumvent the password protection and log in to the computer," Zhang says, speaking directly to Wei. "And I found the software client he's using for email, but everything in it is encrypted. We can't see the contents without a key."

"Is there anything else on the hard drive?" Sun asks.

Zhang shakes his head. A disappointed quiet settles over us, and the sounds of tiny fans, whirring drives, and fingers clacking on ergonomic keyboards fill the small room as Zhang looks up at us expectantly. Tired, tired, tired is all I feel, and I wonder if we've come far enough: Ouyang dead, Ice halted, and us here at this impasse. Unless—how do I put it politely?

"Is this kind of encryption completely unbreakable? Or are there people who could do it?"

Zhang nods and blinks. "Probably a small number of people

with superior resources and experience," he says, and I silently bless him for his nerdy lack of ego. "Those people are not often available."

"Say I wanted someone to look at it in the States—could they try remotely?"

"I could take a capture of the drive and send it."

"Do you have Skype?"

Victor! Holy fuck, man! Are you okay?"

The call quality is full bars, but my Skype window is solid black.

"Hey, Eli." I dig around in my head for the English language. "You've got a Post-it over your webcam."

"Oh, right." He peels it off and his dorm room fills the screen, familiar, distant. Eli looks genuinely concerned but also thrilled, and he's bouncing up and down on the baby blue yoga ball he uses for a desk chair. The bookshelf behind his head is carefully staged with parent-pleasing props: Hanukkiah, tefillin, *The Path of the Just.*

"Dude, you are not looking your best right now," he says.

"Yeah. I got in a scuffle. Sorry I haven't answered your emails. I'm actually coming back really soon. I just need your help with something. You got a minute?"

"Sure, sure, of course I do! What's going on? Is Sun there?"

"Yeah, he's right here with me."

I tug on Sun's sleeve. He bends into webcam range and waves.

"We figured out who's behind Dad's—behind what happened to Dad, and now we're trying to find evidence that connects them to the people in charge. So we have this guy's computer, but his email is encrypted. Can you help us read it? Or, like, someone you know?"

Eli stops bouncing and the smile fades off his face. I can tell he's thinking, because he isn't talking.

“What makes you think I can do that?” he eventually says in a quiet voice, his brow furrowed.

“I don’t think you can do it, necessarily.” I sigh, and another wave of fatigue crashes over me, the riptide dragging at my legs. “I just thought I would ask.”

Eli is scribbling on a piece of printer paper with a Sharpie. “Well, sorry to let you down, man. That’s way out of my league,” he says, then holds up the sheet of paper with two hands:

SFTP TO: 213.114.212.118

I grope around for a pen, scrawl the number onto my hand. “Okay. Sorry to trouble you.”

“No worries, get home safe.” He flips the sheet of paper over and scowls in concentration as he tries to make his wretched handwriting legible, then holds it up again:

←WHO’S THE MEGAFOX?
DID YOU BONE

I cast a glance over my shoulder at Wei, who’s visible in profile chatting with Zhang in the background.

“I’ll let you know when I have my flight. Lots of stuff to talk about.”

Eli makes the “A-OK” sign with one hand, then looks surprised as the first two fingers of his other hand come along and start penetrating it. I shake my head and click the little red phone in the Skype window. The application plays its “end call” chime, and everyone looks over to me.

“I think he can help. Just one more call to make.”

Unlike Eli, Jules isn’t constantly available on Skype, so I call her phone first and ask her to get in front of her computer. Thus she has a solid minute to prepare a barrage of vitriol for me, and she unleashes it as soon as we've got the video call going. Her vocabulary would impress a panel of scholars and sailors, her allusions are startlingly eclectic, and her enunciation crackles like a cattle prod. Pretty soon Zhang, Wei, and Sun have dropped their side conversation and gathered around the screen. As she enumerates to me the myriad ordeals I have brought upon her, since birth in general and particularly in recent days, I do feel guilty, but I have to fight back a tiny smile, because I've missed my sister.

". . . Okay? And think a little more critically about the ramifications of your actions. And most of all, you—hey, who the fuck are these people doing all the hovering? I can see your sleeve, dickbag!"

Sun ducks into view. "Hello, Lianying," he says, smiling hopefully.

Juliana's eyes and mouth go round, then narrow to slits. "You! You are waaay deep in the shit with me! None of this would have happened if you hadn't lured my idiot brother to China with your tall tales and Shaolin Temple charisma. Look at him; you *promised* me he wouldn't get hurt, and his face is all fucked up now! What happened to his face?"

"Jules, my face is going to be fine. Look, you're totally right, okay? I'm sorry. I fucked up, and I owe you big-time. Have you spoken with Lang? Did he find anything in Dad's computer?"

She shook her head. "The hard drive had been wiped. Lang hasn't gotten anywhere, no DNA, no leads, nothing. And he's getting curious about your whereabouts."

"I'm booking a ticket home as soon as I get off this call. I'll be on the next flight. Lang can't solve this unless we help him, Jules. There's just one thing I need you to do."

"You're in no position to ask for favors right now, Victor."

"I know, I know, just listen to me. You have to go to the Quad and help Eli look at some files he's decoding. You have to read the

Chinese for him and see if there is any information about Rou Qiangjun, Zhao—what's his name?" I turn to Sun, lowering my voice.

"Zhao Chongyang. *Chong* like *Chongqing*, *yang* like *yin-yang*."

"Okay, Zhao Chongyang. And Dong?"

Sun shakes his head. "It's not even his real name."

"Well, any references to Zhao Chongyang and a guy called Dong. Jules, these are the guys who called the hit on Dad. I'm coming home now, okay? I'm not in any danger. Please just do this one thing."

On the screen Jules looks small, deflated. "Victor, I tried to file the claim for the insurance policy, and then Perry Peng called me up out of nowhere. He said there was a mistake and the premiums weren't paid. He told me there's no insurance money."

My head plunges like a stone into a pool of frigid water. I had forgotten about the insurance policy. Four million dollars slipped my mind, and now it's gone. It disappeared in one sentence. Not that we ever had it, not that it ever sat in our hands. Did it really exist? Was it important? More important than what we've done? I have no idea.

"Jules, that was blood money, okay? We don't want that dirty money. You don't want to know what those people are doing to make money, because it's seriously the most awful shit you can imagine."

"This is too fucked up. It's all just way too fucked up."

She's crying now, and the bubble of pain inside me just bursts, and I start crying, too, and for a minute there we are, finally, two heartsore orphans bearing a load that's way too heavy. Sun turns away, Zhang is staring, and Wei gently puts her hand on my shoulder.

"I know. It really is. I—I'm sorry." My voice quavers through salty tears. "Just this last thing, okay? I'll be home soon."

She puts her hands on her face, shakes her head, takes her hands away, and exhales.

"Send me your flight info and then I'll go."

29

I'm sitting at the table in the main room with my laptop in front of me, but Wei won't let me get to it yet. She's hovering over me with a washcloth and a bowl of warm water. She's also got a little tin of root-based Chinese salve that smells like ginseng and menthol had a baby, and the baby took a dump.

"*Ow,*" I say.

"*Shh,*" she says.

"Young Wei," says Sun, "we have to talk. Ouyang is dead. Zhao will find out soon. He doesn't know that Old Ai helped us, but there is a chance he will suspect something. He'll probably suspend all Happy Year's operations. Old Ai will be isolated, and this place may become unsafe."

"Big brother," she says without looking up, "would you please boil some water for tea?"

Sun stares at her for a beat, then turns away and walks to the kitchenette.

Wei steps between my legs to get a better angle at the tear on my earlobe. She puts one hand on the back of my neck.

"Tip your head back," she says.

I obey. "Sorry I don't smell so good right now. There was some peeing."

"Mmhmm." She dabs the salve on the tear with a Q-tip. "There. Now, no fighting for two to four weeks, okay?"

She rests her hands on my shoulders and gazes down at me, her lips slightly parted as she smiles the secret smile. I meet her gaze and nod. Then she straightens up and steps away.

"You'd better get that ticket," she says.

"Right." I scoot my chair forward and call up a discount airfare site on my laptop. Sun is arranging the tea things on the table. Wei perches on a chair with one leg folded beneath her and plucks two tea canisters off the tray.

"Wulong or chrysanthemum?" She turns to Sun. "So early, it's the appropriate time for wulong. But you've been out all night playing games, haven't you? So perhaps you would like to drink some chrysanthemum tea and have a nap."

Sun sits up very straight in his chair. "Young Wei," he says, "Ouyang came after us. He kidnapped Xiaozhou. You know we had no intention of seeing him at all."

"Yes, of course." Wei narrows her eyes at him. "But you were ready for him, weren't you?"

"I have to prepare for every contingency," Sun says. "You know that better than anyone."

"And so you knew when you came here that maybe you would kill Ouyang and jeopardize Ai's position. And you came here and asked for his help anyway."

"If Old Li's original plan had worked, it never would have happened."

"Stop hiding behind Old Li," Wei snaps. "You always know how things will happen."

Sun looks down at his lap. "That's not at all true," he says quietly.

We sit there in a silence so tense that I just stare at my screen, not daring to touch the keyboard. Then the tea timer goes off and Wei stands up. She pours two cups of chrysanthemum tea and places them in front of us. Then she walks out of the room.

I sit on the side of my bed with my computer in my lap and book a flight from Beijing to LAX that leaves just after 9:00 P.M. That more or less maxes out my only credit card, so I pay down the balance with the last of the money in my student bank account in case I need to buy a couple more tickets back to Los Angeles. In case Sun and Wei say yes to my proposal. I realize that it's a good thing I'm not enrolled this semester, because at this point, I wouldn't be able to afford textbooks.

No insurance money after all. At least I have the cash Dad left me. I check the orange shoebox under my bed, and lo and behold, Sun has already returned the forty grand we were going to give to Feder. We haven't used much of the Chinese currency. It's enough to tide us over until we can sell the house or figure something else out.

So Perry Peng was closer to Ouyang and Zhao than he was to Dad. He could even have been the one who did the killing—Peng, Rou, Ponytail, or someone else working for the wrong brothers. Maybe it was some poor sap who had no choice. Maybe I don't care anymore. Like Sun said, Ouyang is dead, and Gregoire will help us expose Ice. I want some more answers out of the laptop, but what I really want is to get the fuck out of Beijing and bring Sun and Wei with me. Leave this cycle of lies and violence and start something new.

Once I've cleaned myself up and put on some urine-free clothing, I find Sun still drinking tea at the kitchen table.

"Did you reach Gregoire?" I ask him.

"Not yet."

"Maybe he's still sleeping."

Sun nods to his tea. Lowered head, submissive posture. Sun and I were a lot alike in a way. We were cast in our roles by the same charismatic leader. Sun, a stand-in for Dad's past, and me, a vision of his future. *Playing sports, watching MTV, and disrespecting your parents, haha.* Dad must have been referring to Juliana when he wrote that line of his letter. I didn't give him much trouble. Sitting against that wall as he timed me on his watch. Choosing a practical major, one of the ones he approved. Hopping on a jet to China to go wrestle with his past.

Don't you even care who you become? Jules's words echo in my head.

"Sun, would you come back to the States with me? I've been doing some thinking. It's not about Rou Qiangjun or the head-of-security guy—I want to put the police onto them if I can, and if you can help me, that'd be great—but that's not the point. Look, you could stay at the house. Maybe work at the restaurants or something, and start teaching martial arts."

Sun is looking at me with wide eyes. Finally: the cat caught by surprise. "I just have a tourist visa. I don't have a green card. I couldn't stay."

"We'll figure something out. I thought about this. Jules can marry you so you can get citizenship. She's got a bleeding heart; I mean, when she's heard how Dad treated you, she'll do it in a second. He owed you this and a lot more. I understand if you want to stay here, but I'd really like it if you could come back with me."

Sun looks back into his tea and knits his brow, but I can't read him—did my offer move him, or just remind him of all the things he's been denied?

"Just think it over, okay?"

"No, no. I'm sorry." Sun shakes himself out of his reverie. "I do not need to think it over. Of course I will go. You don't know how tired I am of this place, this life. I want to crawl out of my own skin, some days, I—thank you, Xiaozhou. Thank you."

"I can't begin say how welcome you are." I round the table to put a hand on his shoulder. "Just think about all those tacos you're gonna eat."

Sun pats me on the back. There's a lot of heavy sentiment weighing on his voice. "Xiaozhou, I am grateful to know you. Even though you are so quiet, I can see you are a loving person. You have really changed me. I wish we could have met in different circumstances."

"I feel the same."

A moment of silence catches us in this way: me standing beside him, my hand on his shoulder, his hand on my wrist. I let it seep all the way to where it belongs inside of me before I tell him that I'm going to ask Wei the same question.

He nods knowingly. "So you lost the no-games game?"

Wei's room is a lot more deluxe than mine, which makes sense given her seniority in Ai's branch of the Happy Year family. It's spacious, with a full bathroom en suite and a walk-in closet. She's got a big circular bed that seems to have one pillow on it in every size they make pillows. Xiaofang, her slow loris, is sound asleep in his own little round bed on the floor next to hers. Everything is done up in shades of blue, from the plush navy rug to the summer-sky sheets that match her pajamas.

"I can't go to America," she says. I'm just inside her door and she's standing in front of me, very still, her arms crossed over her chest.

"Look, Sun says he can get you a tourist visa within forty-eight hours. I can pay for your flight. We'll meet you at the airport, and there's a place for you to stay. Maybe you can claim asylum. All of it, we can figure something out."

She looks down and smiles slightly, as if to herself. "I know you like me. But it's not possible for me. You would not be happy."

"No, no, that's not it. I mean, of course I like you. But I don't want anything from you. I just want to be your friend. To help you. To make things right. You shouldn't stay here."

"This is who I am," she says with a hint of frustration. "I can't just go to the United States and become a waitress or a nanny. People are a certain way. They can't change as much as you think."

"Okay, well." This isn't going the way I thought it would. I fish around in my tired brain for something persuasive to say, but nothing floats to the surface. I walk over to her formidable vanity and snatch up a pen. "Sun and I are leaving tonight. I'm going to write down my email here, in case you want to get in touch. Tomorrow, six months from now, a year, whenever. It's a standing offer."

I scribble down my email address on a scrap of paper and put the pen down, but terrible fear keeps me from walking away: fear that as soon as I leave this room, I will never see this person again. I rest my weight in my hands on the vanity and take a deep breath.

Wei walks over and stands beside me. She tips her head onto my shoulder and my mind is filled with the smell of expensive shampoo. "Did you see this?" She plucks a black tube of lipstick off the vanity and twists the two halves until something clicks. A round hole in the side of the lid exposes a tiny nozzle.

"Not lipstick?" I ask.

She rolls her lips inward, holding in her secret smile, and shakes her head. "Pepper spray."

"Yikes," I say in English.

"I have to prepare for every contingency," she says in a spot-on impression of Sun's woodenness, still holding in her smile, until our eyes meet and we both burst into laughter.

"It's not funny," I say, holding my stomach, gasping for breath.

She nods big, her shoulders shaking.

After our chuckles subside into sighs, she says, "What will you do now?"

"I dunno. We're still waiting to hear about the laptop. And

Sun is trying to get ahold of Gregoire, but I'm guessing he sleeps late. I'm really exhausted. Maybe I should do like you said and take a nap."

She pushes the disobedient bangs out of her face. "Do you want to take a nap with me?"

My jaw must be hanging open because she quickly annotates this thunderbolt with two stern words: "No sex."

"What? Uh, right. Yes. Yes, I do want to take a nap with you," I say quite formally, and we both laugh giddily again.

"Okay." She walks over to the big round bed and starts tossing pillows onto the plush rug. "You turn off the lights."

After I hit the switch by the door, I'm reminded by the pitch-blackness that these rooms have no windows.

"Uh," I say.

"Follow my voice," she says. "Come here. Come here. Watch out for the pillows."

"You have too many pillows," I say when I finally reach the bed.

"Mmhmm," she says, and starts pulling my clothes off. All of them.

"Whoa."

She takes my hands in hers and presses them together in front of us. "The rule is, these hands do not touch me," she says. "Do you understand the rule?"

I close my eyes and nod obediently. Nothing happens.

"Did you just nod? I can't see you," she says.

"Oh, right. Sorry. I'm so tired. Yes, I understand."

"Good."

Then we are lying in her bed. She rolls me away from her and snakes one hand under my neck and onto my chest. She puts her other hand on my stomach and presses herself against my back, and I can feel that she is naked, too, her breasts against my shoulder blades, her pubic fuzz against my lower back, her lips directly behind my ear.

"Are you comfortable?" she whispers, and I truthfully answer that I've never been more comfortable.

"Good," she says. "Remember the rule."

We rest like this for a while, and I'm almost asleep when her fingertips start to roam from my stomach to my ribs, then my hip and my thigh, then back to my stomach. I feel her breath get a little deeper in my ear and her nipples tighten against my back. I'm rock hard by the time her hand gets there. I seem to hear her smile as she lets me go and gives me a pat on the butt before reaching her hand up to her mouth and licking her palm. She does this a few times in the long minutes that follow, methodically using her hand to bring her saliva to me until I'm slippery and slick.

I feel drunk with tiredness and excitement. I try to take stock, to tell myself this is happening, but the pleasure is too overwhelming for me to process and file away as thought or memory. She fondles me, lingers, retreating to caress the rest of me whenever I get close to the edge, all along breathing into my ear and holding me to her chest with her other hand, rocking me ever so gently front to back until I lose all sense of time, place, and self. How long does she touch me? Twenty minutes? Thirty? My mind shuts down, and all I know is this endless moment in which I more or less become pure bliss, and she becomes the god of a little world defined by her fingertips. And then her hand quickens; she slips her tongue into my ear; she wraps her hand around the tip of me, and I explode, a pulsing wet ecstasy, into her palm. She claps her other hand over my mouth as I tremble and convulse.

After I'm soft and my heartbeat returns to the sane range, she kisses my cheek and then rests her head behind mine on the pillow. I try to roll toward her, but she commands me to stay put with a wordless murmur. Then I feel the back of her hand moving along my back and spine, and her breath against my neck becomes a rhythmic panting. It dawns on me in my tiny animal brain that she's rubbing my come over her stomach and breasts. The hand moves down and speeds up, and the other hand moves from my chest to my mouth. I part my lips and accept her fingers with a grateful tongue, and somewhere deep in my abdomen the hint of another erection stirs and I almost laugh aloud in my exhaustion.

After bringing herself off in a series of gasping shudders, she wraps herself back around me with both arms and gives me a sticky squeeze. It's then that I finally teeter over the threshold into a slumberous void, my last thought really genuinely being that I am content never to wake again.

—

"Do you not understand the rule?" Holly said, a triumphant smile on her face. "I can explain it again."

"That's such—but—okay, I'm just saying, we won, like, four, five games in a row just now," Andre said. "And nobody has said shit about no NBA Jam rule."

Sophomore year, the weekend after the end of the basketball season: Holly and Jeanie had just knocked us off the table in a hard-fought beer-pong match, and Andre's competitive nature was getting the best of what he liked to call his General Mellow.

"Did you play anyone else who lives here?" Holly asked, faux sweet. "Because it's a house rule, ask anyone. But I really don't mind, we can run it back and beat you guys again."

"Umm, *excuse* me?" Janelle Pearson leaned over the table and popped her gum. "But Tyler and I have been waiting for, like, an hour?"

"Fine, who cares? We won five straight, we can retire, right, Victor? *Kobe.*" Andre shot a high-arcing fadeaway with the remaining Ping-Pong ball; it caromed off the edge of Holly and Jeanie's last cup.

I said, "Good game," and shook hands with Holly and Jeanie, provoking a smile, giggles. Because I'm sweet or because I'm a pathetic dork? Another mystery to me. Who shakes hands after beer pong? I shook my head at myself as we retreated to the back porch, where Eli was sitting on a musty couch, smoking a joint with a girl I didn't recognize.

"Y'all finally lost?"

"Yeah," Andre said. "Victor, you fell off."

"Too much beer. Plus, Holly makes me nervous."

"C'mon, man." Andre shook his head at me. "When are you gonna stop pining and make a move?"

The girl put a hand on Eli's knee and leaned over to kiss him on the cheek, then staggered off in a kegward direction. Eli blinked down at the spot on the couch that she'd vacated. "Shit," he said, then looked back up to me. "So, Holly Michaels, huh? You like that in-charge, alpha female thing? Think she'd strap one on for you?"

As usual, Andre came to my defense. "You got it all wrong, Eli. Our man Victor here is a true romantic *and* a postchauvinist. So he's naturally drawn to strong women such as the lovely Holly. Right, Rice?"

I didn't respond, just tipped my head onto the couch cushions and tried to exhale away some drunkenness. It didn't matter to me if Andre thought I was a romantic or Eli thought I wanted a good pegging. What mattered to me was that I'd been in college for eighteen months, and the optimistic box of Trojans under my bed was still covered in shrink-wrap.

"Andre all *day*! What it is, nigga?"

"You already know, son!"

Snapback caps and tapered fros loomed over me. I tipped myself upright in time to see Andre bounce off the couch and exchange elaborate daps with three brothers of Omega Phi Pi. Back during Freshman Rush, Omega had heavily courted Andre, who managed to fend them off without stepping on any toes; now, he came and went freely at their parties, usually without bringing Eli and me along.

"Why does he hang out with those guys, anyway?" I said to Eli after Andre and the Omegas had drifted away from the couch with nary an acknowledgment of our existence. "That's not, like, who he really is."

"You mean, black?" Eli drew on the joint, spoke in a high whine as he held smoke in his lungs. "I'm pretty sure he's black."

"You know what I mean. We live with this guy who reads bell hooks and makes pierogis from scratch, but they hang out with some slick brother who says things like 'this nigga be like' and 'what's Gucci, my killa?' So why does he have to front like that when he's with them?"

Eli nodded skeptically and tried to pass me the joint, but I waved it off. Finally, he exhaled, a thin stream of smoke vanishing up into the warm sky. "He's just code-switching, V. You think those other guys talk like that all the time? That guy Rashid, in the Clippers jersey? He's magna cum laude, man. In *physics*."

"Seems a little phony to me," I said. "That's all I'm saying."

"Yeah, sure, dude, like we can always be perfectly honest about who we really are, that's super-realistic," Eli said, waxing stoned. "Look at me, I have to pretend to my parents that I don't eat shellfish and constantly wear a skullcap to acknowledge the divine presence above my head. Victor, sometimes we've got to be who people want us to be. And when we do that, yeah, we're protecting ourselves, but we might also be protecting the other people. Man, most people are just playing roles most of the time. Trying to get something: love, sex, money, respect, whatever. And it's great that you're not like that. But."

"But?"

"But it's ridiculous that you expect other people to be like you. And hey, you don't even speak English with your Dad."

He kind of coughed, gagged, and snorted at the same time.

"You show me someone who's the same person in every situation," he said, "and I'll show you a psycho killer."

I might have pressed my point if Janelle hadn't flopped down onto the couch on the other side of me. Janelle Pearson had been in my Finance 100 section, and we were once paired together to make a presentation for which I ended up doing most of the work. By custom she sat among a gaggle of her sorority sisters, but she occasionally caught up with me after class to borrow my notes and ask with a sly smile if I was "still on the basketball team."

Janelle was wearing a white skirt and a pale pink crop top that showed plenty of her amber skin. Her sun-streaked hair was pulled back into a half ponytail; her eyebrows were plucked to near extinction.

"Hey, Victor!" she said.

I responded in kind and introduced Eli, who offered her the joint.

"Oh my God, no, thank you. I just pounded so much beers. Those volleyball lesbos really know how to throw Ping-Pong balls, I'll give them that."

"So you lost, too, huh?" I said. "Another victim of the NBA Jam rule?"

"The what?"

"Nothing."

A silence. Eli elbowed my ribs. Then Janelle laid a finger on my forearm.

"I'm gonna go take a shot. Wanna come with me?"

"No, thanks."

Once she was gone, Eli said, "Dude, you know Janelle Pearson?"

"We had a class together, that's all," I said. "How do you know her? I thought you just met."

"I follow her on Instagram. We've met, like, four times, but she has never once remembered me. I can't believe you just blew her off like that. I'd be more angry if I weren't still in shock."

"What, 'cause I didn't go take a shot with her? Dude, Janelle

Pearson and I have zero in common. I don't think she'd really go for a guy like me."

Eli stared at me for a minute, shook his head, and then pulled out his phone. "Victor, we're not talking about *marriage.* Look at these photos. She's either in a bikini or drinking or both. She just pounded some beers and then asked you if you want to take a shot. I doubt she cares how much you have in common."

I took the phone out of his hands and scrolled through Janelle's admittedly sexy feed as Eli continued to scold.

"She's half Puerto Rican. Look at her belly button, dude! You're telling me you don't want to go find out what she smells like? You know, Victor, you're always complaining about not getting any, but seriously you wouldn't know pussy if it hit you in the face. You're obsessed with this weird notion that girls think Asian guys are nerds. You're not a diminutive gamer from Daegu, you're a racially exotic college athlete. I'm an uncoordinated programmer with eczema and freckles, and you have the nerve to complain to me about your girl problems?"

#happyhour. #beachbody. #YOLO. Maybe Eli had a point. Maybe I needed to loosen up. Our second season of college basketball had just ended, and I continued to escape notice from the coaching staff despite practicing harder than anybody else. Maybe my disappointment had led me to be a little too hard on myself. Like everyone was always telling me.

"Fine," I said. "I'll go find out what she smells like."

"Don't do it for Eli." He produced a pack of gum from his pocket and offered me a stick. "Do it for Victor."

I popped the gum into my mouth and stood up from the couch. "*Nǐ de yánxíng hé nǐ de nèixīn bù kěnéng suíshí yízhì de*—It's impossible for your conduct to always align with your heart," Dad once said, a grim look on his face.

I found Janelle in the kitchen, and pretty soon we had rinsed out a couple of Solo cups and located a handle of Bankers Club. What's your major? Where are you from? What's the best part of being in a sorority? I asked questions, listening, being careful not to make jokes or open up about myself or anything silly like that. She brushed her hand against mine, she leaned close to me, she had gotten a C in Finance 100.

She smelled like coconuts.

Should we do another shot? Had it always been this easy, and where had I been? Pretty soon she was leading me up the stairs, pushing me onto a bed, pulling off my T-shirt. She was doing slurpy kisses on my belly, telling me she'd heard I worked out a lot, but wow. She was pulling at my belt, and I was praying I'd be hard by the time she got there, when Holly walked in with three or four people behind her.

"Uh, wow. That's unexpected!" Holly said, wheeling around, herding people back into the hallway.

"Don't you knock?" Janelle exclaimed.

"Not usually on my own door," Holly called over her shoulder.

I was on my feet in an instant, halfway after her, telling her I didn't know, I thought—

"Don't sweat it," she said, and pulled the door closed in my face.

I turned back to Janelle. She had kicked her shoes off and lain down on Holly's bed. "Don't worry, she doesn't care. Come back over here." She licked her lips. "I need to see the rest of that ripped bod."

I blinked at her a few times, then turned back around and headed out the door. Holly was just disappearing into a room down the hall.

"Wait," I said. "Holly. Can I talk to you for just a second?"

She squinted at me, came back out into the hallway, walked over slowly, folded her arms in front of her. "What's up?" she said.

My face went hot. Saliva pooled in my mouth. It vaguely occurred to me that I was rip-roaring drunk. I said I didn't know it was her room. I wouldn't have gone in there with Janelle if I had known it was her room.

"Look, I already told you, don't sweat it."

"I know you did, I just—there's something else I wanted to ask you. Would you like to have dinner together sometime? Or lunch? You don't have to. I mean, maybe I could call you about it."

Holly looked away, blushed, traced a shape on the wall with her fingers. "Victor, I—"

Some dude poked his head out of the doorway behind her. "Holly, babe, can't find a lighter," he said.

"Okay, one sec," she said. The head disappeared. Holly turned back to me, reached out, and rested a hand on my shoulder.

I noticed that I wasn't wearing my shirt.

"Victor, you're a sweet guy," she said. "I like that about you. But you really don't know the first thing about timing, do you?"

Then she turned and walked away.

30

"Xiaozhou? Wake up. Xiaozhou? Wake up."

I open my eyes, then shut them again, gradually returning to my body after a journey to the most self-annihilating depths of sleep. Where am I? *Who* am I? Someone named Xiaozhou whose face hurts, I guess. Someone who saw a man die with a knife sticking out of his face. Someone who had his consciousness erased by five deft fingers.

"Where's Wei?" I ask.

"She is gone," Sun says.

"What? *Gone* gone?" I open my eyes again, prop myself up on my elbows.

"She took Xiaofang and a suitcase. She told me you were sleeping in here." Sun says this slowly, like he's going out of his way not to imply anything. "We have to meet Gregoire in an hour."

"Oh." I drop back into bed, close my eyes. "Okay, I'll be up in a minute."

After Sun leaves, I pry myself out of bed and discover that every single muscle in my body is sore. I fish Dad's Casio out of my pants pocket and check the time: 11:30 in the morning. So I got about three hours of the sleep of the dead. Better than nothing.

Someone thoughtful left a full glass of water on the bedside table, and I down it with a thirst that seems to originate in my legs. I rinse off in Wei's shower and dry myself with a supersoft blue towel. I poke through her remaining toiletries. Shower puff, leg razor. Surprisingly ordinary stuff for a highly evolved sex-angel from Planet Orgasm. No supersecret love perfume or mind-numbing opiate pills. Or maybe she took that stuff with her. *Gone gone, with no goodbye.* If I had more than a quarter inch of hair, maybe I could pull some out in anguish. Instead, I splash some cold water on my face and poke my puffy left temple hard enough to wake myself up. More time later to mope over love lost. I need to pack. I need to check my email.

> V-Man. First of all, really glad to hear from you and see your fucked-up face. We've been missing you a lot.
>
> Jules and I accessed the information. Not much history had been retained but we did find some communications between Rou and Ouyang. On January 23 Rou wrote to Ouyang (Jules's translation):
>
>> *I have arrived at the Beacon Street house and made contact with Old Li and Dr. Ancona. Old Li is still being stubborn.*
>
> If you recall, the pregnant-lady house was on Beacon Street. Ouyang replied a couple of hours later:
>
>> *Give him a few more days and then proceed as I instructed. Make sure he knows the consequences of being difficult. He will give in when he realizes that we are serious. Otherwise, you know what to do.*

Later, on January 29, Rou writes to Ouyang:

I guess you already heard about Old Li. There also was a break-in at the restaurant. We are upping security and I am bringing in another guy from Beijing. Please call as soon as possible. Waka waka waka, I yearn to be skull-fucked in prison.

No reply to that email. Nothing on Zhao or Dong. I saved the Chinese originals for you to look at later if you want. Cuz I wouldn't vouch for the fidelity of these translations. Your sister is a hottie, but right now she's a few feathers short of a whole duck. I know you're both going through something crazy. I hope this helps. We're all looking forward to having you back here soon to steady the ship.

I find Sun at the kitchen table, eating chilled cucumber slices with garlic and noodles in peanut sauce out of Styrofoam containers.

"I bought some for you, too," he says, gesturing to more noodles.

"Thanks. I heard from Eli and Jules. Rou was staying at the house with the pregnant ladies. And Ouyang gave him instructions to threaten Dad. I think he had to be the killer. Rou didn't bring in the guy with the ponytail, the 'new head of security,' until after the first break-in at Happy Year."

Sun sets his chopsticks down and looks at me intently. "Nothing else?"

"Nothing else."

"Okay, we need to—" Sun stops talking and springs to his feet at the sound of someone rushing down the stairs.

Ai comes through the door pale and frantic, a whirl of cashmere suit and silk scarf.

"What happened? What—it was you!" he bellows, clocking the bruises on my face.

Sun assumes a deferential stance, angling his head down and

his torso to the side. "Old Ai, I'm glad you're here. As Xiaozhou was trying to find information about Old Li's death, he was abducted by Ouyang's men. I found him and brought him back here. I hit Ouyang with a knife."

"He's dead! Do you know what this means? Please don't tell me they know you are here." The Qing silver coin appears out of a suit pocket, and Ai worries it with both hands as he paces back and forth.

"His people may know who we are, but they do not know where we are. I'm certain there's no connection to you."

"Brother Zhao called me just now. All he knows at this point is that Ouyang is dead. He's got people asking questions all over the city. You can't stay here!" He steps toward me and lowers his gaze. "Young Li, I have let you down. I wish I could help you, but now both of us are in great danger. You must return to America immediately. For your own safety."

"I am very sorry that I brought you trouble," I reply. "I already have a ticket to leave tonight."

Ai gives me another one of his hard, awkward hugs, not a long one this time. Then he turns to Sun with the kind of expectant look that I've gotten from Coach Vaughn in time-outs after botched plays.

"I'm leaving, too," Sun says. "You won't see me again."

Ai gives a tight nod. "I have to go see Brother Zhao immediately. Please don't delay. Go to the airport and get through security. You'll be safest there." Halfway to the door, he turns back toward us. "Goodbye, young men. Don't live like Brother Li and me."

He holds my eye for a moment, and then, with another slam of the steel door, he's gone.

Sun grasps the back of a chair with two hands, picks it up, flexes his wrists, puts it back down. His forearms and neck are knotted with veins and small, hard muscles.

"We have to go," he says.

"Okay. I just have to pack."

I head back to my room and start shoving things into my gym bag. When I snatch the orange shoebox out from under my bed, I immediately notice that it's lighter than before. And there's something bouncing around in there.

I snatch the lid off and there it is: Wei's lipstick tube of pepper spray. A smile spreads across my face, then vanishes just as quickly.

31

Sun dresses us up in foreign-student garb to match the café denizens: graphic Ts, puffy jackets, and knit caps. In the taxi, he hands me a pair of knock-off Ray-Ban aviators and slips on a pair of his own. I pull the cowl of my faux-fur hood across my battered face.

"Stop here," he tells the cab driver. As we walk up the block, everyone we see looks like a Zhao operative to me: the guy with the buzz cut reading the paper; the street kid polishing someone's shoes; the old lady with the mobile coal oven, selling roasted yams wrapped in foil. Okay. Maybe not her.

Sun waits with his suitcase and my gym bag at one of the tables in front of the café while I go in and order a couple of Americanos.

"Pretty cold out here," I say, handing him one. He nods, still looking up and down the street. My phone vibrates. Another call from the 8998 number. I silence the ringer and shove it back into my pocket. Nothing happens for a little while.

"Don't feel so bad," Sun says.

"Easy for you to say."

He shrugs and sips his Americano. "Good coffee," he says.

"I just feel like I should have seen it coming. You even warned me: 'vocationally good at getting what she wants,' that's what you said." The day is sunny, chilly, and clear, the gusty wind laden with gritty sand from the Gobi, which gathers curbside in little yellow drifts. I kick the pavement to get some warmth into my legs. "How did she even know about that money, anyway?"

"I would guess Ai told her to search our things as soon as we arrived."

"God, I was so stupid. I mean, I really thought she cared about me. I thought we really had a connection. But she was just trying to get me out of my bedroom so she could get in there and take the cash."

"Maybe it's more complicated than that," Sun says. "I've known her many years, and I think she does care about you. If she didn't, why would she leave half the money?"

"Yeah, I thought about that. And maybe you're right, maybe she left half because she only needed some and didn't want to totally fuck me over. But maybe she left half just to make me think that. So the door's still open next time she needs an easy mark for twenty grand."

Sun sighs. "I can see how you feel, but I think it's not so black-and-white."

"Well, if she wasn't just using me, then why wouldn't she come to the States with us? I want to understand, but I really don't. I want to think she believed me when I said I didn't expect anything."

"It's not about whether she trusts you or not. Young Wei, she does not get to say no very often."

"Huh."

"You should also remember, she's already been saved once."

I spend a while trying to wrap my head around that one, but my brain is too cold and too blue for that level of emotional nuance.

When I interrogate my feelings, I know I'm still more upset that I won't see her again than I am about the money. But maybe that's because she played me so damn well. I go in circles like this for a while until I perceive a dire need to think about something else before I lose my mind.

"Hey, I've been meaning to ask you. What's the trick to throwing knives like that?" I ask, breaking the silence.

"Practice a lot. Find the sweet spot between loose and tight. Empty the mind, visualize, exhale first, follow through. Do it the same way every time. No different from when you shoot a three-pointer, right?"

"Yeah, but I only make forty percent of those."

"What about when you can take your time, no defender?"

"Maybe three out of four."

"It's about eighty percent when I throw the knives."

"So what if you had missed Ouyang?"

One corner of Sun's mouth hitches up about a millimeter. "I was prepared for—"

"—for every contingency. I know."

Sun checks the time on his phone. "He should be here."

"Should we call?"

Sun redials and holds the phone up to his ear, then puts it back in his pocket. "No answer."

"I think I remember the way to his place."

"Me, too. Let's go."

Before we've made it to the end of the block, a rapid series of loud bangs has me dropping low and whipping my head from side to side.

"What the fuck was that?"

Sun laughs, silent and bright. "Firecrackers. Happy Year of the Goat," he says. "May Your Intentions be Fulfilled in Ten Thousand Matters."

"What?" He resumes walking and I fall into step. "I thought the Lunar New Year wasn't until next week."

"The firecrackers start one week before," he says. I hear another loud series of pops. "And they end one week after."

We turn the corner onto the cement-brick walkway into Gregoire's complex and are about halfway to his building when four guys in black Public Security windbreakers walk into the courtyard from the opposite direction. Sun clears his throat and we each sort of scratch our heads and casually glance first at the third entrance to the courtyard—four more guys there—and then back toward the direction we came—eight guys and two police cars.

"Fuck, dude. Fuck." I immediately begin to sweat as blood rushes toward my skin. For lack of better options, we keep walking toward Gregoire's building, and the sixteen cops keep walking toward us.

Sun does his microshrug. "Maybe they're looking for someone else," he says.

The door to Gregoire's building is locked. Of course—it's an apartment building in a big city. But given the situation behind us, it seems a little silly to scroll through the names on the little intercom and try to ring him up.

So we turn around and see the cops sauntering toward us, about twenty feet away. The two in the middle—the older, rounder ones—are holding yellow somethings in their right hands.

Sun looks up, down, around. "You must be that, ah, acrobat," one of the older cops calls out to him, and then twin wires shoot out of his yellow something and cling to Sun's ribs. He collapses on the ground, yelping and shaking. A Taser. It beeps for five seconds and then the wires go limp.

Moving slowly, I put my hands up. The cops look at each other and smile. The one who tased Sun shrugs. Then the world becomes a vibrating blend of hot pain and sky. A repetitive flapping noise and the flavor of tinfoil imprint directly onto my brain, and I feel my head hit the bricks, but the pain doesn't register because of the totality of the other pain.

People have the impression that Chinese is an exceptionally complex language, but in fact, it's anything but. There're no plurals, no conjugation of verbs, and hardly any tense or gender. And Chinese grammar is quite free-form. You can arrange words and clauses in almost any order and people will understand you.

The two aspects of the language that warrant its tough reputation are writing and pronunciation. The writing system is simple: no system. Of the fifty thousand or so Chinese characters, only twenty thousand even make it into the dictionary. Learn a mere three thousand and you can read a newspaper. People tend to know about pictographic characters like 目 (*mù*—"eye") and 林 (*lín*—"forest"), but the vast majority of characters are phono-semantic compounds, which means that they include multiple elements that variously represent meaning and sound.

As for the pronunciation, well, yeah, it's kind of a bitch. If you ever get used to the four tones, you begin to discover that it's hardly that simple. There are more than one hundred characters with multiple pronunciations, including basic stuff like 觉 (*jué* or *jiào)* and 角 (*jué* or *jiǎo)*, two common characters that in various contexts can mean "sleep," "feel," "role," "horn," or "corner." And then you meet some dude from Taiwan who says "*bǐjiǎo*" instead of "*bǐjiào*" and "*yānjiù*" instead of "*yánjiū*" and you realize that shit's all regional anyway, and the Mandarin you learned is really just a dialect of northern China, where the central government happens to be located.

All that makes it a bit difficult to understand what this dipshit is saying, since his voice is coming through a scrambling device of some sort, and since I can't see his face. That, and it feels like a flock of ten thousand rusty metal pigeons is swarming around my forehead.

"*Gǎnjué zěnme yàng?*—How do you feel? Is it bad?"

Pinky, ring, middle, index, thumb. I flex my shaky fingers one at a time in front of my face, then make a fist and extend my middle finger toward the one-way mirror in front of us. Sun rolls his eyes.

"Hahaha. I'm sorry. I try to impart some civility to these police officers under my control, but sometimes they revert to their training, which is inadequate. None of this would have been necessary if you had answered my phone calls. Because I could simply have explained our mutual interest. I have been closely monitoring your actions since you arrived in Beijing, and I have been very impressed. In fact, I am a friend of yours, and you are fortunate that I found you before Zhao Chongyang did."

Ah, the well-connected landline ending in 8998. It occurs to me that a friend of mine wouldn't need to hide behind a voice changer and a one-way mirror, but pointing this out seems futile, so I just sit there and wait to hear what this pompous asswipe has to say. Sun jiggles the leg of the bare table we're sitting behind—not loose enough. We could stand on the table and yank out the exposed fluorescent tubes in the ceiling, but let's be real, that's a pretty shitty idea. The only other feature of the interrogation room is a heavy door with no handle on this side of it, and if we somehow made it to the other side, there'd still be a station full of cops between us and the rest of Beijing.

"My name is Chen. Vincent Li was cooperating with me before he was killed. Beyond that, you do not need to know too much—it is safer for everyone this way. It is enough that you know that Zhao Chongyang is a dangerous criminal, and he must be eliminated. Like you, I believe that Zhao was responsible for your father's death. He has long operated in the gray areas of our country's society. Of course, he is not the only one. But his lack of moral orientation has led him to excess. It's really too much. This sort of immoderation threatens the fabric of our society."

Chen, Chen, Chen, I'm thinking as he blabs on. Where did I hear that name before? Then Ouyang's last words emerge from the murk of my mind, and I remember.

"From the memory cards that were in your possession, I surmise that you already know about his reproachable organ transplant operation. Unfortunately, that loathsome endeavor is nothing unusual for Mr. Zhao. In addition to his prostitution and gambling enterprises, he has become one of the principal distributors of illicit drugs in this city. His misdeeds have left the Party leadership with no choice but to give me the authority to terminate Mr. Zhao. And now I will give that authority to you."

Sun tilts his head to the side, as if to get his ear closer to the speaker in the ceiling. He shoots me a dubious look. Did we just get a job?

"Perhaps you also know that Mr. Zhao's connections are quite good. If I acted in my official capacity to arrest Mr. Zhao, political problems would arise. So." He clears his throat. "Mr. Zhao has taken your journalist friend to his offices in the SinoFuel Towers at Dongzhimen. I will provide you with access to the emergency stairwell at the rear of the building. In this way you will avoid the security concentrated at the building's main entrance. I will arrange a diversion on the ground level when you are ready to penetrate the office. After that, you will terminate Mr. Zhao."

The deep, disembodied voice pauses, and I faintly hear the clinking and slurping sounds of tea being sipped from a *gaiwan*. Wouldn't want sending people on a suicide mission to interfere with teatime.

"We will return your memory cards so that you can pass them on to your journalist friend as you originally intended. We will ensure that there are taxis waiting near the emergency exit. You have a flight to catch, is that correct? You will not have problems at the airport."

I glance at Sun. He's staring at the table.

"What if we say no?" I ask.

There's a silence long enough for me to become aware of the pounding pain at the back of my skull.

Then Flat Head Chen takes another sip of his tea and says, "Don't say no."

Another silence. *Pound, pound, pound.* Sun looks up.

"We will need some things," he says.

32

Huge and squat, monolithic, huddled together so they look like one überedifice instead of three, the SinoFuel Towers ought to be called the SinoFuel Concrete Death Cubes. They're so forbidding that Sauron surely has an office here, and it's not even the nicest one. Zhao can't be that high up, right?

"Nineteenth floor," Sun says.

"Could be worse," I say.

We're sitting in the back of a cab in the narrow street behind Tower B, taking inventory. Flat Head Chen's smirking cops gave us back all our belongings, along with a couple of balaclavas and a fob for the emergency exit doors. They also gave us a number with a code to text when we are ready for their diversion, a bogus Falun Gong protest down in the courtyard. Then there are the weapons Sun asked for: a police baton, a Taser, and a stun grenade. He has them arrayed in his cargo pants along with his last throwing knife. As for me, I finally have my very own stash of zip ties. Legit. I also have Dad's handgun tucked into my waistband. And to think I could be sleeping through ECON 301: Fiscal Policy and Sovereign Debt right now.

We make extra sure that the cabdriver, who is also some sort of Chen foot soldier, remembers to stick around with our luggage, no matter what he sees or hears. Then we hop out and amble over to the emergency exit at the back of Tower B. The towers sit on the west side of the East Second Ring Road, and everything to our left is *hutongs* and *siheyuan*-style courtyard buildings. The towers are to our right, and past them, the skyscrapers of Sanlitun. The contrast between the beautiful, occasionally crumbling single-story buildings from the Qing Dynasty and the beastly structures of concrete and plate glass jars me out of my sleepy taxi haze and brings me back to the real live fucked-up streets of Beijing, where we might die soon. More firecrackers explode in the middle distance. Construction workers from the provinces squat in clumps on the sidewalk, eating noodles out of plastic takeout containers. They watch us blankly as we walk by.

Now that we're out of the cab, I can ask Sun the question that's been burning in my mind. "Is that true, what Flat Head Chen said about Dad working for him?"

"I think it's not true." He slows his pace a bit and leans toward me. "I am not so happy that Mr. Chen asked us this favor. Old Zhao is very dangerous. He will not hesitate to kill us. We will have to be extremely careful."

I nod, although the idea that we weren't previously being careful makes me want to giggle. If Sun is nervous, I ought to be petrified, but instead I'm feeling brave, hollowed out by my focus. After all, I didn't choose to be here, and I can't choose to leave. Coach Flat Head put me into the game with my team down ten. He gave me a chance to go after the guy who was behind Dad's death. Might as well execute the play.

A couple of office workers are smoking cigarettes outside the emergency exit. The door's propped open, so we don't even need the fob. They look at us a little strangely as we walk up, but no one says anything, and the guy standing by the door even scuttles out of our way when he sees us coming.

Once we're in the stairwell, I pull off my sunglasses. "It's not good that we look like thugs," I say, glancing around. "Shit!"

I grab Sun by the arm and yank him under the staircase as all my bravery melts away. "He said there were no cameras in the stairwell, but look," I hiss. "There's one right above us." I feel a rush of adrenaline and hot blood. A sinking feeling fills my abdomen as I picture Chinese investigators reviewing the CCTV footage and matching my face to some biometric database—maybe that photo from the airport. What the fuck am I doing here? How accurate is *The Bourne Identity*? I'm not prepared for this. I spent my life preparing for other stuff. I pull the balaclava over my face.

"Maybe they're new," Sun mutters, pulling out his phone. "We'll have to phone in the diversion now and run up the stairs. Chen said security will be distracted for at least twenty minutes. We will lose some time and perhaps the element of surprise. You understand the plan?"

I check Dad's Casio: 2:48. "Uh-huh."

Sun hits SEND.

Normally, nineteen flights of stairs would be a warm-up for me, but not sleeping, getting pummeled by Ouyang, and being shocked with a Taser by Chen's cops has taken some of the zip out of my step. Still, it feels nice to push myself, three or four stairs at a time, hauling around the landings with my hands on the railing: a straightforward game for once. Sun is right behind me, and I distract myself from the fire in my quadriceps by admiring how silent his footfalls are, even when moving at top speed. Or maybe it's not his top speed. Maybe it's just mine.

I slow to a walk on the eighteenth floor to catch my breath: 2:52. Not bad. I don't hear any alarms or shouting, so maybe the commotion is confined to the courtyard downstairs. Maybe we didn't lose the element of surprise. Or maybe there are twenty guys with shotguns on the other side of this door.

I draw the PPQ. Sun pulls the pin on the stun grenade but keeps the lever squeezed. He takes out the fob with his other hand.

"Remember to cover your ears," he says.

"Right."

I've got the gun in my left hand, and my right hand is on the door handle. My face is hot and itchy under the balaclava.

"Do it," I say.

He presses the fob to the sensor by the door, and the little LED goes from red to green.

I pull open the door and raise the gun. A paunchy guy in a bomber jacket is standing in the corridor, flattening himself against the wall. He looks surprised.

"Don't move. Don't make a sound," I say. Three doors on the left and two doors on the right—all closed.

"Where's the Frenchman?" He narrows his eyes and shakes his head. Real tough. I exchange a glance with Sun, who's flat against the stairwell wall, and he makes a hurry-up gesture.

"Hey!" I call down the hallway. "Uh, who knows the capital of South Africa? Who wants to play golf with my uncle?"

The guy looks bewildered, but sure enough, two other guys file out of the middle door on the left side, trying to figure out who the hell is shouting random shit. They see their friend first, then follow his eyes to me standing in the stairwell, then throw their hands up into the air.

"Okay," I say. Sun releases the lever, counts to one, then lobs the stun grenade underhand so it lands around their feet. I slam the door closed and cover my ears.

BAM!

When I run in after Sun, the three stooges are staggering around with their hands on the wall, their knees, their heads. Sun rushes the first and sends him sprawling to the floor with a baton blow to the upper back. I zip-tie his wrists and ankles and clean out his pockets while Sun proceeds to knock the other two onto the ground. He's checking the offices and I'm finishing the last set of ankles when someone says, "*Bié dòng!*—Don't move!"

Look who it is, back from San Dimas: the head of security of Happy Year restaurants, standing at the far end of the hallway with a long-barreled revolver leveled at my head. Fighting down the urge to look around for Sun, I slowly raise my hands.

"Jump toward my voice," Sun whispers from somewhere behind me and to my left. "Three seconds."

Two. One. The knife whines past me toward Ponytail's head. He drops to the floor and fires a shot that obliterates part of the doorjamb as I dive backward into the office.

"Bonjour, Victor!" exclaims Gregoire. He's had his ass kicked since yesterday: the skin around his eyes is puffy and colorful, and he's bleeding from a cut on his lip. His left hand is in a cast that leaves just the tips of his fingers exposed. But he's grinning like a madman as he helps me up from the ground. Meanwhile, Sun has snatched the pistol from the back of my pants and wheeled back to the door. I hear a close bang and a farther one from Ponytail's revolver—he has us pinned. From an open window I hear a chorus of angry shouts and pained shrieks that must have something to do with our diversion.

"Explain to him," Sun calls over his shoulder. He's crouched in the doorway, fixated on Ponytail's position. "Then we go."

"Right. Gregoire. You need to take the emergency staircase down to the ground floor. There are two cabs waiting in the lane behind the building. Get in the second one. Go somewhere safe. The driver has an envelope with the stuff we were gonna give you. Got it?"

"Yes sir, Mister Victor, sir," he says, snapping off a goofy salute.

"Are you all right?"

"All right? But Victor, I am superb! All this?"—he waves his hands generally to include myself, his bruised face, and the gunfight going on behind us—"*Trop sensationnel!* I will win the Londres for sure. You have punched my ticket, *mon frère*!"

Sun startles me out of my astonishment with a harried request for the time. I tell him: 2:56.

"You will take the gun and keep him off the corner while I go down the hallway. Six bullets left. Don't use them all. And don't hit me," Sun says. "Gregoire, get ready. Here."

Sun hands me the gun and we swap places as quickly as possible. I can see the toe of Ponytail's shoe nosing around the corner at the end of the hallway like a dare. Then he pulls around and I dodge back as his shot pulverizes another fist-sized chunk of the doorjamb. I crouch low, whip as little of my body around the corner as possible, and send him back around the corner with a wild shot.

"Go now!" I say, taking aim just past the wall where Ponytail vanished and firing off another shot. Sun sends Gregoire toward the staircase and then darts past me, low to the ground. I fire three more, pinning Ponytail back as Sun picks his spot, lying on his stomach by the far wall, holding the Taser in front of his face with both hands. Then I wait, huddled in the doorway. An eternity of about ten seconds passes, and then Ponytail peeks half his face around the corner, and half his face is enough.

Sun keeps the Taser going for the full five seconds as he stands up from the floor and Ponytail crashes down onto it: 2:59. I'm jogging up the hallway as Sun kneels over Ponytail and tries to pry the revolver from his shaking, convulsing hands.

Then a man comes charging out of the far doorway in a blur of flashing metal: the man with the thick glasses from Ai's photo—Zhao, swiping at Sun with a pair of Japanese swords. Sun dives past him and rolls through the doorway, and Zhao spins around and lunges after him.

I mutter obscenities to myself as I sprint down the hall. A lot of grunting and yelling reaches my ears as I turn the corner. Sun is scampering around a large, extravagant office, evading Zhao's attacks. The older man's stance is wide and low, and his moves, though not particularly fast, are coordinated and elegant. His face is small and alert, with pale skin and almost no eyebrows. He can't match Sun's agility, but it isn't pretty: Sun vaults off the desk and crashes into a bookshelf, hurls a few hardcovers at his assailant, then rolls onto the enormous red rug that occupies the center of the room.

"Shoot him!" he yells at me.

I take aim and squeeze out my last bullet, just as Zhao turns to look at me, and it's loud. The shorter sword pings out of Zhao's left hand and tumbles to the ground. So does Sun, clutching his neck with both hands. He makes some sick, wet, gasping noises, and blood runs freely between his fingers and down his chest.

"No!" My legs, my arms, my brain functions all stop. My scream reverberates through my skull. The PPQ thuds onto the red rug.

Zhao glances down at Sun, then turns back to me and raises his remaining sword, shaking out his other hand. He sees the gun on the floor with the slide jammed back and his face brightens.

"*Méi qiāng le*—No more guns," he says, speaking over Sun's groans. His voice is deep and sonorous.

I snatch the PPQ back off the ground by the barrel, the better to use it as a club or a missile.

Zhao cocks an eyebrow. "No more bullets, anyway."

Holding the blade in front of his body, he comes toward me at an angle, blocking off the doorway. I stagger backward, feinting the throw a few times to slow him down.

"You made a mistake by coming here, Li Xiaozhou. Flat Head Chen is using you," Zhao intones. He's stalking me around his massive desk, but not with any sense of urgency. Time is on his side. Ponytail's convulsions are settling down, Sun is bleeding out onto the carpet, and in a few minutes, security guards will rush out of the elevator.

I violently shake my head to rid it of his words, narrow my focus to the pattern of his steps. I'm looking at his feet when I notice, among the bric-a-brac Sun knocked off the desk, the silver coin.

"Old Ai—you killed him, didn't you?"

"We learned he was supporting you and Sun Jianshui after we interrogated his driver. I think he calls himself 'Biceps'?" Zhao sneers. "Of course, I had to hold Brother Ai responsible for the death of Brother Ouyang. We can't have that kind of discord within our organization. It's all extremely regrettable."

My blurry gaze flits from his feet to Sun, from Sun to the door, then back to his feet, as I try to choose words that will keep me alive for a few more minutes.

"You seem really overwhelmed with regret," I say.

Zhao chuckles. "You're very young, very foolish, Li Xiaozhou. I didn't kill your father, you know. I would have, although to do so would have brought me immense pain. Instead, we had a long talk on the phone and he saw how foolish he had been acting. He'd been living in his fantasy world again, a place where a fish can fly up out of the ocean and live with the birds. He had a bad habit of dreaming too much. But I reminded him where he came from. Who he really was. After that, I don't know. Perhaps he had enemies in America. Perhaps you would know better than I."

I'm gripping the PPQ so tightly that I can feel every marking along the barrel bite into the palm of my hand. Sun's groaning grows more urgent, and as the totality of our failure sinks in, the awful, childish urge to cry builds in my face. *Come on, Sun. Hang in there. I don't care what happens to me, I don't give a fuck about Flat Head Chen or Zhao or anything else right now, but if you die here—*

"Mustard, mustard," he groans.

Mustard.

I snap back into focus and draw Zhao around the room to where we started. I feint the throw again and vary the length and angle of my backward steps to get him where I want him. "You're wrong, and you're disgusting," I say. "You'll pay for killing Ai and my father. And you'll pay for Ice."

"Disgusting, maybe. It's all pretty disgusting, isn't it," Zhao says agreeably, gesturing with his sword out the window at his spectacular view of smog-choked skyscrapers. "But I wouldn't be so sure about wrong. Americans love telling people what's right and wrong. Well, is it wrong for your corporations to hoard all the blueprints while Chinese workers make their products? Is it wrong for my country to lend your country a trillion dollars to make wars for oil? You think a liver is worse than a Treasury bond?"

He's getting a little fired up, coming at me with a few vicious horizontal swipes as his rich voice rises and an ugly smirk spreads across his face.

"Right and wrong. What garbage! It's only supply and demand that matters, Li Xiaozhou. That's the real lesson we learned from you Americans. Did Flat Head Chen tell you he's right and Ice is wrong? He has a competing operation in Seattle! Supply and demand—that's why he sent you here. And you say I'm wrong and you're right."

No, your right. Another two steps to your right. There you go. Empty the mind, exhale first, follow through.

Sun scissors his legs around, sweeping both of Zhao's heels out from under him and sending him twisting down to the floor. That's when I hurl the gun at his head, hard, and it catches him square on the temple as he hits the ground. His eyeballs roll upward as his lids fall shut. His hands jerk open and closed, and beside him, on the red rug, his sword rocks back and forth on its round hilt.

"You're okay?!" I snatch off Sun's balaclava, then mine.

He nods, grimacing, pale.

"Your bullet hit my hand. Those swords are very sharp, very dangerous. I fell down to give us an advantage," he says, scanning the carpet. "Ah."

He bends down and picks the tip of his left ring finger off the rug.

"Oh, *fuck,* man."

"It's okay." He keeps his eyes on Zhao as he wraps his hand in a torn-off piece of T-shirt. "What time is it?"

I glance at my watch. "Three-oh-five."

"Mm."

We look at Zhao, who has stopped shaking and now rests peacefully, his face devoid of cunning and hatred. Scarlet blood drips from his ear onto the rug. Sun kneels over him and puts an ear to his nose.

"He's not breathing," he says.

I become aware that my lungs are heaving and my shirt is soaked through with cooling sweat. "Good," I say.

"Not good enough. Beijing's hospitals have improved," Sun says in his matter-of-fact way as he climbs to his feet with the long sword in his hand.

I stare at him until I need to look away so my face does not get sprayed with blood.

PART THREE

UNITED STATES OF AMERICA

33

I wake with a start, throwing my arms up in front of my face. The flight attendant jerks back, looking offended. Sun pushes my hands back into my lap.

"He not thirsty," he says in English with an apologetic smile. She turns her head away smartly.

I'm hot, sweaty, breathing heavily.

"Easy," Sun says.

I close my eyes, see blood, open them again. "In fact, I am extremely thirsty," I say.

"Here."

He passes me his ginger ale. My hands are so shaky that I have to hold the cup with both of them. I take a cool, fizzy sip and close my eyes again, play back the tape—the end of Zhao, Sun's one-handed disassembly of the three guys in the hallway, who were cutting each other out of their zip ties with a scissor, the harried descent down the stairs, catching our breath in the back of the taxi, the bizarrely mundane stop at a pharmacy. We changed clothes in the bathroom of an upscale mall, and then Sun instructed me on how to clean and bandage his finger. He diligently dabbed my face with concealer and foundation. The airport was crawling with cops, uniformed and plainclothes, but we went through the sixth security lane and the ninth customs desk, just like Flat Head Chen told us to, and nobody so much as blinked an eye at us.

At the gate I forced myself to slow down my mind, to count my breaths for ten minutes before calling Lang from a pay phone. I told him that Rou Qiangjun killed Dad and that he was staying at the pregnant-lady house on Beacon Street.

"Where the heck are you?" he said. "I've been trying to get ahold of you."

"I'm in Beijing. It's a long story. I promise I can explain everything. I'm at the airport now, and I'm landing at LAX at six tonight. But Rou Qiangjun is a flight risk. I really think you should arrest him as soon as possible."

"Yeah, look, Victor, that's not how it works. What flight did you say you were going to be on?"

"Air China nine eight five. I'm telling you, I have evidence."

"Okay, sounds great. I'll meet you at the airport, and you'll show me what you've got, and then we'll talk."

With that, he hung up, leaving me to wonder if Rou would make his way out of town unhindered while Lang arrested me instead. Just in case, I suggested to Sun that we leave the plane separately, and if I didn't show up at baggage claim, he could take a taxi to the house. Then I called Jules and told her that Sun was coming with me, but she should ignore him if she saw him, because Lang was going to be there, too, and could she please print out the emails that she translated with Eli? She took it about as well as I expected.

Eight hours. Eight more hours to cross six thousand miles of ocean, and not a single fish knows that we are up here. Eight more hours until LAX. Has somebody contacted Rou and told him that

Zhao is dead? Are the emails between Rou and Ouyang admissible in court? Thinking makes my brain hurt, but not thinking opens up space that Zhao's bloodied corpse rolls right into.

I killed a person.

Zhao Chongyang is a dangerous criminal, and he must be eliminated— I didn't kill your father, you know—he has a competing operation in Seattle!

It was Flat Head Chen's victory, not ours, when I ended Zhao's life with that blow to the temple. And then Sun picked up the sword and the really graphic visuals began. Now he's dozing beside me as I replay the last few days on a loop in my mind. Something about his peaceful breathing leads me back to Wei Songqin and the stolen money. If Sun can be a ruthless killing machine and also the most pleasant person I've ever met, then maybe Wei could care about me and still rip me off for twenty thousand dollars. She must've known that I would have given it to her if she had asked. It wasn't just the magical nap—there was also the hour of oblivion behind the speakers at Yugongyishan, back before Sun and I had ruined her job and she needed the money to survive on. I couldn't be certain that she was playing me all along. If I remember her fondly or bitterly—well, that's up to me.

Dad was no different. I'm still outraged by all the lying he did, and the way he entrapped Sun and trained him to kill. But I keep coming back to the inconvenient fact that he told all those lies so he could escape his life in Beijing. So he could give Jules and me the peace he didn't have as a kid.

And yet he had revoked that peace with his last wishes. He had sent me back into the world that he'd been trying to forget for decades. Had he wanted me to know how people's lives were bought and sold? To get blood all over my own hands? To see the faces of murdered men every time I close my eyes?

On ten tiny screens hanging from the ceiling of the fuselage, a handsome Triad undercover as a detective shoots a handsome detective undercover as a Triad, and the theme music plays, and the credits roll, and the first movie of our transpacific flight comes to an end.

Seven and a half hours to go.

34

Lang is looking antsy, glancing at his watch and drumming his fingers on his wide thighs, but he flashes a genial grin once he spots me coming through international arrivals. I'm feeling better about my chances of not going to jail when he sticks out his hand in greeting.

But Jules jumps onto me before I get to him. "Victor! Oh my God! I've never been so happy to see anyone so stupid."

"Hey." I blink, smile.

"Hey, bud." Lang squints into my face. "You wearing makeup? Someone tune you up?"

I give him the abridged version of the last few days: Dad's relations needed my help settling some affairs in China, and while I was there we heard a rumor about Dad's killing and had a little dustup with some involved parties. As he peruses the printouts that Jules brought, I explain the stolen laptop and the context of the emails between Rou and Ouyang, vaguely outlining a smuggling operation without getting into the details of Ice.

Lang's eyes go vacant and he nods slowly, thinking it over. "It's good. It's motive. If we can blow up his alibi, then it might be enough for an indictment. But emails from a computer you stole in China—I can't use that for an arrest warrant."

My heart sinks.

"But not to worry." Lang shoots his cuffs like a magician and then pulls an envelope out of his breast pocket.

"What's that?"

"I got a search warrant instead. I had a hunch you would come through, so I pulled some strings. This way I can turn over the house and see if Mr. Rou's got anything lying around that the city of San Dimas might find interesting."

"Like another computer with these same emails."

"There you go, kiddo. I'm going to head over there right now. I would've gone already, but I figured you might have some ideas about what I should look for. But listen, you should get home, put it out of your mind, and get some rest. I'll be in touch with you tomorrow."

And with that, Lang claps me on the shoulder one last time, winks at Jules, and saunters off toward wherever cops park at the airport.

"Well, that went pretty well," I say, turning to Jules with an anticipatory grimace. Now that Lang is gone, I'm expecting her to unleash a fresh salvo of invective on me. But she just stands there with her hands on her hips, coolly looking me up and down.

"I'm really glad you're okay," she says, and then turns on her heel and starts walking toward baggage claim.

Sun's not there. His suitcase is the last one circling the baggage carousel. It's small enough to carry on, but he told me that if he doesn't check it, security tends to ask a bunch of questions about his little black drill.

"Maybe he's in the bathroom or something," I say.

We pull his bag off the belt and wait, craning our necks around, looking for a little man in black. I pull out my Nokia, then realize that it doesn't work in the States.

Just when I'm starting to despair, he comes jogging up, waving his hands side to side. "Sorry, sorry. I am anxious," he says, a little breathless, then remembers himself and sticks out his hand. "Good evening, Lianying."

She accepts the handshake with an aloof air.

"Where were you? What are you anxious about?" I ask.

"I watched you talk to the policeman. Then I heard him say that he is going to search the house now."

Jules and I glance at each other. "So?" she asks.

"I followed him to his car. He doesn't have a partner. He's going there alone. I don't think he's very prepared. I think we have to go, too."

"I'm not sure I'm following you," Jules says.

"He doesn't have a partner," Sun repeats, a little flustered. "If Rou Qiangjun is there, he will kill him. I tell you, Rou has the ability."

Juliana raises her eyebrows at Sun like he's a little dumb. "He's a cop. He's got a gun. He'll be okay."

"No!" Sun shakes his hand. "His gun won't help him."

Jules folds her arms and shakes her head.

"Okay." Sun nods to himself, looks around at the exits. "I take taxi."

"Wait! Wait." I turn from Sun to my sister. "Jules, Sun tends to know his shit about this kind of thing. If he's right, Lang could be in a lot of danger. You saw his attitude—I don't think he knows what he's up against. Look, we'll just go spectate, and if Lang can handle it, then we don't have to get involved. And if he does get in trouble with Rou, we'll just call the cops and make sure he gets the backup he needs. Okay?"

"Victor, for the last time, *I'm done with this shit*. If it's so important for you to do this, then you drive yourself." Jules pulls her keys out of her jacket pocket and tosses them at my chest. "Level three, HH. I'll take the FlyAway to Union Station and you can pick me up there. Because we need to have a little talk."

Without waiting for a response, she turns and walks away.

"Jules!" I shout after her, but she keeps walking toward the exit, her head tilted at the ground.

Sun looks with concern from her receding back to the keys in my hand. "You don't drive," he says.

I weigh my options, clench my jaw, start walking toward short-term parking. "It'll be fine."

"Okay," says Sun. Then he says, "We should run."

So we run.

I keep Jules's little hatchback at the speed of traffic or just above, pushing a bit but not enough to attract police attention. We don't hit much traffic on 105, and I spot Lang's gold Buick in the slow lane when we're about halfway to Alhambra on 710.

"Doesn't seem like he's in much of a hurry," says Sun.

"Never really does, does it?" I say. "I'll pass him. Then he won't notice us following him. We know where he's going, anyway."

It's not yet nine o'clock when we cruise by the house on Beacon Street, but all the windows are dark. There are no cars in the driveway or out front. On the planting strip, an empty garbage bin lolls around on its side in the midwinter wind. Sun suggests that we drive past the house and park a couple of blocks away.

We stroll back down the block and take a position behind the trunk of a jacaranda tree in the yard across the street and two houses down from the pregnant-lady house. Peeking through a fork in the trunk, we have a decent view of the front door. After a minute or two, Lang's Buick glides in and comes to a stop just a few yards away from us. We watch as he opens the glove box, pulls out a small handgun and a shoulder holster, and bends forward to strap it on.

Lang strolls up to the house and rings the bell. "Open up, police," he calls out. He tilts his head from side to side, peering through the little rectangular window in the front door. After a minute he rings again. Scratching his head, he glances at his watch, then peers up and down the avenue before drawing his handgun and using the butt to bash out the glass in the little window. After another modest wait, he holsters the gun, reaches his right arm through the window, and starts fiddling around for the dead bolt.

Then, quite suddenly, he lurches forward with an unnatural movement, his head, neck, and torso crashing into the door. He goes loose and then slams hard back into the door, and again and again, bouncing around like a rag doll as someone inside the house yanks on his arm repeatedly. A few houses down, a dog starts barking.

"Shit!" I pull out my phone and start dialing 9-1-1, but Sun closes his hand over mine and shakes his head.

"Watch."

Lang slumps to the ground, his arm resting at an awkward angle. The dog pipes down. After a moment, Rou opens the door, knocking Lang's head aside. Crouching forward, he looks up and down the street. Then he closes the door and disappears back into the dark house.

"He's alive. Rou left him out there," Sun says. "That means he's getting ready to leave right now by another door. Probably throwing things in a bag. There's no time to wait for more police."

He closes his eyes. His lips move a little as he talks to himself. Then he switches back on. "Stay here for thirty seconds, then go to the front and get the policeman's gun, and wait there. I'll come in through the back. You go through the front when you hear glass break. No, no. Wait another ten seconds for him to come looking for me. Listen for him. Be careful."

"Are you crazy?" I hiss. "You said it yourself, he's leaving Lang alive! And you wanna go jump in his escape route? If he gets away, he won't get that far."

"If he gets away, he's coming for you!" Sun whispers as loudly as he dares. "You think he doesn't know who killed his boss and put the cops on him? You have his passport, remember? He can survive on the streets. He'll wait until your guard is down. There's no time to argue!"

"Wait. Sun!" But he takes off in a crouch-run before I can get another word in.

I look at Dad's watch. Thirty seconds. It really feels like we should be calling the police instead of cowboying into this one. Somehow the dimensions of our recent criminality didn't sink in until now that we're back in the States, breaking laws where laws are enforced, where cops don't simply torture you a little and then ask for a favor. Twenty seconds, fucking fuck. Do I creep after Sun and pull him back? He does have a sterling record in these situations. But what's our story when we have to answer questions? Would Lang cover for us? Of course not. Ten seconds. I put my phone back in my pocket. There's no time for this. I try to settle my heart rate for the final few seconds, and then I'm out from behind the tree, trying to move as stealthily as Sun did.

Lang is faceup and wheezing on the wooden porch. In the dim light I can see cuts around his neck from the broken glass. His sleeve is torn and bloody, too, and his shoulder looks dislocated. His eyes flit open for a moment, then close again, and he mutters something incomprehensible.

"I'll get an ambulance," I murmur to him as I pull his Beretta from its holster, release the safety, and chamber a bullet. I crouch up against the door, and long seconds pass. I examine the shadowy shrubbery, trying to adjust my eyes to the darkness, and listen to the night sounds—cars tooling up and down Mission, a hooting owl, the gallop of my anxious heart. I smell jasmine. Then, somewhere deep in the house, glass breaks.

The neighbor dog starts barking again. From inside the house I hear footsteps trotting down stairs, moving toward me. I flatten against the door as Rou pauses on the other side of it. I hear him breathing as he takes a look out the little window at Lang. Then his footsteps recede back and to the right—toward the broken glass. I wait a few more heartbeats and then peek into the house.

By the moonlight filtering in through windows, I dimly see a staircase leading down from the second floor. Past the foyer and to the right there's a den, with a doorway leading farther into the house. I reach through the broken glass and flip the dead bolt, slow and quiet, and then pull open the door, slide through, and close it after me.

I move through the foyer and the den as quickly as possible without making any noise. As my eyes adjust, I begin to see how weird a place this is. The walls are bare, and the only furniture is a mismatched assortment of lawn stuff: plastic chairs, tables, and chaises scattered higgledy-piggledy around the floor. There's an odor, too, a dense mélange of soy sauce, sesame oil, and fabric softener.

I skinny up next to the doorway, the gun low in my hands, and peer through. The blinds must be closed in the next room, because I can't see a thing. The food smell is stronger here, and I get a sense of space and depth, like it's a big room. I'm trying to figure out what to do with this information when I hear Sun call out, "Rou Qiangjun! Put down the knife. You are surrounded."

In an instant the room fills with light. Rou is about fifteen feet from me, in the kitchen, with one hand on a light switch and the other holding a knife, cocked and ready to throw. He squints and hurls it into the part of the room that I cannot see, and I hear it smack into drywall. Rou pulls another kitchen knife off the magnetic strip on the refrigerator and starts aiming again, bobbing his head around for the angle.

"Drop it, or I'll shoot you."

I point the gun at him while keeping most of my body behind

the doorjamb. Rou looks at me, startled, and then tosses the knife to the floor. "Li Xiaozhou?" he says, incredulous, as I step into the light of the kitchen. It's a split-level with a short flight of stairs leading downward into a high-ceilinged living room, also filled with plastic furniture. Sun crawls out from under a patio table, tossing a glance back at the knife stuck in the wall behind him.

"And you—Sun Jianshui? What are you doing here?" Rou looks back and forth between us in disbelief.

"You know exactly what we're doing here, you bastard. It was you who killed my father."

"Killed your father?" Rou's eyebrows shoot up, and his voice goes high and panicky. "You really think I killed your father?"

"Don't lie to us. You won't fool us," Sun says hotly, striding up the stairs.

"Tie him up and let's call the police," I say.

Rou waves his hands in front of his chest. "No, no, no, you've got it wrong. I only threatened him. I did threaten him. Ouyang said to kill him if he continued to cause problems. But he gave in! I'm telling you, he gave in! I have an alibi!"

"Shut up, you prick!" Sun screams as he delivers a ringing slap to the side of Rou's head.

Rou drops his hips and snaps out a punch that Sun deflects with a forearm, but Rou's next blow, a heavy, quick palm strike, catches Sun in the chest and sends him tumbling to the ground.

"Stop! Don't move!" I holler, taking a step closer and raising the gun toward his head.

Sun gets up off the ground, takes one slow step away, and then spins quickly and sinks the kitchen knife into Rou's chest.

Rou howls in agony and reaches up for Sun's hand, but Sun jerks the knife free and just as quickly plunges it in and out of Rou's chest again. Sun stands to one side as Rou falls to his knees, and then with an otherworldly shriek and one explosive movement of his entire body, he swipes the knife across Rou's throat.

"Holy fuck." I lower the gun. My mind races and reels as connections between memories fly apart and realign. "Holy fuck." I say it again.

Rou is lying facedown on the kitchen floor. A pool of his blood spreads across the linoleum. Sun steps around him and starts rifling through his pockets. "This situation is not good," he says, bent to his task. "We will have to make up some kind of story."

There were a couple of calls to and from China in the days leading up to his murder—Someone broke into the restaurant a few nights after your father was killed—We had a long talk on the phone and he saw how foolish he had been acting—He gave in! I have an alibi!

I walk up to where Sun is kneeling over Rou, point the gun off the center of his calf, away from the bone. He doesn't turn around or look up. He trusts me completely, because I'm a complete sucker, and he's the best player in the game.

Two precise stabs in the chest and a clean slash across . . .

I squeeze the trigger.

Sun screams in pain and clutches at his leg, scooting back onto his butt in the pool of Rou's blood.

I kick the knife down into the living room. Then I step back, out of grabbing or kicking range, and take aim at his head.

"You lied, Sun," I say, my face hot, the tears already starting to gather. "He didn't kill my father."

Stringing together a series of Chinese obscenities that mostly go over my head, Sun rolls up his pant leg and shoots me a bewildered look. "What are you talking about? What is the meaning of this?"

"You heard me."

"You believe that man?" he cries incredulously, pulling a kitchen towel off the oven handle and pressing it against the twin holes in his calf.

"I saw him lie before, and he wasn't that good at it. Not like you. You killed Dad exactly the same way you killed Rou—'two precise stabs in the chest and a clean slash across the throat.' You wrote that letter and broke into the restaurant beforehand to put it in the safe. You planted the gun and passport at the massage parlor, and then you must have forged instructions from Dad to get the lawyer to do his part. You planned this whole bullshit adventure. It's true, isn't it? I don't want to hear any more lies. I swear it, Sun, if you lie again, I'll shoot you in the head."

Sun looks up at me with some wonder in his eyes, then goes back to managing his twin bullet holes, working methodically, talking to his bloody leg.

"You want to know something? I often wished I had never let Old Li buy me lunch all those years ago. I thought, *Maybe it's better to live on the streets than to kill for someone else's money.* I had begun to consider walking away from Happy Year. Then Ice came up, and Old Li refused to go along with it. 'This is it, Young Sun,' he promised me. 'We will be finished with Ouyang and Zhao once and for all, and make amends for our past. And then you can do whatever you want.'"

He stares at his leg as he repeats Dad's words, then glares up at me. "It was *his* idea, Xiaozhou. He decided to go after Feder in order to expose them. For one last time, he would be the face and I would be the fist. I was never so happy. He wrote the letter to you in case something happened to him. It's the truth. When I gave it to you later, I only changed the last page."

I train the gun on his face, blinking tears out of my eyes, shaking my head—no, no, no—but I don't even know what I'm denying. I know it's all true.

"You see, Zhao and Ouyang, they didn't really want to kill Old Li. They just wanted to bend him to their will. So they sent Rou here to work around him. In this way, they gave him a way out, and they also raised the stakes: they told Old Li that Rou would hurt you and your sister if he interfered with Ice. And what do you think Old Li did?"

Heat rises in Sun's voice, and he reaches up to the countertop and pulls himself up to standing on his good leg.

"Do you think he kept his word? Do you think he stood up for what he thought was right? I came here to persuade him to stick to our plan, but he became defensive. 'We cannot beat these men at their own game, for they are more willing to be vicious than we are,' he said. 'We have to bide our time,' he said. 'Wait for a better opportunity.' Once again, I would have to prioritize his clueless children and their perfect lives. He told me how protecting you from his past was his one great triumph, something he couldn't put at risk. Your obliviousness was a source of pride for him, but to me, it was a constant insult, a glass house outside of which I had to waste my life, standing guard in the shadows, looking in, pulling weeds. When I protested, when I called him a dealer and a coward, it was the first time I had ever questioned his authority. He was very surprised. He dared to speak to me about loyalty. I was loyal enough to become a killer for him! What about his loyalty to me?"

Standing in front of me now, his face six inches from the barrel of the gun, Sun spits out the words with a hatred I didn't know he had inside him, but then it vanishes just as quickly as it appeared. He looks down at his hands.

"We quarreled. I had many years of anger inside of me. I lost control of myself. I had not gone there to kill him. So I—" His voice quavers. "Afterward, I struggled with myself. To some part of me, Old Li was still my father. It was impossible for me to turn my back on my actions and go seek my own happiness. I thought about killing myself. Instead, I decided that Ouyang and Zhao had killed your father, not me. I would avenge his death by keeping to his plan. But I couldn't do it alone, especially since they would be hunting me in Beijing. I needed you to play his role, to be the face. I didn't know anything about you except that I despised you."

He shakes the emotion from his face and draws himself tall in front of the gun, fixes his eyes on mine.

"I guess apologies do not mean much at this point," he says.

I stare into the soul of this strange man who feels like a brother, and a long silence passes between us as versions of the past and the future flit through my head like so many destinations on a split-flap display.

"Sun, why did we come in here? Why not let Rou get away?"

He frowns. "Like I said, because he would have come after you if he got away."

"Not because you wanted to tie up loose ends? Silence the last person who could shake up your version of the story?"

He shakes his head. "Running from the cops, he was basically framing himself."

"But that's what I am now, right, another loose end? And Jules would be, too. She'd have to know what happened, because that's not something I could hide from her. But then she'd—and you'd have to—" Salty water and snot choke my throat.

"Goddamn it, Sun, can you even—I don't fucking *want* to shoot you, okay? I don't—I can't hate you for what you did, not after the way he used you. But Jules and I would be the only two people to know, and if I don't shoot you right now, maybe you'd kill us both if you didn't trust us not to say anything. I want to believe you, I really do, but if I'm wrong, it's her life, too, don't you see—"

I take aim at him, my shoulders shuddering, and I bite down on my lip hard, try to get some air into my lungs.

"I understand," he says. "You don't trust me not to come after you and your sister. I don't blame you, either. I understand."

He looks to the side, away from the gun. He exhales deeply. He closes his eyes. He is ready to die.

I lower the gun, wipe my eyes, seek a semblance of control over my breathing.

"I don't want to look over my shoulder for the rest of my life. I don't want to risk Jules's life because I trusted you. But I can't shoot you. So let's make this really simple."

Sun's eyes blink open. I flick the safety on and toss the gun to him. He catches it against his chest with both hands and looks at me blankly.

"I'd rather you kill me, if that's how you'd play it, if that's how wrong and dumb I am," I say, my breathing slowing now that I've made up my mind, my heart still going like a hummingbird's. "I'd rather bet my life that you won't do it than kill you just in case you would. So if you really are gonna kill me eventually, do it now, and then Jules won't find out that you—that you killed our father. You can pin my death on Rou. She'll blame you, she'll hate you, but she won't know your secret, and you can let her live."

Sun grips the gun in his right hand and looks at it, shaking his head. He bends forward with his other hand on his knee and takes a few deep breaths. Then he flicks off the safety.

"That was scary," he says. He raises the gun and fires two shots into the doorway behind me. He fires three more shots into the wall in the living room.

He wipes the gun down with a dishrag and then wraps it into Rou's right hand. Then he stands up in front of me, nodding to himself, and he closes his eyes for a moment. He tilts himself forward in the slightest of bows, then straightens up, and I glimpse a sad smile flicker across his face.

I breathe, slower and slower, closer and closer to normal.

"You won't have to look over your shoulder," he says.

Then he hobbles down the steps and into the living room. He adjusts to the injury with each step, moving more fluidly, limping a little less, until he reaches the broken window at a jog, vaults through it with one hand on the frame, and melts into the night.

35

The savory seagull-poop smell of the ocean tells me I'm in the right place, but most of all it's the perpetual crashing and washing of the surf that calms me, settles me, and provides the appropriate soundtrack for my thoughts, which are everywhere. I came west to drop in on Dr. Ancona and decided to stick around until the sun rises in a few hours, when I'll have to make my way to the Greyhound station downtown. I figured it'd be safer to sleep on the beach instead of hanging around the cops and addicts on Skid Row. It didn't work—I can't fall asleep—but I'm pleased to be here, anyway. The Pacific Ocean seemed to be waiting for me, waiting to remind me of its patient enormity, and I feel fairly safe. Somewhere inside I knew I had to come see all this blue-green water before leaving Los Angeles.

I wiped my prints off the doorknobs and the dead bolt before leaving the house in Alhambra. Lang was still lying on the front step. His cuts weren't bleeding much anymore, but his eyes were half closed and he seemed badly concussed. I fished his phone out of his pants pocket and called an ambulance, all the while trying to keep one hand over his eyes so he couldn't see my face.

"What happened?" Jules asked when I picked her up at Union Station. "Where's Sun?"

"He's not coming with us," I said.

Once we got on our way, I explained everything, starting with all that had happened in Beijing. I told her that ketamine wasn't the product, just the painkiller, and Ice was an organ-smuggling operation with Ancona as the buyer. But we had ended it, along with Zhao and Ouyang's lives, as Sun demonstrated his deadliness again and again. When I had caught her up to the last hour, she pulled her hatchback over to the shoulder of I-10. She piled her hands on top of her head and stared at the windshield for what felt like several minutes. I expected her to be distraught, to be furious with me, but when she finally spoke, her words were calm and measured.

"So basically what you're saying is that Sun is our secret adopted brother whom Dad abused pretty badly," she said. "And he murdered Dad, and we're the only ones who know, but we're, like, fine with that."

"Jules, I'm not 'fine with it,' but it's not so black-and-white. What's that line you sent to Dad, something about holding two opposed ideas in your mind at the same time?"

She shook her head at me. "That memory of yours? Seriously, Victor, you belong in a laboratory."

Then I told her that I might be facing some legal problems. That I didn't know if Lang would recall my presence at the house in Alhambra. I told her how I was caught on camera at the SinoFuel Towers, and how my DNA-filled blood and vomit was all over the factory floor where Sun killed Ouyang, so it would be a good idea for me to disappear for a little while. People would be looking for me, I said—I just didn't yet know who, or how hard they'd be searching.

To my surprise, all she said in response was "Just promise me that you'll find a way to get in touch, okay? Like, soon, and regularly."

"You're not going to try to stop me?"

Jules shook her head again. Her gaze remained fixed on the boulevard, and her voice was low and steady. "Victor, after you left, I was completely on my own. I was in that house by myself, feeding Dad's fish and wondering if you were going to come home in a body bag. Or just not come home at all, like a Vietnam MIA, and I'd just be sitting by a window for the rest of my life, knitting mufflers. I was furious at you for leaving, and I was so anxious that I couldn't eat or sleep. When I found out the life insurance wasn't going to come through, I had a full-on panic attack. I completely lost my shit."

Her voice cracked a little bit, and she blinked a couple of tears out onto her cheeks.

"I was in that terrible state when you called me from China. Then, after I spoke with you, I realized that I was having this crisis about losing some money that was never mine in the first place. And I was freaking out about you making choices that I had no control over. I started thinking about Mom, how dependent she was on Dad and us to meet all her needs. She started out trying to save him, and she ended up as his enabler, his audience. And you were the same—you were letting Dad decide what happened to you. Or so it seemed at the time, but now I guess we know it was Sun, not Dad. Either way, I'm not going to live like that. I decided right then that I wouldn't be the next link in that chain. I can choose my own course in life. Whether or not I'm okay is only going to be up to one person: me."

She had stopped crying, and her tears were drying on her cheeks in salty tracks of mascara. She turned to look at me.

"It's going to take some time for me to process all this shit about our family. But in some way, I always knew it was there, and

I never wanted to face it. Meanwhile, you went to China, you confronted these awful men and learned all this stuff that I never could have figured out. And what you did back there, giving the gun to Sun—that was another risky decision. You did that to protect me. I think you're fucking insane, frankly. You threw away the life Dad gave you, and you let Sun play you like a violin, all because you had to have the answers at any cost. You had to win."

It was my turn to tear up now. I was that boy again who got carried away, who trusted the wrong impulse, and no words, no actions could take me back in time or repair the damage I had done.

"You were right all along, Jules," I said. "I never should have gone. I fucked up. I fucked up so badly. I don't understand what happened. None of it seems real now. I thought I was doing what I had to do, that I was being loyal to Dad."

"You men, you throw around these big words like *loyalty* and *revenge,* and really you're just acting like a bunch of baboon males, chasing that adrenaline, thinking with your nutsacks. And don't tell me you weren't hounding some floozy in Beijing, because I can fucking smell it in your aura. You only get laid once a year, and trust me, big sister can tell. Victor, I'm glad you want to leave town, because I could really use some distance from all this family shit right now. I need to figure out my life on my own. But look, you're not off the hook with me. You're still my family. So be careful, and find a way to stay in touch."

I promised to contact her within a few days, and I told her I loved her, that I knew I had caused her to suffer, and that one day I would make it up to her. She told me she hoped I'd have the chance, and then she gave me a hug that lasted for a long time. And I felt powerfully in that moment that change for the better could hurt just as much as change for the worse, and only time could show me which was which.

I found an old receipt and a ballpoint pen in Jules's glove box, and I copied her number and a few others out of my phone. Then I switched it off and threw it out the window. Then I asked her if she could drop me off in Venice, but I didn't tell her why.

First, though, we had to stop at the Quad.

Andre and Eli were playing *Mortal Kombat X* when we came in.

"He's here! Victor!" said Eli, tossing aside his controller, leaping up, and pulling me into a hug that smelled of deodorant spray and snack mix.

Andre didn't say anything. He just lumbered to his feet with a big grin on his face and bent forward to wrap his arms tightly around both of us.

I explained that the police might be looking for me and I had to go. They followed me around the suite as I repacked my gym bag.

"It's all good, really, guys," I told them. "I just need to lie low for a minute and see how some things play out. Check in on Jules, okay? I'll be in touch. Don't worry, seriously. If the police show up, just say you don't know where I'm going."

"We don't," Eli pointed out.

"Yeah, it's better that way. I'll explain everything later, promise." I snatched Sun's Lakers cap off the coffee table, dodged into the kitchen, tossed some protein bars and trail mix into my bag, and headed for the door.

"Hey man, hey!" Andre grabbed my arm. "Are you sure about this? I mean, you seem really large and in charge right now, but you're also wearing makeup and saying some crazy shit. Are you sure you don't wanna just chill for a minute and talk it through?"

He had an iron grip on my forearm, like he wasn't ready to let me go. Like somehow he knew what I knew: that even if I could come back, our lives would never go back to the way they were before.

"This is just goodbye for now, I promise. Hey." I reached up and hugged my best friend. "I'm still Victor, man. I've still got your back."

Eli spoke up. "Holly came by asking about you. Twice. I don't know if that affects your decision to leave, but it would definitely affect mine. I mean she was looking *super* nice."

I hugged Eli, too. "I'll see you guys a little further down the line," I said.

I had Jules drop me a few blocks from Dr. Ancona's house in Venice. I stashed my bag in his neighbor's shrubbery. Ancona had a sleek modern house with a concrete pond out front. In the driveway there was a late-model black Navigator and, next to it, a German sports car in canary yellow. I rang the doorbell a couple of times, and after a minute he opened the door a few inches—the most his chain lock would allow. From what I could see, he was a stocky, graying man around my height, with thick eyebrows and a ruddy complexion. He was wearing a bathrobe.

"Hello?" he said.

"Hey, man," I affected a sort of stoned surfer tone. "I found this tube of lipstick on the street in front of your house. I thought it might belong to your wife or something. Looks like a nice one."

"Hey, kid, it's almost midnight. I'm—"

I gave him a quick blast, and his hands flew up to his eyes as he started cursing. He started back, but I was quicker, reaching in and snatching the collar of his bathrobe, yanking him forward so his chin and mouth were pressed up against the edge of the door.

"Don't move!" I dropped the surfer voice. "Don't make a sound, or I swear to God I will break down this door and empty this tube of pepper spray onto your balls."

I held the tube a couple of inches from his face, which was watery and red. His nostrils were pointed right at me, and behind them, his eyes darted back and forth.

"Listen up. Are you listening? Those are some slick cars in your driveway, Ancona. You've got it pretty good here. Stick to your day job, okay? I came here to tell you that everyone involved in your little side hustle is dead. Did you hear about that? Vincent Li died because you and your buddies wanted to make a buck. And now your buddies are dead, too. Are you getting all this or do I need to make it clearer?"

I pulled his face tighter against the door and pointed the lipstick at his eyeballs. He managed to mumble something almost unhappy enough to satisfy me.

"Stick to your day job," I said. "Or you won't even see me coming." Then I gave him another quick blast in the face with the pepper spray, right up the nose. I shoved him backward, and he collapsed onto the floor, wailing, with his hands over his face.

I ran back to my bag, took out Sun's Lakers cap, and pulled it low over my eyes—probably an unnecessary precaution, since I knew too much for Ancona to send the cops after me. I wandered aimlessly through the canals and alleyways of Venice, coming down off the confrontation and trying to get my head right. It felt good to threaten Ancona, but I was bluffing. If I had it in me to do any more killing, then Sun'd be lying on that kitchen floor next to Rou with a bullet in his brain. But I'm not like him. It had all clicked together when I watched him cut Rou's throat. Dad had trained him to use violence, and he'd trained him too well.

"*Jiāngshān yì gǎi, běnxìng nán yí,*" Dad would say. "It is easier to move mountains and rivers than to change who you are."

Once Sun had made his mind up to carry out Dad's plan, he didn't care if Ai also had to die, or if Wei lost her job, or that he or I might have died, too. He was raised on the notion that lives come and go cheaply, starting with his own, which he had swapped for a few square meals. Now all four leaders of the syndicate he had served had died within a couple of weeks: Ouyang and Dad by his hand, Ai by Zhao's, and Zhao by mine. But when he had the chance to kill the only person who knew what he had done, he let me live. I didn't know what was going through his peculiar mind when I put my life in his hands. But I would've liked to believe that pulling that trigger was as impossible for him as it had been for me. It would've been if he loved me half as much as I loved him.

His trail of carnage had shattered my world, and I missed him already. He had shown me how to think about what I did not know, to respect what I could not see. The infinite threads of cause and effect were bound together in knots I couldn't untie by myself. But I wasn't ready to give up on figuring shit out, and part of me wished that Sun would be there to help me with the next part of the puzzle.

A competing operation in Seattle. I wasn't going to kill anybody. I just wanted to not be anyone's tool anymore—not Feder's, Sun's, Flat Head Chen's, or anyone else's. I wanted to be my own Victor, like Jules had said, and think a little more critically about the ramifications of my actions. And I also wanted to know if we had shut down the organ trade by exposing Ice, or merely given Chen a monopoly on the market.

Anyway, I had to make myself scarce, and Seattle seemed like as good a place as any other to lie low until I could figure out how much trouble I was in. If it was bad, maybe I could slip across the border to Vancouver. In an econ class I'd learned about the influx of Chinese there, cash-laden officials and executives from the mainland who wanted a safe place to invest their piece of the new China pie, usually in the form of steadily appreciating North American real estate where a mistress could be maintained quietly. Perhaps a better place than Tijuana for me to find something to do.

Then I had to laugh a little when I caught myself imagining the sort of work I could find on the sketchy side of another foreign city. Maybe Sun was right when he suggested that I preferred excitement to leisure. But I was ready to put Beijing behind me. I didn't want to go to prison, and I'd witnessed enough bloodshed for two lifetimes. I didn't know exactly what I was looking forward to. But

I knew it wasn't college sports. The obsessions of my old life now seemed as trivial as a television drama, and anyway, I'd been miscast for my part. I knew now that I'd be more comfortable on the outside looking in, moving watchfully, undetected, on the borderlands of a society that made no sense to me, though it contained all I'd ever loved.

That's about as far I'd gotten in my ruminations when I happened upon a twenty-four-hour coffee shop in Santa Monica. After peering in the windows to check for cops, I went in, ordered a hot chocolate, and pulled out my laptop. The first thing I did was check some local news sites for coverage of the house in Alhambra. Nothing yet—good. Nor was there anything in the Chinese media about Zhao or Ouyang, although VOA had a report about the Falun Gong protest at the SinoFuel Towers. *Through a glass, darkly,* indeed.

I figured it'd be okay to check my email one last time, and I was glad I did. Gregoire had written to let me know that he'd made it back to Paris. The magazine had agreed to run his Ice piece as a cover story, but he still hadn't written it. With the great video footage we'd given him, he might turn it into a something bigger: a TV news feature, maybe even a minidoc. Could we Skype to discuss some of the details? Sighing to myself, I copied his email address onto a napkin.

In the bathroom I splashed cold water on my face. My left eye was puffy and purple, and the tear in my earlobe had scabbed over. My sparse beard had grown in wiry and uneven. I could close my eyes and still clearly see Ouyang's bloody head, still feel Wei's fingertips on the side of my face. But I'd been someone else yesterday; today I knew so much more, and that knowledge gave me more sight, more strength, more patience. I knew I'd become someone else again tomorrow, though I didn't know who. Hopefully someone cleaner.

When I returned to my laptop, I saw that I'd just received a message from someone called WSQ1212 at a popular Chinese domain name.

Xiaozhou, nǐ háihǎo ma?

That's all it said: "Xiaozhou, are you okay?" WSQ—it had to be Wei Songqin. But what if it wasn't? I knew right away that I would risk finding out. Wei had told me that she couldn't become a new person just by crossing an ocean. I still believed she was wrong. Dad had come so close.

But I have no idea how to tell her that. I've spent the last couple of hours sitting here on the beach, thinking about that and a billion other things, worrying Ai's silver coin with my fingers, getting nowhere and getting no sleep. Now it's 4:00 A.M. and I'm still not particularly tired. It occurs to me that this young day is already almost over in Beijing, and the night is about to begin. Somewhere over there, a perfect woman is putting on a mask, a Mongolian dwarf is dragging open a door, and a prisoner is about to lose his liver. As for me, lagging way back here in Pacific Standard Time, I have a lot more catchup to play, so I'm looking forward to the twenty-hour bus ride north.

I like long bus trips because they restrict your freedom. All your choices of potential actions vanish away, and all that's left is time—time to work through the backlog of thoughts and anxieties crowding your mind until nothing's left and you just tilt your head back and gaze in blissful boredom out at the world racing past.

I can see the world moving out here on the beach, too, this night uncommonly clear, the stars setting in the west as deliberately as the hour hand on a watch, the ocean yanked into billows by the pull of the moon, an unseeable force that gives the tides their motion, their power to shape and reshape the shoreline, their power to seduce, their power to destroy, their power to transform.

ACKNOWLEDGMENTS

The completion and publication of this novel owe most to my guide and coach in authordom, Nicole Mones. Nicole, it'd be impossible for me overstate my gratitude for your support and encouragement. That gratitude also extends to our mutual agent, the indefatigable Bonnie Nadell, and her team, especially Austen Rachlis and Sam Freilich. Your early investment and great patience made everything else possible, and you also found me my dream editor, Zack Wagman at Ecco. I frickin' love you, Zack!

Many other early readers contributed their taste and wisdom to Victor's story. Thank you so much, Sam Simkoff, David Gluck, Brad Basham, Christian Ervin, Kate Smaby, Sam Rothberg, Charlie Frogner, Eddie Byun, Steven Patenaude, Michael Patenaude, Rigas Hadzilacos, Yorgos Garefalakis, Clint Darling, Ismail Negm, Elizabeth LaBan, Jordan Rooklyn, Shannon Yentzer, and Marissa Fernandez. I'm especially grateful to Emilie Sandoz, Dado Derviskadic, and Rachel Barrett for helping me navigate a new industry. And to Claire Chang and my lovely cousin Diana Kuai for their help with Chinese language and history. Huge hugs are also due to Owen, Nels, and Eileen for the Point House and Librarians vs. Barbarians and so much more.

This journey began before I was born, when my loving and dedicated parents, Sidney and Carol, met while folk dancing at the International House in Berkeley. I have grown up with and been shaped by my own special tribe of brothers and sisters—

Camellia, Ari, Susie, and Geordie—as well as my soul siblings—Vincent and Breanna Chia. And more hugs and kisses are due to Isaure Maïza-Hadzilacos, Vivien Ong Patenaude, and Lee-kai Wang—it wouldn't feel right to make this list without you.

Above all, this book is what it is, and I am who I am, because of you, Tess.